Hold

Hold

Book 2 in the Fieldings Series

Kimberley Ash

TEA ROSE
PUBLISHING

Dedication

For you strong single moms out there. You know who I mean.

I love you.

Contents

Prologue

Being Audrey Hepburn sucked.

"Cat!" Thea Fielding shouted from the back porch, into the pouring rain. "Caaat!"

The gutter leaked a steady sheet of rain onto her head. She almost welcomed it for its cooling effect on her headache, but it was sending icy drops down the back of her neck, making her shiver and curse.

"Cat!" she yelled again. "Goddamn, flea-bitten, ratty old caaaat!"

Through the back door behind her, an unholy wail started up. For a few seconds, three-year-old Benji had forgotten his tantrum in his shock that his mother had turned her back on him, walked out of the kitchen, and slammed the door, leaving him alone. But apparently he'd remembered his grievance.

"Shut up!" another voice called down the stairs, breaking into a squeak on the last word. "Shut up, shut up, shut up!"

"Nooooooo!" Benji wailed at his brother, Jake. "Youuuuuu shut uuuuup!"

"God, Benji, quit it!" She could imagine Jake's angular body bending down the narrow staircase to shout through the railings. "You're so stupid!"

"Cat!" Thea called, hoping she could drown them out. What did she care if the damn cat didn't come in, if it got soaked and lost and run over by a car? They hadn't even named the thing. It would be one less thing for her to have to take care of.

Benji was thumping something, or maybe hammering his heels against the kitchen floor. Jake echoed the sound with his feet running back upstairs, no doubt to jam his earbuds into his head so he could tell the truth later when he said he couldn't hear her. Thea put one hand on the peeling porch post, which moved a little, and leaned farther out into the rain.

Now she really was Audrey Hepburn, crying and yelling at the end of *Breakfast at Tiffany's*. If Audrey had had Thea's dull brown hair, awkward height, and exhausted, dark eyes, that is. And if she'd had two boys and a useless ex who'd left them all with no warning, left *her* with nothing but what she'd scrounged and kept for herself for fifteen years. Which, from this end of a leaning porch at the wrong end of this Boston suburb, didn't look like a whole hell of a lot.

She scrunched her hand into a fist as Benji's yelling passed beyond misery and into anger. He was probably rubbing his head into the macaroni and cheese he'd just thrown on the floor. Which she would now have to clean up. Benji *and* the floor.

Dammit, this was not how her life was supposed to go! She was the smart one! She was going to beat them all! All her teachers had said so. So how did she end up with two kids and a crappy job and–

"Mooooommmmm!" Benji's voice had transcended anger; now it was hitting her where it really hurt: her heart. He sounded lost and pathetic, his sobs body-shaking to both of them. Thea knew how he felt.

She turned back to the house. As she opened the back door, a black streak of matted fur dashed past her into the house, smearing a wet line along her calf. But Benji was crying too hard to touch the cat as it went past.

Thea sat down on the floor, picked Benji up, and deposited him in her lap.

"Okay, buddy," she murmured, wrapping him up as tight as she could in her arms, mac and cheese be damned. His hot, wet face leaned into her chest, and she felt a juddering sigh escape him. "It's okay."

"I want Daddy," he said.

Thea squeezed her eyes shut, more of her own tears falling down her cheeks. "I know, sweetie."

Jake didn't say these things. He didn't ask for his father. He knew Gabriel wasn't coming back, and that broke Thea's spirit more than Benji's endless hoping.

They'd been like this for a month: the shock of Gabe's final voicemail, sent from his mother's home in Ireland because he was too chicken to call her until he was well out of reach. The three of them held in this limbo, waiting for something to happen, for something to get better.

Benji's head got heavier against her, his sobs subsiding into gulps. She loved him fiercely, and her love for Jake bordered on obsession. He suffered more, and would suffer more, from his father's desertion. Thea sighed, her fists clenching on Benji's back.

This has to stop. We have to change. I have to change.

The solution came to her between one heartbeat and the next. As soon as her mind formed the words, she felt the change in her. A thrill of energy that wasn't anger or fear or panic. She pulled Benji away from her so he was facing her, and began wiping his wet cheeks. His birthmark, which spread down his cheek and would probably need surgery one day, was even darker against his red face.

"Ben-ben," she said, giving him a big smile that made his eyes widen, "Mommy's going back to school."

♦

Liam McConnell stood in the vestry of St. Barnabas's church, running his hand over his close-shaven chin and feeling at once sick and elated. His father, next to him, was dressed in the same morning suit as Liam but with a more subdued waistcoat—Avery had put Liam in a lavender vest because it and ivory were her colors. He had a suspicion the purple clashed with his hair, but he wasn't about to say anything.

"I don't have any great speech for you," his father said. Like Liam, Pat McConnell had red hair, but his had turned white over the last few years. Dad always said he'd gotten it watching his only son swan off to college when he had a perfectly good job waiting for him at home.

"You don't need a speech, Dad." They didn't see eye to eye on much, but today Liam loved everyone. He had exactly what he wanted: Avery, a career in teaching despite his dad's best efforts, and a house that would pretty soon be worthy of his new wife. A future doing what he loved, with the woman he loved by his side. "I just hope I'm as happy as you and Mom."

His father scrubbed his chin the same way Liam did. "What your mom and I have doesn't come along very often."

Huh. But Liam was sure his dad didn't mean that the way it had sounded. "I know it's a lot of work, keeping a marriage going."

"You got that right. And your Avery here, she's used to the finer things." Dad waved a hand at their boutonnieres, which were sharply sculpted calla lilies in a darker purple than Liam's waistcoat.

Liam ignored the uncertainty in his voice and the implied criticism of his fiancée's style. He was more a wildflowers and straw kind of guy, but wasn't every man? "She's the same as me, Dad. We'll be working for those things together. She knows two teachers' salaries won't stretch to fancy cars or exotic vacations. We talked about it."

Pat grunted. "Good. Well, I hope you're right, son. 'Course, if you'd stayed with the business, you'd have—"

"Dad." Liam scrubbed his chin again. "Not today, okay?"

His chin was cold. And it *itched.* But Avery had asked him to shave his beard, just for today.

"You don't like the beard?" he'd replied. "You could have said something sooner!" They'd been together for three years.

"I love you, hon, and the beard is... well, part of you, I guess, but I just thought for the wedding you could, you know, be kind of a little... groomed."

It wasn't like you could nest birds in his beard; he kept it cut pretty close. But if it was what she wanted for the wedding, who cared? He only had to look at Avery's perfect Cupid-bow mouth and big blue eyes, fringed as they always were by impossibly long, dark lashes, and he knew he'd give her anything she wanted.

Because she was giving him everything he wanted.

Chapter 1

Two years later

The first class in Thea's master's in education program covered language immersion theory. Of which she had exactly zero experience. Couldn't they have started with something more comprehensible like, maybe, neuroscience?

She clutched her hobo bag to her more tightly and walked into the class. About twenty other students were already here. They were sitting, she always thought, according to their intensity of will to pass the class. The front row people with their laptops out already, fingers at the ready. She avoided them; she couldn't stand the sound of other people's fingers on keyboards. The back row held kids who planned on teaching relative arts. Counter-cultural symbols, nose rings, giant holes in ears—boy, were they going to regret those in a few years—tattoos, etc. Much too cool for school. For Thea, anyway.

But in the middle sat a group she was content to dump her bag next to. She'd expected a room full of students fresh out of their bachelor's degrees, so she was pleasantly surprised to see that at least three of the people on her row were her age or older. A tall, pale woman with thick ginger curls had a richly decorated notebook in her hands. A purple hijab framed the face of another woman with tawny skin; her paper was in a binder, and she had four different colored pens in front of her. Two men sat next to each other; their blond hair was short and spiky, and they each wore horn-rimmed glasses, one in a jade green, one in royal blue. They looked like The Proclaimers, except that when she looked more closely, they weren't twins. They carried ordinary spiral-bound notebooks, like the one Thea used, but had pulled out beautiful jewellike fountain pens.

She sat down, nodding politely at everyone. The woman in the hijab gave her a bigger smile than everyone else, and somehow Thea knew that they recognized each other as mothers. A coloring book sticking out of the woman's bulging bag at her feet confirmed it.

"Zahra," the woman said, holding out a hand.

"Thea," she said, shaking hands.

"I'm Chloe," said the redhead. She was very tall, taller even than Thea.

"Nice to meet you," Thea said. "Are you already a teacher?"

"Nope," Chloe said. "Hey, did either of you bring a granola bar or something? I skipped lunch, and this damn class happens right through dinner."

Thea and Zahra both opened their bags. Under the layers of tissue packets, wet wipes, travel-size tubes of ibuprofen, Band-Aids, and hairbrushes, they pulled out snacks: goldfish from Zahra, a protein bar from Thea.

They smiled at each other. "How many kids do you have?" Zahra asked.

"Two. Fifteen and five and a half. He wouldn't want me to forget the half. You?"

"Three. Ten, eight, and one." The two women exchanged exhausted looks.

"God, thanks," Chloe said, chowing down on the protein bar. "Yay for GMO soy," she added with her mouth full.

"Do you have any children?" Thea asked politely. They sat at their table, and she began shoving the rest of her junk back into her bag. The answer to her question seemed obvious, given Chloe's lack of purse, but still.

"No. I'm way too high-maintenance. Couldn't make a kid suffer having me for a mom."

Thea was about to introduce herself to The Proclaimers when another man came over to them. She couldn't determine his age; his eyes looked young, but he had a beard that aged him. Against his dark-red hair and beard, his eyes were a piercing blue. She was glad he kept his beard trimmed; she wouldn't have to spend all her time wondering if he'd missed bits of fried egg in there.

He was tall, though probably not any more so than her five-ten.

Finely carved biceps were highlighted by his T-shirt, which had the name of a plumbing company on it: Pat the Plumber. Was it a hipster thing?

He caught her looking at him. Thea gave him a small smile. He scowled.

Ookay, then.

Being offended at her looking at him—okay, checking him out; he had biceps all the way to next Tuesday, for heaven's sake—didn't stop him from taking a seat in their group, next to Chloe. *Figures. Redhead for redhead.*

"Hi!" Chloe said.

"Hello," he said, his mouth a thin line in his beard, and reached down into his bag. He had a dark-green backpack with a BU patch sewn on it, from which he pulled a notebook like Thea's.

You can stop looking now, T.

Chloe lifted her eyebrows at Thea over his head. Thea shrugged one shoulder a fraction but held back a laugh when he straightened and looked right at her again. At her, not Chloe.

You're just in his line of sight. Don't get any ideas.

The professor was at the front of the class already, plugging in her laptop and checking the projector. She was of medium height and wore a long skirt with a long tunic over it and a long, diaphanous scarf draped over that. She looked like a floating rectangle, but her smile was genuine as she took everyone in.

"Good evening!" she said in a carrying voice. Thea noted the teacher's tone and figured she'd better learn how to do that. Then again, she was hella good at yelling at her boys. That'd probably do it.

"Welcome to the next year of your life," the woman continued with a sardonic smile. "I'm Jeannie Havilland. Our main focus in this degree is to get you to become *teachers*—better teachers than anyone getting their certificate right out of college." She smiled at them. The bearded man next to Thea seemed to be bridling a little. "That's not to say that you haven't been excellent teachers, those of you who did just that. But you're here because you want to be better—possibly to move into supervisory positions."

Pat the Plumber relaxed. Okay, so that was his career track. But what had brought the rest of them here?

The class was more than three hours long, so they took a break halfway through. The crack of chairbacks against tables accompanied groans as everyone stretched cramped legs and hands.

"Thank God," Zahra said. "I gotta pee so bad I can't even look at a water fountain."

"What do you want to teach?" she asked Thea and Chloe as they came back from the bathroom. The men were coming back to the table too, the twins and Pat the Plumber in some intense discussion that paused them on the way.

"High school English," Thea answered. "I also minored in film studies, so I'd like to find a school that offers that."

"Where did you get your bachelor's?"

"Right here." Thea smiled. "The ink's still drying on my diploma."

"Really?" Zahra looked impressed. "With two kids?"

"*Because of* two kids. Because I'd be in the funny farm if I'd sat around waiting one minute longer for my ex to come back."

She stopped. They were all looking at her, even Beardy McPlumber, whose gaze pinned her to her seat worse than any of them. Thea cleared her throat and tucked a nonexistent piece of hair behind her ear. "Uh. TMI. Sorry." She really had to get out and talk to adults more.

"That's okay." Zahra gripped her hand briefly. "You go, girl." Then, in a gesture that made Thea love her even more, she took the spotlight off her by saying, "Chloe? What do you want to teach?"

"Special needs," Chloe said. "The neuro-spicies? My wife's nephew is autistic and it's tough to watch him negotiate the world. Then these poor kids with ADHD who can't sit still, and then they take away recess so they're even itchier..."

Professor Havilland joined them. "That's great that you're focusing on special needs kids," she said. "Though you're all going to have to know your psychology class back and front. The jury's still out on mainstreaming versus giving the kids room to study their own way–"

They talked for a little while longer. Thea and Zahra showed each other pictures of their kids, and Beardy and the twins finished their argument and sat down. Beardy pulled out an apple; the twins sucked on what looked like iced coffee.

Beardy ate that apple as if it had done him a personal injustice. She'd never seen someone devour a piece of fruit so fast. Four bites, tops.

He caught her staring. *Those eyes, though.*

Well, since he wasn't looking at her for any other reason than that she was looking at him, Thea felt brave enough to say, "Hungry?" and pulled out another protein bar.

He looked at it, at her, and then took it. He had broad hands and heavy forearms. Not that she was noticing. "Thanks," he grunted.

Wow. One word. She felt so honored.

"It's just a two-bite brownie for you, probably," she said in the voice she used to tease Jake out of a funk. As she said it, he ripped off the wrapper and bit into at least a third of the bar. "Three bites, then," she said to herself, though loud enough for him to hear.

He swallowed, which must have hurt–had he even chewed?–and grimaced. "Thank you," he said, "again." Then he stuck out his hand. "Liam."

"Thea," she replied, shaking his hand. It was warm–and ever so slightly sticky from the apple core.

"Crap," he said, and let go to rub his hand on his pants. Thea laughed, which helped dispel the tingle in her fingers from touching him. She wasn't sure without staring at him even harder, but she thought he might have gone a little pink above the beard.

"You're already a teacher?" she asked.

"Yep." He bit off the word the way he'd taken bites out of that apple.

She waited.

"Technically," he said, and there was a heavy weight of story behind the word.

She opened her mouth, but Professor Havilland called them all to order at that point, moving back to the front of the class. Thea reached into her bag one last time and handed Liam a wet wipe. He sheepishly took it, and she grinned at him, which for some reason made him scowl again.

Jeez. Can't even laugh at himself.

She had no more interaction with him during that class. As it ended, Thea's mind was already on how quickly she could get home and see how much ice cream Jake had let Benji eat tonight. But Zahra put her hand on her arm, stopping her from turning away from the table.

"Do you think...?" she began, biting her lip. She tried again. "Are you looking for a study partner?"

"Yes!" Thea said with enthusiasm, just as Chloe chimed in, "I sure am!" and one of the twins said, "We are. We know nothing about teaching."

Beardy McSticky Hands was hauling his backpack onto his shoulder and didn't say a word.

"Oh," Chloe said. "Let's set up a group. Can we? I don't know what the hell I'm doing. I haven't studied for about twelve years, and I was always crap at taking exams."

"But how are we going to coordinate everyone's schedules?" Thea asked.

"If it's in the evenings, I can do it," Zahra said. "My husband'll watch the kids."

"Evenings work for us," said the twins.

"And me," Chloe added.

"Well," Thea said, "Then you'd better come to my house, 'cause it's just me and the boys, and if I ask Jake to babysit his brother one more night, there'll be a full-scale rebellion."

The idea of her house didn't seem to bother anyone. She took a quick mental inventory of it, with its scuffed walls, old furniture, and general smell of boy. Then she shrugged. She wasn't going to apologize for her life anymore.

"If you all really don't mind traveling to me, let's get together next week. Just give me this week to bury the dead bodies and wash the cat and stuff like that."

♦

When everyone else had left the room, Liam dropped his backpack with a crash before sinking into a seat and lowering his forehead to the table next to it. *Damn. That is so inconvenient.*

That was a line from some movie. Avery had watched it with him. Well, she would know all about inconvenient. She'd apparently found their marriage pretty incon-freaking-venient, hadn't she?

Yeah, your marriage that you just got out of. That lost you your job. That screwed up this degree for you.

He raised his head and scrubbed his beard with one hand, looking at the door she'd left through. *Thea.* Huge, tired eyes. Long, thick, dark hair that looked too heavy for her slim neck. She'd given him a protein bar, but she was the one who looked like she could use a few meals.

And she barely looked at you. Never even looked your way when they were all talking about the study group.

He'd probably scared her off. But he'd seen the surprise on the faces of their group when she'd talked about her ex, and he sure the hell didn't want to get into his own horror story and see the same look on her face.

Luckily, one of the two guys—David, Liam thought his name was—had come up to him after the women had left and asked him if he wanted in.

No, you don't want in. You want to run as far and as fast from that woman as possible.

But he did want to take this class. He needed to understand it backward and forward before he started his next job. He was moving to an urban school where the ratio of non-native speakers was around forty percent. So anything that would help him with that would be good, right?

He banged his forehead against the table a couple more times.

His phone rang. His father. "Dad," he said into the phone.

"Liam," his father said in the same cold tone. "You'll be at Dunning Road tomorrow?"

"Of course."

"The guys will be there at seven."

"So will I, Dad." God, every conversation they'd had since he'd quit his job at the school had gone like this. Except the one after he'd left Avery, when the conversation had been Pat saying, "I told you so," and his mother hugging him and crying. That had been fun.

"Well, I know you're not used to the hours," his father said.

"Dad, I spent half my weekends working for you, even before I left Central. I know what time to get to the site."

Pat dropped the subject. Went onto another of his oldies but goldies. "Good thing you got your plumbing license, isn't it? Glad I made you get it?"

"Uh-huh." *Yeah, Dad. I'm thrilled that I had to put what I wanted on hold for five years while you scored a point.*

But Liam couldn't deny that earning money was a hell of a lot better than not earning it, and while he'd gotten another teaching job fairly quickly, it didn't start until the fall.

The money he earned from his dad wasn't going to pay for his master's, and the divorce had eaten through what he'd saved. He could just about pay for this class, the college giving him special permission to take it while he deferred the rest of his studies.

"How was class?" Pat asked after an awkward pause.

Surprising that he remembered. "Class was fine. Good." If only it weren't a crumb instead of the full master's degree he'd been hoping to start.

"All right." There was another pause. "See you tomorrow, then."

"Yep. Bye."

That was Dad. All heart.

Chapter 2

Thea was fluttering. That was the only word for it, and no matter how often she told herself to get over herself, that she didn't have to prove anything to anyone, she'd still spent all the time she'd had at home cleaning, preparing for the study group. Putting on a Cary Grant movie while she cleaned had helped her relax, but she'd kept stopping to watch and so she had to rush the last half hour.

The early June day had been warm, and she'd opened all the windows to try to make the house seem bigger. Jake and Benji were fed and in their rooms—at least, she hoped Jake was; she was afraid to check—Audrey's litter box was fresh, and the store-bought cookies were warming in the oven. Not that Thea was pretending she'd baked, although she'd shoved the box deep into the recycling bin. Of course not. She just liked warm cookies.

Chloe was first. She swept in, seeming to take up a lot of space in Thea's small living room with her big hair and her height, and hugged Thea. "Smells amazing in here," she said.

The twins—Seth and David, though she'd forgotten which was which—arrived next. They'd brought their own iced coffee but were happy to have a cookie with it. Zahra had already texted that she was going to be late, so they started without her.

But the doorbell rang sooner than Thea had expected. "Oh, Zahra's husband must have gotten home early," she said to the others and opened the door.

It was Beardy—uh, Liam.

She hadn't thought he was coming. When the group had swapped phone numbers, he hadn't said anything, hadn't gotten his phone out. So she'd assumed he didn't need a group. He was the only one who was already a teacher; he probably knew this stuff.

Also, having him sneak up on her like this, as it were, she was unprepared for his height. He was an inch or so taller than her in her bare feet, and standing in front of him, she became aware of the breadth of him.

It was probably that detail that made her want to adjust her hair, like she was messy and not put together. Not his bicep, thrown into full glory by his hand looped into his backpack strap.

"Wrong night?" he asked in his cranky growl when she didn't move.

"Oh, hey, Liam!" one of the twins said, hearing his voice. "You found us, then." The twin stood to see Liam in the doorway. Since Thea was still blocking Liam's way, the twin squinted at her through his blue frames and added, "He was invited, too, right?"

Liam was still looking at her. "No! I mean yes!" Thea said. "Of course. Come in!" Dammit, she sounded breathy. Out of control. *Get it together.*

The others welcomed him loudly. Thea went to get another chair from the kitchen table and waved him to the one remaining comfortable seat. But he took the hard chair from her, shaking his head, and before she could protest, he was seated by the kitchen entrance with his ankle over one knee, looking completely at home.

Since he hardly said a word at first, her stress level lowered and the group got going. They worked well together, with an easy camaraderie she had never had with her fellow undergraduates—perhaps because she'd been so much older than them. But she did wonder why Liam was here if he wasn't going to say anything.

About half an hour into the session, though, he suddenly growled, "Dammit, I can't stand it anymore," stood up, and marched into the kitchen.

Everyone stared after him. He had been so still during the meeting unless they asked him a specific question that they'd forgotten he was there. And now he'd changed the dynamic of the room simply by rising with such speed and almost storming out.

Thea followed him. "What?"

"This damn faucet." He was already on his knees in front of the sink, opening the cabinet and throwing things onto the floor. Old scrubbing sponges, a dishwashing brush coated with soap from a leaking detergent bottle, rubber gloves that had perished and lost a few fingers when he pulled them off the sticky cabinet floor: all appeared at Thea's feet. She felt her cheeks flush. Was that how bad it had gotten under there?

"Hey!" she exclaimed, catching a can of Comet before it spilled. "Do you have to be so—"

He didn't even seem to have heard her. "Doesn't that drip bother you? Bothers the crap out of me, and I've only been here twenty minutes."

She dropped to her knees herself, gathering up the items as if she could hide all of them from her guests. She looked behind her. Yep, they were all in the doorway, gazing at her and Liam as he got farther into the cabinet.

"Woah, Thea," Chloe said. "You didn't say you were going to put on a show. Nice butt, Liam."

He didn't answer. Thea hoped he at least had the grace to blush. An old drain plug, stuck inside a plastic tub that might once have held deodorizer, rolled out of his hands and came to rest at the feet of the crowd at the door. *See, I did at least try and make it a little less stinky in there.*

The inventory of Thea's messy life finally stopped. Liam grunted with satisfaction and turned the tap to stop the water supply. The dripping, which had been magnified by the cookie tray she had thrown into the sink earlier, ceased. Liam got up, hit his head on the cabinet frame, cursed, and rubbed his head as he examined the faucet. His hand still on the back of his head, he turned to Thea.

"Got a wrench?" he growled.

"Yeah," she snapped back. "You want me to finish what that cabinet started?"

His eyebrows lowered, eyes turning dark. "You want this fixed or not?"

She folded her arms in defense, but he had her and he knew it. She ignored their audience and stomped out of the back door.

Even though he hadn't lived with them for two years, most of

Gabriel's things were still at her house. When he'd so unceremoniously left them, he'd left all his tools behind. They were in the basement, which was dank and smelly and leaked every time it rained. Thea had thrown all his crap on the floor one day and left them there. She still had to go down to use the laundry, but she went nowhere near the table Gabe had laughably called his workshop.

She threw open the double door entry from outside and steeled herself against the spiderwebs and cave crickets. It was dark in there, and the light from two bare bulbs slung from the ceiling was pitiful.

Sure enough, inside the ancient space, lined with nineteenth-century stone and badly clad pipes, a canvas bag of tools sat rotting in a puddle in the corner. "Ew," she said, her voice deadened in the damp air.

"Thea?" Zahra's voice came through the floorboards right above her.

"Yeah," she called back, lifting her head—but still watching for spiderwebs. "Be right there."

She approached the tool bag as if a snake were about to leap out of it, but it just sat there, dark and pathetic and ignored. She used the mere tips of her finger and thumb to open the flaps. They were slimy and moldy, and her fingers were instantly filthy. "Ew," she said again. *Oh, and for the eight hundred and ninety-sixth time, fuck Gabriel.*

The tools might have been sodden, and some of the rubber coatings might have turned to powder in her revolted hands, but they were made of steel and there was still a faint sheen to them. Thea saw something with a wrench at one end and a round hole at the other sitting at the top of the pile. Gratefully, she pulled it out, again with finger and thumb, and hightailed it out of the basement.

With a certain pride, she held it out to Liam, who was now standing in front of the sink. His audience hadn't moved.

His mouth was a thin line. "What am I supposed to do with that?"

She pulled back her hand. Now he was really starting to piss her off. "Uh, fix my faucet? Or I can think of another place you can put it."

Suddenly, he was right in front of her, so close she had to look up to see his eyes and smell the mixture of whatever deodorant he used and the bleach he'd dislodged in the cabinet. *Damn, those eyes.*

They bored into her as if searching for something in her own. A tingle began somewhere behind Thea's navel. She might have parted her lips.

"Do you think," he said, his breath brushing her cheek, "that you could go find me an *adjustable* wrench? One that has some hope of fitting your antiquated pipes?"

Her new friends were watching them, crowded into the doorway like the Keystone Kops, Seth and David somehow managing to appear one head on top of the other. And the wrench sat heavy in her hand, obviously too big and heavy to do any good against a kitchen faucet.

Thea burned with humiliation. She'd never wanted to be wrong-footed by a man again, and here she was, the first time she'd let one in the house since Gabe. Not that Liam was here to... Not that she was thinking of...

Shit. She turned around and climbed back down to the basement.

Cursing Gabe, Liam, and the perished pair of rubber gloves upstairs, she dug deeper into the bag, found an adjustable wrench, and took it back to Liam. Everyone except Chloe had gone back into the living room. Thea shoved the wrench at him and pushed past Chloe, who barely moved, her gaze riveted by Liam's fine jean-clad butt again sticking out of the cupboard.

"Aren't you gay?" Thea said from behind her.

"I can recognize a work of art when I see one, can't I?" Chloe said. Thea pulled her away from the door, but not before they heard Liam give a snort of laughter that echoed a little in the cabinet. *Hey, look at that. A sense of humor after all.*

"Come on, I need to outline this paper," Zahra said—bless her understanding heart—and the four of them went back to work.

In a few minutes, Liam, wiping his hands with paper towels, came in, said, "I'll be back," which made Chloe almost spit out her soda, and swept out of the house.

"'Come with me if you want to live,'" Chloe said.

"Uh-huh," Zahra said.

"Excuse me," Thea said to avoid her knowing look. "I have to go put Benji to bed."

Benji had been remarkably self-sufficient tonight. Putting a movie on his tablet had held him in one place. Jake had been doing his homework, of course. She hoped to God.

Now that he had his mother's attention, however, Benji was not about to relinquish it. "Come *on*, Ben-ben," she growled as he changed his mind for the fourth time on which pajamas to wear. Then he whined and groused like a two-year-old when she tried to help him brush his teeth, and she told him so. So he grizzled and whined and wouldn't pick out a book. Thea finally got pissed and said, through gritted teeth and in a quiet but furious tone, "Fine! I love you! Go to sleep!" and she left the room.

Benji started crying louder. *Goddammit. This whole fucking thing is to help me be a better mother, and the first time I have people over, I screw that up, too.*

"Mom?" Jake was right behind her.

"What?" she snapped. Would her fellow students think she was a terrible mother if she opened a bottle of wine?

Jake took her tone in stride. Which made her heart sink as well. *God, all I've done for years is bitch at these kids. They didn't ask for the dad they got.*

"Sorry," she said in her least crazy-mom voice. "What is it, hon?"

Jake looked so much like his father when he got that shifty look in his eye. "Um, a few of the guys are meeting up for pizza. Can I go?"

"Pizza? You just had dinner!"

"Two hours ago."

"And it's a school night."

Jake looked up at the hallway ceiling. "It's still early. 'Sides, there're only like three weeks left of school."

"Nice try, big guy. No going out on a school night. Go take out the garbage and bring Audrey in. Benji," she raised her voice to cut through the closed door and his crying. "Quit it."

"Jeez." Jake pushed past her and went down the stairs.

In the kitchen, he looked at the mess Liam had left on the floor. "I got to clean this up, too?" he said in an aggrieved voice.

"Crap. I forgot about that," Thea said. "No, just do the regular garbage." Her sister, Cat, would have told him to throw this stuff out too. But there was Comet powder on the floor, and she didn't have any other rubber gloves. *And why do I always have Cat's voice in my head, judging my every tiny decision?* "But come say hello, first."

Jake reluctantly turned to the living room, a hand going to his hair, to make sure it was spiky enough, she assumed. He stopped on the threshold, blinking at all the new people.

Thea squeezed past him. "Jake, this is everyone. Everyone, my eldest son, Jacob."

She couldn't help the pride that sat in her voice when she looked at him. He might look just like Gabe, but that meant he was beautiful.

Everyone chorused a hello and then, seeing how awkward Jake was feeling, politely looked away from him.

Liam walked in the front door at that moment, carrying a paper bag from the hardware store. He assessed Jake coolly.

"Donaghy," Liam said unexpectedly. "Freshman basketball?"

Jake looked as though he'd just seen the headlights of the car that was going to kill him. "Mr. McConnell?"

"Uh-huh. How are you?"

"Umm, I'm good."

"One of your teachers?" Chloe asked. Thea was so surprised that Jake knew Liam, her voice was gone. She should have asked him that.

Liam replied first. "I coached varsity. At Central."

That was Jake's school. Jake's look of horror had rearranged itself into something Thea couldn't name. "But you quit," he said.

Liam looked as if the conversation had gone to a place he really didn't want it to. "I left, Jacob. Big difference. You trying out for JV this year?"

"Uh…" Last season, Jake had told her that he wanted to quit. That had been a fun conversation. "Maybe."

"You should. You're good. Good layups."

Jake flushed and looked everywhere but at Liam. Thea giggled, and she didn't get to do that very often these days. A teacher! In his own home! Talking to him like a normal person! No wonder Jake looked so confused.

"Um, okay," Jake finally said, and nearly fell over his feet getting back into the kitchen.

Thea grinned at Liam. "You must have been a pretty terrifying coach."

Did he go that adorable shade of pink again? It clashed with his hair and beard. But he shrugged. "To a fifteen-year-old, anyone who tells you what to do is a tyrant."

"Or a mother," Thea added.

"Same thing," Zahra said.

"So, hey, Thea," Chloe said. "You got any wine?"

Liam walked past them without saying any more and began banging around in the kitchen. It sounded as though he was pounding the leaky faucet into submission. Thea followed him to find the wine. Jake had pulled the garbage bag out of the bin and hustled out the back door so fast it had to be a record. Benji had quieted down, and the kitchen was strangely peaceful as she opened the bottle—next time she was going to buy wine that cost more than eight bucks—and Liam assumed the position under the sink. Then Jake banged back through the door, carrying a disgruntled Audrey, whose expression he echoed. He looked warily at Liam's legs, then at her, and took the cat upstairs with him before Thea could ask him to do anything else.

Figuring silence was the way to go, she left Liam to it and went back to the others.

The wine wasn't bad and gave them all fresh heart to keep going with the assignment. An hour later, Zahra stood, stretching. "I'm sorry, I have to go. Gotta get lunches made for tomorrow."

"And I have to drive back to the city," Chloe said, standing with her. Seth and David also took their cue to leave. They hovered for a moment, looking uncertainly into the kitchen, where the water was now running.

"Thanks, guys," Thea said. "I learned so much more today than I ever could on my own." *And had an entire conversation with grown-ups who aren't related to me.* Her ridiculous throat closed up.

"Me too!" Chloe exclaimed. "Same time next week?"

"And we'll see you in class." said Zahra, hugging her. Zahra, in particular, was a woman Thea wanted to get to know.

"You want me to stay a minute?" Zahra said low into Thea's ear. She loosened the hug and gave a side-eye to the kitchen.

"No, I'll be fine," Thea said. Liam was confusing and probably a pain in the butt, but he wasn't dangerous.

Unless you count that rocking ass and the way he looked at you before.

"Holy shit!" she heard from the street. And five seconds later, Seth and David had walked back through the house into the kitchen.

"Is that your truck?" Seth asked Liam.

"Uh-huh," she heard.

She looked out the window as Seth said, "Damn, dude, you should have told us!"

At the curb outside Thea's house sat a 1950s, powder-blue behemoth of a pickup truck, with a hood like something out of *Rebel Without a Cause.*

"When would I bring her up?" Liam's voice said. "You like old cars?"

"Uh, yah? Have you seen Seth's hands?" David said. "He's the mechanic, I'm the accountant. Erikson's? On Route 9? It's our dad's garage."

"What have you got under the hood?" Seth interrupted. Liam replied with a series of words Thea knew were English but made zero sense to her. The twins seemed impressed, judging by their low whistles, and Seth said, "That was what I heard. I thought it was just a truck going past with a sweet rumble, but it was you and that 'Vette engine."

Thea looked out of the window again. The truck was nothing like a Corvette.

The twins came out of the kitchen and said goodbye to her again. Then they stood in front of the blue monster—actually, it was kind of adorable, like a big blue baby—and shook their heads a couple of times before getting in their own much more ordinary car and driving away.

Well, damn if she was going to go into the kitchen until Liam came out. She arranged the plates and wineglasses in the middle of the coffee table and opened her textbook, pretending to read.

He finally reappeared in the doorway. His jeans were wet, and there were smudges of dirt on his pale-green T-shirt. Which, she noticed, he filled out quite nicely.

"Um," Thea said. "Thanks?"

He nodded and grunted. "Waste of water." Obviously whatever joviality he'd had with the twins wasn't about to extend to her.

Thea bristled. "I know. I meant to get to it—"

"Not with the state those tools were in."

Was that smudge on his T-shirt... mold? "Oh my God, did you go in the basement?"

He shrugged. "You should treat your tools better."

Thea went into the kitchen, Liam making room for her. All Gabe's tools were cleaned off and laid out on a kitchen towel on the table. The floor was empty of all the detritus from the cabinet. The last of the June evening sun shone through the back door and glinted off the clean tools and shiny sink.

The first thing Thea felt, and the scariest, was relief. Someone had helped. Someone had done something she couldn't do. She hadn't been alone. For this moment, the millstone that was this house was not her burden alone.

Then, fast on the heels of that feeling, was terror. She backed up until she hit the refrigerator, knocking off a few magnets. "I'm not interested," she said past a tight throat.

Liam, who had folded his arms while she examined his handiwork, unfolded them again. "What?"

"I—I'm not interested. In a relationship." Relying on someone, the way she had Gabriel? Aw, hell no. She wished Liam had left the damn faucet alone.

He shook his head, moving away from the table he'd leaned against. "Jesus, woman, I just fixed the faucet. Don't flatter yourself."

Thea's cheeks burned. "S—Sorry," she stammered. "I just... want to be clear."

"I'm clear," he said, spreading his hands.

"Thank you," she said again. "For the faucet."

He rolled his eyes and went out to the living room. Picking up his backpack, he said, "Think you can let me come back to the group next week without worrying I'll jump you?"

Her cheeks actually hurt, she was blushing so hard. "Yes, fine. Goodbye."

She was too embarrassed to watch him leave, but when she heard a grumbling roar from the street, it was instinct that drew her eyes back to the truck. The street echoed with its vibrating growl. It did sound like a Corvette.

Thea glimpsed Liam's outline through the window as he paused for a second, perhaps to let the engine get over the shock it seemed to be in at being inside a seventy-year-old truck. Then he shifted into gear and the behemoth pulled away, without the plume of black smoke she would have assumed that kind of antique would produce.

A teacher with a penchant for old cars. Or a plumber who wanted to get out of the business. Correction: who had gotten out of the business but was back in it again. Thea didn't know what to make of him.

When she'd finished cleaning and went upstairs to bed, she was surprised to see Jake open his door. "Mom."

Her mind immediately raced through all the things he might have told her about his schedule the next day that she'd probably forgotten. "Yes?" she said warily.

"That Mr. McConnell," Jake said, not meeting her eyes. "I just thought... thought you should know what he did."

Oh, God. What? What did that good-looking lumberjack plumber/ teacher/motorhead do? A hundred scenarios flew through her mind, all of them involving smitten schoolgirls.

"He quit his job right in the middle of the school year. Left Mrs. McConnell—she's a teacher there too—and just quit. He was supposed to coach basketball camp this summer. The team's pretty pissed. And Mrs. McConnell always looks kind of... sad, and she yells at the students now. Well, kind of."

Okay, phew. No schoolgirls. "He didn't give any reason? That you know of?"

Jake shook his head.

"Well." Thea pondered the news. "He must have had a reason." But he seemed cranky enough to just drop everything if it pissed him off enough. "Shame about the basketball team."

"Yeah. Mr. Price is going to run it now, and he's not nearly as good as Mr. McConnell was."

She cut her eyes sharply to him. "Not that you care, right? Because 'you don't care about basketball anymore.' Right?"

Jake rolled his eyes at her. "Right." And he went back into his room and closed the door.

"Good night!" Thea called.

A sound came from within that might have been *good night*. Thea put her hand on the door, said, "I love you," in a voice low enough not to carry, and went to her own room. She'd given Jake the master and Benji the next largest room, so hers was barely big enough for a double bed and a chest of drawers. She kept her hanging clothes in Jake's room, which had the largest closet. The house had only the bathroom downstairs for the three of them.

Thea fought her way past the drying rack with her bras hanging over it and climbed over to her corner of the bed. Audrey had already taken over the other three-quarters. Thea had to change in bed because there was no floor space for her to do it.

The house was a mess, yes. Still, it was her mess, and she didn't appreciate smug, redheaded ex-teachers coming in and pointing out what a mess it was.

She pulled the cat to her and buried her face in its back. "Maybe he was so horrified he won't come back next week," she told Audrey. "Maybe he can go back to ignoring me in class again."

Audrey yawned and rolled onto her back, her front paw batting Thea's nose. Thea had gotten used to going to sleep like this.

Those eyes, though.

Chapter 3

The toilet was unwieldy and wanted to drip down his jeans, but Liam corralled it with a garbage bag and carried it down the stairs. Strictly speaking, this was the apprentices' job, but Liam wasn't going to give anyone a chance to suggest he was sticking his nose up at his former profession.

Outside the house, he heaved the toilet into the dumpster, enjoying as always the satisfying *crunch* of porcelain disintegrating against the other debris, then began to walk back to tackle the floor tile. But the name on the side of a van caught his eye, so he changed direction.

The driver was on his phone but finished up as Liam approached. "Liam, my son," the man said, sticking a hand out of the open window to shake. "I saw your truck, knew you'd be around here somewhere." He nodded at the powder-blue Chevy, which stuck out like a fairy among beetles in the row of workers' trucks at the edge of the property. "How the hell are ya?"

"Good, Sean, how are you?"

"Booming, thank you, bloody booming. All these flippers buying up dumps and getting in over their heads renovating. We get paid more to fix it than if they'd had us in to do it in the first place!" Sean O'Brien cackled, his ruddy face open and his eyes sparkling.

"Good to hear it." Sean, who, if Liam wanted to guess, was about fifteen years older than him, was the general contractor on this house. Liam's father and Sean had done a lot of business together over the years. Liam had overheard Sean tell his clients that they could trust Pat's work, and when Sean had built his own house, Pat and Liam had done the plumbing work together.

"What are you doing here? I thought you'd left the business."

"Yeah." Liam had an answer ready. With the right amount of self-deprecating shrug, he put a hand to the back of his neck. "Between jobs, let's say. My dad's taken me on temporarily."

"Well, it's good to see you. Never thought you'd set foot back on a jobsite." Sean looked up at the house. "Look at this poor darlin'," he said in his Irish brogue. The house was a Victorian that had been manhandled so many times over the decades, there was now nothing for it but a complete gut job. Sean loved houses and talked about them as though they were his children.

"You'll fix it," Liam said.

"Yeah, but we lost most of the original moldings and the chimney can't be saved and all that hardwood got termites." Sean shook his head. "It's a bloody shame."

"Speaking of which," Liam said, "I have to get back in there and rip up century-old tile."

"All right, son, I'll let you go." They shook hands again. "I had a good look before we started the demo, but if you see anything worth saving, let me know, won't you?" Sean kept a salvage yard as well as his contracting business.

"If I don't steal it myself." Liam grinned. He'd renovated a similar old house by making good use of the salvage yard.

Except you'll probably have to sell the house now.

The smile slid off his face before he could stop it. "Y'all right, son?" Sean said.

"Yeah, sure." Liam hiked some sort of cheerful expression on his face and waved goodbye, turning his back so Sean wouldn't see how fake it was.

Liam lived on the middle floor of a Gothic Revival house that had been so badly renovated before he got there, the town had condemned it. He'd bought it with money he'd earned working for his father and called in every favor he'd gained from five years of friendship with other contractors to fix it up. He could now put a price on those years he'd promised to his father—the cost of a complete replumbing of a hundred-and-fifty-year-old house. The pointed gables and stained-glass windows had been saved. He'd found wide-plank flooring and old bricks to revive the place inside and out and had paid a local millworker to recreate the elaborate trim in the eaves.

Another thing Avery had taken from him, that house and the promise he'd felt in it. Once, he'd thought he had everything he wanted. Now, he just wanted not to lose anything else.

♦

Thea's house, the second week, and everyone came back. This time they brought food and a bottle of wine. Zahra brought sparkling apple cider.

Even Liam came back, though he arrived after everyone else, fidgeted for fifteen minutes, and then went into the kitchen. Thea heard the bathroom door close.

Ten seconds later he was back. "Your toilet's running too? Do you know how much money you're literally flushing away?" Before she could answer, he added, "And what's with that window? Your heating bill must be through the roof. Literally." And he stomped out to his truck where, they saw from the front window—to which, yes, they'd all rushed—he pulled two toolboxes and a toolbelt out of the back seat and went around the back of the house. Judging by the cording on his arms, the toolboxes were heavy.

Not that Thea was interested.

"That man is going to fail his exams," Chloe commented.

"He already knows all this," Zahra said. "Haven't you noticed?"

"Don't tell him that," Seth begged. "He's our best resource for real-life classroom stories." He held up the wine bottle to Thea. "Pretty obvious why he's here, you ask me."

"Nuh-uh," Thea said, who was blushing again. "You think I like having all my crappy housekeeping skills pointed out? And I told him to quit it." At least, she thought she had. Yet he'd brought his own tools this time. "He's just an interfering, grumpy old—well, young—hipster, and we can do without him."

"I can't," Chloe interjected. "I think I might go watch him bend over the toilet."

"Gross," David said.

"You know what I mean."

"Stay where you are!" Thea commanded in a hiss. "No one is going to ogle him in my bathroom."

Chloe leaned back in her chair as if it were a throne. Her Titian curls helped her general impression of a queen. "Okay, then, Miss I'm Not Interested, go tell him to stop."

Thea closed her eyes. "Fine. I can't do that. I've been fighting that toilet for six years. And I *did* try to fix it myself," she added, begging them with her eyes. "I just always seemed to buy the wrong size O-ring or something."

Chloe spat wine all over the coffee table.

"It's a legitimate term," Seth reminded her.

"I know!" she choked. "Sorry! My innuendo meter is very sensitive!"

"Let's get back to work," Zahra said, handing her a napkin.

◆

Liam joined them again half an hour later. He'd changed his T-shirt and added a plaid button-down over it. Hanging open. Of course.

"You know," David said, "you want to play Joe the Plumber, the bathroom at the garage could use an overhaul."

Liam sat down and pointed at the bottle of wine, raising his eyebrows in question to Thea. She poured him a glass and didn't, did not, watch his big hand grip the delicate stem.

"Not playing," he said. "My dad's Pat the Plumber."

Everyone except Chloe, who lived in the city, said, "Ohhhhh." The vans were common in the area.

Thea looked at Liam. The man would not stay in the boxes she set up for him. First, he was some hipster, bearded kid who thought he could teach. Then he was a selfish quitter who'd leave his team in the lurch. Then he was a frustrating know-it-all plumber who made her feel like crap about her house. Or a macho pain in the ass who drove around in a baby-blue truck. Or a sweet man who knew that she was alone and wanted to help. Or a source of serious discomfort every time he looked at her with those old-soul blue eyes.

They weren't looking at her now. "So why are you a teacher?" she demanded. Why wouldn't he stay put?

"Because I didn't want to be a plumber," he said simply.

"Duh," Chloe said.

"Okay," Thea conceded. "So why the master's? You already know how to teach."

He scowled at her in a way she was becoming quite used to. "I want the master's degree to get a raise, okay? And maybe to go into administration one day. Happy now?"

"But you know how to… to plumb," she said.

"It was the only way my dad would let me go to college," he said. "Now can we get back to work. *Please?*"

They turned back to their laptops, but Thea wasn't done. "You said you quit at Jake's school. Sorry," she added when he opened his mouth, "left. Do you have another job lined up?"

He gave a dramatic sigh and folded his arms. "Yes. But it's in a school with a high percentage of immigrant and refugee kids, and I need this—"

"Ooh!" Zahra interrupted. "Where?"

"Jamaica Plain." He didn't scowl at her the way he did with Thea. Bastard.

"Where?" Zahra's face had lit up. "Are you going to English?"

"No, JFK. You live there?"

Something came over Liam's face then. The scowl was gone; he leaned forward in the hard chair he still insisted on taking. His face softened, but his eyes were keen.

"Yes! Oh, this is awesome!" Zahra clapped her hands together, and Liam smiled. Only a slight curve in the thin line of his mouth, but Thea noticed nonetheless. "I'm involved with the Somali refugee community there." Zahra glanced around at the others. "My parents brought me over when I was five. It's a good-sized community, and there are more asylum-seekers coming all the time. We need teachers like crazy."

"Well," Liam said, putting up his hands, "I haven't had a class with a majority of non-native speakers since I was a student. I'll have some catching up to do."

Zahra waved that away. "Pssh. You've got it. You know this stuff cold. Would you like to come and meet some of the kids before school starts? Oh!" She sat back and gazed at him, her brown eyes shining, sparks of gold appearing in them from the color in her hijab. "I know two kids at least who'll be starting high school in the fall, and it would mean *so much* to them if they met you before school started!"

"I'd love to meet them," Liam said, and damn him, he sounded serious. And happy. And focused. He was right; he didn't want to be a plumber. *This* was his passion.

"Can we all come?" David asked. "Do you think any of them want to come out to the garage?"

"Are you kidding?" Zahra looked at him with even more stars in her eyes than the ones she'd pointed at Liam. "We're *always* looking for people to help them get acclimated."

"And they could come to the gallery," Chloe said, then quickly added, "if the collection that's up is age-appropriate, anyway. Steph's had a vagina phase that takes some getting used to."

There was a mic drop instant of silence, and then they collapsed into laughter, Seth and David falling off the couch to curl up on the floor, Chloe as red as her hair, and Zahra holding her sides and yelping, "Ow! Stop! No, really! It hurts!"

Thea had tears in her eyes but saved some energy to look at Liam. He'd thrown his head back with a bark of a laugh that Thea felt through her chair, and he'd gotten that hint of pink along his cheekbones again. But he was still holding himself in, sobering long before the others, long enough to notice that she was looking at him.

For some reason—the same reason that had made him scowl at her and no one else for the past two weeks, she assumed—his smile was wiped clean off his face, and he gave her the full blue stare of which he was capable. Beyond the two of them, the sounds of the others coming down from their laughing fit seemed to be happening outside the room. Thea wondered why he didn't like her, and he frowned and raised an eyebrow and looked away, as if dislike were too strong a term.

◆

At the end of the session, Thea followed everyone out to their cars. She waved to Chloe and the twins and hugged Zahra but hovered near Liam.

"See you tomorrow," he said, opening his truck door, which required a bit of a lift and a jimmy before it would cooperate.

"Liam," she said as the others drove away. "How long did your father make you wait?"

He paused with the door open. She couldn't see his eyes in the dwindling light. "Five years," he said. "It's a five-year apprenticeship."

Five years. Five years to wait, to live someone else's dream before you were allowed to follow your own. "You could have quit."

He shook his head, still looking into the car. "I'd promised."

She'd given up on hearing more than a few words at a time from him, so she was surprised when he said, "He was hoping I'd change my mind. And I'd be making more money if I'd stayed in it. Especially after—"

He seemed to notice that he'd put a couple of sentences together in front of her. He threw his tools in the bed of his truck. "Bye," he said abruptly.

"Wait." Thea put a hand on his arm. She didn't know why; there was just some vague feeling that she would like to know what it would be like to have him smile at *her*.

Mistake.

His arm was bare, exposed by the shirtsleeve he'd rolled up—which couldn't go up a whole lot, the shirt being tight and his forearm big. There was something about the muscles in his arms that just *got* to her. Unbidden thoughts of what he could with his hands flooded her. Her eyes went from her office-job white hand on his tan skin to his eyes.

He raised one eyebrow. One *excuse me, what the fuck do you think you're doing, touching me?* eyebrow. Thea jerked her hand away as though he'd caught fire.

"Sorry," she said. *Argh! Never apologize!* The whole point of asking him this was to stop herself feeling so wrong-footed around him.

"What is it?" he said. Dusk was falling around them, throwing his face into shadows and planes of light from the porch light. She wished she could see more than the outline of his face.

"Uh..." *What was it again? Oh, yeah.* "Next week, could you come a few minutes early? Will you teach me what you did to fix the faucet and the toilet?"

A white slash of a smile in his dark-red beard. *There.* "Sure. I'll show you."

He slammed the passenger door closed, which required him stepping closer to her. Thea nearly didn't step away. He didn't seem to notice but went around and got in the driver's side. The truck started up with its 1950s roar.

Thea was breathless and worried that she'd come across as too needy. The only way she knew to cover it was to be sarcastic. "You got a hazardous goods license for that exhaust?" she called over the din.

"You got one for that mouth?" he replied through the open passenger window. Then he cracked a laugh. A proper, good, loud laugh. A laugh that buzzed through her head to her chest to some other quickly awakening parts of her.

"Bye, Thea," he said and pulled away, leaving her standing on the sidewalk.

Chapter 4

But after their next class, Liam regretted his decision.

He'd convinced himself he was merely helping out a single mom who was overwhelmed and needed it. The faucet and the toilet were small potatoes, hadn't taken more than ten minutes each. It was the tidying up afterward and the trip to the hardware store that had added the time. He could take twenty minutes out of his nonexistent life to help out the mom of a former student, couldn't he?

And she'd asked him to teach her how to fix the plumbing herself, which meant she wasn't some helpless chick used to a guy doing everything for her, and he wasn't being a macho asshole by doing those small things. She'd overreacted the first time, but now that they were clear on the parameters, there was no reason for him not to teach her how to help herself. Maybe he could relax a little when he was there next time. Talk to her kids. Learn how to be sociable again.

Then she came into their classroom the day before he was supposed to go to her house, and he caught himself making a sound under his breath reminiscent of his truck.

Thea had her hair down, one long, beautiful sheet of chestnut brown that highlighted her dark eyes and had a curl at the ends he wanted to wrap around his wrist. She was wearing a dusty pink T-shirt that made her look healthier than she had that first night and a brown skirt that swung around her hips.

She saw their group and smiled big, and now Liam was really glad he was sitting down. She had that kind of artless, toothy grin that only Julia Roberts should be allowed. It was genuine, unforced, and brightened her tired eyes. It was also vaguely familiar; he'd seen it somewhere before, and not on Julia Roberts.

But she wasn't smiling at him. She was smiling at Zahra and Chloe and then at Seth and David. When she saw him the smile faltered. *What the hell?* What did he do to deserve that?

"Hello, Liam," she said, her eyes sliding off his face. Like he was barely in front of her.

"Thea," he acknowledged.

The best seat was next to him, but she went to the other end of the table and sat between Chloe and David.

Well, fine. If that's the way it's going to be, sweetheart. Bite me.

She reached behind her with one hand to get something out of her backpack, and her breasts strained against her blouse. Nice breasts. Two small handfuls. Mouthfuls.

Shit.

He tried to focus on the class. But he'd remembered a lot more of this class than he thought he would, and his brain wouldn't stay pinpointed on the professor.

When they stopped for break, he went to the men's room with Seth and David. But he couldn't hide in there, and when he came out, she was walking out of the ladies' room with Zahra and Chloe. Chloe's red hair bounced along in front of him, seeming to want his attention, but all he could see was the curl in Thea's hair, which fell halfway down her back.

"How did you meet your husband?" he heard Thea ask Zahra.

They didn't seem to notice him behind them.

"Oh, the usual. Nice Muslim girl meets tattooed biker boy. Nice Muslim girl's mother faints. And they all lived happily ever after."

"Really?" Thea said.

"Really."

"She really fainted?" Chloe asked.

"Yep. Screamed that I had to be pregnant and she was going to die of shame. Turned out, I wasn't pregnant, and he converted." Her smile could now only be described as smug. "I'm waiting on telling her where I got my tattoo."

Thea threw her head back and laughed so hard she had to sink into a chair a row or two above theirs. Liam walked past her, hoping to ignore her shaking shoulders.

I'm not interested.

I'm not interested.

He wasn't sure whose voice he was hearing.

◆

"Hey, girl," Sam said.

"Hey, you." Thea held the phone gingerly between two rubber-gloved hands. Was bleach bad for phones? She tried to hold the phone in the crook of her neck, and it slid out and fell into the wet, bleachy bathtub. "Shit!"

"What the hell?" she heard her younger—and favorite—sister yelp as she frantically pulled off a glove.

"Hold on, hold on!" she screamed at the phone. She pulled off both gloves, reeled from the smell she'd been holding her breath against for ten minutes, and grabbed a paper towel to pick up the phone. "Nearly there!" she called. She wiped off the phone—and then panicked because she'd nearly hit the hang-up key—put the screen to sleep, wiped the phone properly, and finally held it to her ear.

"Good afternoon, how can I help you?" she said in her most professional voice.

"Good afternoon, weirdo. What was that?"

"Phone to bathtub."

"Ah. You're in the bath?"

"Nope. Cleaning it."

"Ooh, fun."

"Well, I have"—how could she classify Liam?—"someone coming over."

Sam, damn her, picked up on the tiny hesitation. "*Someone*, huh? Someone you have to clean the tub for? Come on, T. Spill."

"All right, all right, don't get excited. He's a—"

"He!"

She'd known Sam would react like this. Given how hard she'd hated Gabriel and how thrilled she'd been when Thea had kicked him out—the first time—any mention of a male in Thea's vicinity would make Sam sit up in her Hemingway camp chair. She was an archaeologist and traveled all over the world but had now lived in New Mexico for two years. Two years that hadn't included a trip to Massachusetts, not even when their brother's babies had been born.

"Cool your jets. He's teaching me how to fix a toilet."

"What does he look like?"

"It doesn't matter what he looks like!" And Thea didn't trust herself to describe him in disinterested terms. He'd looked great last night—biceps doing their cha-cha in another Pat the Plumber T-shirt, his hair and beard just hipster enough to be interesting but not so much that you'd start looking for a pair of suspenders and knitted grandad vest.

But he'd scowled again, those blue eyes narrowing against her as if she'd insulted him. She'd half expected him to cry off after that look, but he'd texted her this morning to confirm, asking her what time the boys got home from school so he wouldn't interfere with her schedule. So, once again, she didn't know what to make of him, and she wasn't about to explain that to Sam.

"T." Sam's voice was patient, patronizing. "It *always* matters what they look like."

"I'm too tired these days to care," Thea lied. It didn't bode well for this visit that she hadn't just told Sam a plumber was coming. Plumbers were faceless contractors. Unattractive, the classic plumber's butt rising out of their baggy jeans. Thea's breath shortened at the idea of anything like that happening to Liam around her.

"Look," she went on. "I want to chat, but the timing's bad right now."

"No fair! Since when did you want to know how to fix a toilet? What's wrong with it?"

"I'll call you tomorrow. It's fine. And I should have learned to do this stuff ages ago. I was always waiting for Gabe to do it, which was my own stupidity."

"Well, you got that right."

"Thanks."

"You know what I mean. Still no word, I assume?"

"Of course not." Thea had stopped hoping six months ago that Gabe would come back. She was ashamed that she'd waited that long.

"Good. How are the boys?"

The doorbell rang. "Oh shit." She stank of bleach and hadn't gotten out the tools Liam had cleaned or anything. "They're good. I have to go. Love you, bye!"

"Hey!" Sam was laughing as Thea hung up on her.

There wasn't anything she could do—or should do—about her outfit, an old Fielding Paper polo with the collar falling off and pregnancy khaki shorts. *You're about to crawl around in spaces no human should have to examine*, she reminded herself as she tucked a curl behind her ear and went to the front door. *Get over yourself.*

Wise words.

♦

"God," Thea said, her head in the dank and moldy cabinet fifteen minutes later. "How do you do this all day?"

"I don't," Liam said behind her. "I'm a teacher, remember?"

"Oh, right."

"So look up. You see the nut that goes around the drain?"

"I see three nuts."

"The one closest to the sink. This one." He put his head through the open cabinet door she wasn't stuck in. Despite the sickly-sweet smell of whatever needed cleaning out of her sink drain, she couldn't miss his clean scent. If he came a little closer, she might be able to take a surreptitious sniff of his shoulder or his hair or something.

Damn.

Thankfully, Liam backed out of the space and put his arms in the cabinet instead. "This one," he repeated.

When he seemed satisfied she knew what to turn to do whatever she wanted, they backed out of the cupboard to find two dark-haired figures squinting down at them.

Benji was holding his tablet. Jake had slouched down the stairs, his curiosity overcoming his apathy.

"You want to see?" Liam asked Benji. The boy happily climbed into the cabinet, and Liam finally laughed. "Not all of you, bud. Then you'll have no room to swing the wrench."

Liam patiently showed him what they'd been talking about, adjusting his explanation effortlessly so that Benji could understand but Jake wouldn't feel patronized. Thea was surprised to see Jake asking questions that ended up with Liam taking them all down to the furnace in the basement. Benji, who usually insisted he was terrified of the basement, stood in silence for ten minutes while Liam and Jake talked. That boy was getting ice cream, no doubt about it.

When they'd exhausted the wonder that was the 1920s version of central heating, Liam packed up the tools he'd brought, still talking to Jake. "You got your summer job lined up yet?"

"Uh." The easy mood they'd fallen into shuddered to a halt. Suddenly, Jake's face showed that he'd remembered Liam was a teacher. And a teacher he didn't like anymore. "Oh, well. I've got time."

"My dad's always looking for summer help, if you're interested," Liam said.

To give him some small credit, Jake quickly squashed the horror that came over his face. "Oh, uh. No, thanks. I'll probably just work at the froyo place or something."

"Then you'd better get over there. The college kids are home already, and they're taking up those jobs. The ones that include air-conditioning." Liam turned around at the foot of the basement stairs. "Think about it. You'd be learning a skill. And you could help out your mom more."

That made Jake scowl. "Jake helps out a ton around here, don't you, hon?" Thea said, putting a hand on his shoulder. "He babysits Benji most nights until I get back from work."

Liam shrugged. "Good for you." But he'd also lost his relaxed tone.

"Okay," Thea said. Time to change the subject. "We've put it off long enough. Show me what you did to the toilet."

The boys ran. Literally. She'd never seen them slither up the basement stairs so fast. "Homework!" Jake shouted over his shoulder.

"Homework!" Benji echoed, though he was five and didn't have any. Jake almost certainly didn't, either, with only a week left of school. Thea smiled at Liam, a smile probably full of indulgence and pride in her lazy, faithless sons.

"I'm not surprised," Liam said. "The state of that thing when I first got here, I was afraid to go near it."

"Hey! I clean every—"

"Oh, it was clean enough," he said. "I was talking about the mechanics."

"Show me."

Thea led the way. The first step up from the basement floor to the staircase was higher than the rest, the floor having sunk over the years. "Watch your step," she turned around to say, but he was already there, his hand out, as if he'd thrown his coat over a puddle and was waiting to escort her over it. Such chivalry made her want to laugh and also brought back that flash of fear. It was safest to ignore his hand, but the space was small and she brushed it as she walked past.

Liam took his hand back as if she'd slapped it, and now Thea had a new emotion to add to those that welled up when he was around: guilt.

"Thanks," she said. "I got it." Would that count as an apology? She didn't want to apologize. She didn't want to be wrong. She didn't want to continue to feel the brush of his hand against her side as she preceded him up the stairs to the house.

"Finally!" a voice said as they came in through the back door. "We thought you'd fallen down a well. Hi, Liam."

It was Chloe, followed by the rest of the group, which Thea had completely forgotten about. She hadn't fed the kids, hadn't fed Liam, and there were no snacks for her guests. She had spiderwebs in her hair and work clothes that were definitely not for public view.

Liam didn't seem fazed. "The boys asked about the plumbing," he said, for the first time initiating conversation while blocking the view to the kitchen. Behind him Thea threw everything back into the bathroom cabinet, took wine out of the fridge, and put the oven on. Then she was running upstairs, ripping her clothes off as she went and changing into something that fit and didn't have holes in it.

In one minute she was back to greet everyone, and they sat down to go over their homework. Liam continued to be more animated than they'd ever seen him. He seemed to have given up on his standoffish routine and volunteered information from his experiences so fast, they had trouble writing it down. Thea popped in and out to check the chicken nuggets and feed the kids and put food out for Audrey. Benji, no longer content to be by himself, came and sat at her feet, intent on his tablet until he fell asleep, worn out with his exciting afternoon of plumbing, and allowed Thea to put him to bed.

She half hoped Liam would leave before the rest of them and half hoped he wouldn't. He didn't, but he was close behind Chloe, who winked at Thea, blew her a kiss, and let the screen door shut behind her.

Now they were alone, and she didn't know how to handle him. It'd be better if he left first. Still, she could at least say thank you.

"Thank you," she said.

He stuck one hand in his jeans pocket and used the other to scratch his beard. "You're welcome, Thea."

"Everyone calls me T," she said before she noticed she was doing it. It wasn't true. Only her family called her T. She hadn't asked any of the rest of the group to do that. Her cheeks heated. She should be having him call her by her last name if she was going to put any distance between them at all. More than the couple of feet that separated them right now, anyway.

"Okay," he said. A silence fell over them—if the sound made by the old, buzzing air conditioner in the window could be called silence.

"We never got to the toilet," he said.

"No."

"I'll come over early again next week. And can I fix that a/c unit? It just needs a couple of shims."

She closed her eyes. *Stop helping me.* "You don't have to."

"Oh, yeah, I do." His old acerbity rose back to the surface. "I always have a headache when I leave here."

Her face grew hotter, but she said in a flippant tone, "Sounds about right. This house is one big headache."

He frowned; he was taking her seriously. "Still," she went on, a smile tagging the corner of her mouth, "It's a roof over our head, so I'm not complaining."

"Why did you buy it, with all the work it needed?"

She tried not to take offense. Failed, but anyway. "I hardly saw it before we bought it. I'd just had Benji and dumped my ex—temporarily—and my brother and sister found it for me. I barely remember walking through it before I signed the papers. I just wanted a place that was ours: mine and the boys'. Everything basically worked, it had three bedrooms, and I didn't think beyond that."

He scrubbed a hand through his beard. "It's a nice old house."

Thea nodded at the powder-blue truck that waited patiently at the curb. "You like old things, huh."

That slash of a smile appeared again, and Thea grinned back. "Yeah," he said, his eyes reflecting his smile. "I guess so."

♦

They all had final papers to plan. Thea was sad that the class was coming to an end. After this, they would be doing an online technology in the classroom class, and when fall started, they'd be following their own specialties. She had looked forward to these classes more than any of her undergrad courses because of her new friends—she could call the rest of them friends, even if she didn't know how to categorize Liam, who had yet to show any pleasure in her company.

Everyone was coming to teaching from other careers. Chloe had floated around a few jobs before she'd met her wife, whose gallery she had been running for several years. "But she's being kind, letting me run it," Chloe admitted. "I'm crap at it. Washing the windows, that I can do. Rent agreements and commissions, blech. But when we got the special needs kids in for classes, I felt useful for the first time in my life."

Zahra had been a secretary until she'd stayed home to have her babies. "It was the recession." She shrugged. "You took what you could get."

"The having babies part or the secretary part?" Thea asked with a grin.

Zahra smiled back at her. "Some days I wonder."

Seth wanted to teach shop part-time and get more high school kids into the garage. David was an evangelist for teaching kids financial literacy and had already asked the group if they had IRAs.

Then there was Liam. "Did you always want to teach?" Chloe asked him during the break that night. Zahra and Thea had compared notes to bring snacks they could all share.

"Yep," he said with his usual loquaciousness.

"Wow," Chloe said, which was what everyone was thinking. "How did you know so early?" She indicated the rest of them. "We've all been floundering here, 'finding ourselves"–she did finger quotes–"and you've always known?"

"Yeah," Thea said, speaking before he could. "I can believe it. The second Jake comes in the room, you're like a sheepdog puppy with his first sheep. You just get this… focus around kids."

"Don't tease him, Thea," Zahra chided, while Liam avoided her eyes.

"Puppy?" he said. "How old do you think I am?"

"Old enough," Chloe broke in. "Right, Thea?"

Now Thea and Liam were both blushing. "Chloe, have a heart," Seth said.

"I do!" Chloe shook back her curls. "That's why I'm now dying to know how old Liam is!"

"You know," Liam said, gripping the back of his neck, "if I'd asked you this, you'd have socked me halfway across the room by now."

"Possibly," Chloe agreed. "So, okay, I'm thirty-one. Seth? David?"

"Thirty-two."

"Thirty-one." They said it at exactly the same time, so later, Thea forgot which one was which.

"Zahra?"

"Nuh-uh. I'm a mother. We don't have to tell."

What a great excuse.

"Fine." Chloe pouted. "Thea? That goes for you too?"

Her cheeks were so hot. "Let's just say I'm... older than all of you."

"Liam?"

Liam's jaw looked made of granite, but the blush was still staining his cheeks. "Let's just say I'm... younger than all of you."

Dammit.

Chapter 5

"You've got to slap it on. Like butter. No, not like—Jesus, woman, how much butter do you put on bread?"

Thea put on a terrible British accent. "I'm sorry, guv'na, we wasn't allowed no butter in the orphanage."

Liam rolled his eyes and took some goop off the tile she was holding. "Oh, please, guv'na," Thea begged, "don't beat me again! I'll bring you some lovely gewgaws next time I'm up in Bloomsb'ry!"

Liam pointed at the wall. Thea placed the tile into the space he'd left when he'd chipped out the cracked tiles around her bathroom sink. "Is this how you entertain yourself instead of fixing up your house? And what the hell is a gewgaw?"

Now that she had the accent, Thea couldn't let it go. "It's jewelery, innit? Lovely sparklers."

"The British don't say sparklers for jewelry."

"They might." She made a mental note to watch *Oliver Twist* with her English sister-in-law at the first opportunity, and to ask her which words could still be used in her new and excellent accent.

She picked up another tile and buttered the back of it with a little more precision. "Better," Liam grunted.

"Better butter," she said. Then she said it again. And again. And sang it until he had to leave the room.

British accent drives him nuts, check.

Once she'd found out that Liam could be teased, the dynamic of their... *let's call it friendship*... had changed. The best part of this afternoon, of Liam coming an hour or two before everyone else, was that Thea could use skills she hadn't remembered she had to tease Liam, to elicit a reluctant smile from that surly mouth. She'd found that her own sense of humor hadn't entirely disappeared.

"Get those tiles on," he said from the kitchen. "I'll get started on the air conditioner."

There were only six tiles; she'd been out shopping the weekend before and had bought them on a whim.

"You should have bought porcelain," he said when she'd proudly shown them and the mortar to him, "and did you buy grout?"

But he'd come two hours early today, replaced the innards of her toilet and shown her how to mix the mortar before chipping off the tired old tile around her sink. The boys, now home for the holidays, had greeted him—Benji joyfully, Jake reservedly—and proceeded to eat their own weight in ice cream while she worked.

"Mom?" Jake said.

"Mm-hmm?" she mumbled, catching a drip of mortar. Butter. Not cream cheese. Check.

"Can I go out?"

"Where to, Jake?"

"Just into town. Some friends are getting pizza."

She had no reason to say no. It was just that she had a sneaking suspicion that Jake's friends were the ones with the reputation around town. Perhaps the ones who'd vandalized the kids' playground last weekend. The day Jake had been hanging with them. Thea had cringed when she'd heard the news at the bus stop, and like the ostrich she was, hadn't mentioned it to Jake.

But she was only guessing. "Which friends?"

"Zachary Benedetto, Andrew Gallagher—"

"Oh, Jake." Thea didn't spend much time gossiping with the other moms these days, but those names had filtered through to her.

"They're all right, Mom. Anyway, we're going to look for jobs, too."

She looked at him now. His pale-blue eyes were wide open at her, as innocent as could be. The group was coming in an hour, and she had to feed Benji and get some appetizers put together. It was the last day of school, after all, and most kids were hanging around in town, enjoying their first day of freedom.

He couldn't come to much harm with most of the school out and about, so she said, "All right. Have fun—legal fun!" she called after him as he whooped and began to run back upstairs. "Be home by ten o'clock!"

"Eleven!" came the voice down the stairs as Jake ricocheted off his walls, looking for his favorite sneakers, no doubt.

"Ten thirty!" she said, as he'd known, and she'd known, she would. Thea sighed, crossed her fingers and her eyes, whispered, *please don't let him smoke*, then walked outside to see how Liam was getting on.

He was getting on just fine. The window where the air conditioner sat was empty, the window open. He'd set up a couple of sawhorses in the yard and was five steps up a ladder with a power drill in his hand, making holes in her siding. A pencil was tucked behind one ear, and the back of his navy T-shirt was already stuck to him with sweat on this hot June day. The temperature had quickly reached ninety degrees and climbed from there, yet he'd still come over as he'd said he would, two hours before class met, to either do work on her house or show her how to do it.

To distract herself from the view and Jake's possible descent into vagrancy, she said, "I do a mean Jimmy Stewart, too, by the way."

"I'll bet you a million dollars you don't," he said without turning around. "Hand me the bracket out of the back of my truck, will you? Farther back, Ben." Benji was riding his bike up and down the driveway behind Liam and kept getting his handlebars within the ladder danger zone.

"Benji, back off or you'll have to go inside." When she was sure Benji had changed his trajectory, Thea went over to the blue monster baby and looked in the bed. It was perfectly lined with polished wood and chrome slats, the bracket kept from sliding by a forest of bungee cords. She did her best to undo the cords without scratching the perfect paint job but flinched when she accidentally let go of one end and the hook sprang to the other side of the flatbed with a loud *clunk*.

She threw a guilty look behind her, but by the grace of God, Liam had the drill going and he hadn't heard. She checked for dings in the paint, but didn't see any, and got the bracket out of the truck.

The packaging for the bracket said very clearly on the cover: Installs from inside the house! No drilling needed!

"Uh, Liam?"

"What?" He stepped off the ladder and went over to the sawhorses, where he'd left a handsaw and a small pile of wood.

"This says..." He was looking at her impatiently, his mouth that thin line in his beard. There were two gaps below his lower lip where the beard didn't grow. She wondered what he'd do if she pressed a finger to one of them. "This says, no drilling needed."

She was rewarded for her concern with another long blue look and a frown. "Right," he said, his voice as chilly as his eyes. "So you take the unit in and out every season?"

"Yes! Well, I used to." Another thing that she'd let go after Gabe had left. Honestly, not having a man around the house, or at least someone with bigger muscles than her, was a pain in the ass sometimes. "It's heavy," she finished lamely.

"It's heavy," he repeated, well, heavily. "Okay, then, so since it's sitting there, sagging under its own weight, with only the weight of that almost-rotten window pane holding it down, I figure the bracket's going to need more support than this to make sure it doesn't fall out. Since it sits there all winter with snow and leaves and God knows what on it." He held out his hand for the bracket, already reaching into his toolbelt—and yes, it did make his pants slide down a little, but there was no plumber's butt yet, and yes, she'd checked—for his tape measure.

Thea blushed and handed it to him. "You know, being a know-it-all can get old real fast," she countered.

"You'd better get used to being one when you're a teacher," he said. "Never show them you don't know something."

"That's terrible advice! Setting kids up to think adults are infallible!"

"Teachers have to be or you lose their respect." He was measuring and drawing on one of the pieces of wood.

"But there's no way I'll know everything about every book ever written!"

"Just the books on the syllabus. And you know the plot of more books than you think." He looked up at her through one sweaty curl that hung over his forehead. "Unless you spend all your time watching old movies instead of reading." She thought she might have seen him smile again. "Stand by with that caulk gun when I get these onto the siding."

She picked up the giant squeezy gun thing and shouldered it, pointing the tip at him. "Now, I–I–just need you to stick 'em up, see?"

He leaned back on the ladder and stared at her for a moment. "You owe me a million dollars."

She pouted. "I never watched Jimmy Stewart's Westerns. Benji! Get away from the ladder!"

Without a whole lot more conversation, she helped Liam finish what he was doing, and he came down to her eye level. Kind of a shame, as she'd been enjoying the sight of his arms holding the drill, bracing the shims, his biceps flexing...

"Benji!"

"Sorry!" At least he hadn't ridden his bike into the ladder. Just into Liam's legs. "I wobbled!"

He hadn't fallen off, partly because he'd put his foot out to stop himself and partly because in a split second, Liam had dropped the drill and grabbed the boy's arm.

"Go inside," Thea said in a deadly voice.

"Mommm!"

"I warned you."

"But I didn't–"

"Inside!"

Benji threw his bike to the side and stormed into the house.

"Sorry," Thea said. "I hope your drill's okay." *That was* not *an innuendo. Don't blush, don't blush.*

"Not a big deal."

"He only did it to get your attention, you know."

Liam smiled, this time a gentle smile that lit up his eyes in a whole new way. "He's a good kid."

Thea was warmed by the compliment, but as usual, the next second she was suspicious. "If the next words out of your mouth are *he needs a man in his life*, I will fill up your orifices with that caulk gun."

"Jeez." He held up his hands. "You need to... never mind. I was just saying he was a good kid. That's it."

"Fine."

"Fine." He began to put together his tools. Thea helped him secure them in his truck, and they went inside.

"How many old movies have you watched?" he asked. His beard had some sawdust in it from cutting the wood, and a bead of sweat was running down his cheek and onto his neck.

Focus, Thea! "Most of them," she answered. "When the boys were younger, it was AMC or start hitting the tequila. Cary Grant saved my liver."

Liam picked up the air conditioner like it was a box of popcorn and inserted it into the window. "Go check that it's straight outside." Thea did so, yelled that it looked fine, and came back in as the air conditioner clicked on with a soothing hum rather than the bone-rattling judder they'd all become used to.

"Ahhh," she said, lifting her hair off her neck with both hands. She was wearing a loose T-shirt and felt it rise up above her waistline as she did so.

Liam might have been looking. Or he might have been thinking and just happened to look in her direction. She couldn't see his eyes to check but wondered if she saw his cheeks flush a little.

"You gonna give a man a glass of lemonade, or what?" he said.

Not much of a come-on. Not that she wanted one. "Right, right." She wound her hair around into a bun as she led him into the kitchen.

He sat at the kitchen table and made it look small and insubstantial as he scrubbed at his sweaty hair and beard.

Not part of the deal, remember? Get your eyes off his biceps and those back muscles you could see working when he was up that ladder.

She congratulated herself on her self-control as she went into the bathroom to find a hairband rather than leaning over the table, giving him a good shot down the front of her shirt, and daring him to do something about it.

Quit it, Thea, she told her reflection in the bathroom mirror. *You're just damn horny. He's not interested, and neither are you.*

Something pulsed deep inside her. *Hell yeah, we're interested.*

She pushed at her reflection with a hand as if it were a real person and went back to the kitchen.

Why was the sight of a man taking a good long drink out of a glass of lemonade so hot? This was getting worse. Thea kept her back to him and busied herself around the kitchen preparing food for the rest of the group.

"So I've been thinking," he said behind her. "I want to ask my dad to come and look at your furnace. The banging pipes you mentioned: you've got air caught in there, but the system's so old I'd rather get his opinion before I start bleeding it."

"Oh." She turned around from the refrigerator. "I don't know, Liam."

His eyebrows went up. "Why not? He knows his stuff. He won't tell you that you need something you don't."

How could she explain it? "Look. Having you do this work here and there—and more importantly, showing me and the boys how to do it—is one thing. I should be paying you anyway—"

"I told you, I have a job. I don't need your money."

"I know." She was the one flushing now. Despite their declaration of indifference, Thea vacillated between relief that they'd spelled out the rules, and hope that the reason Liam kept coming week after week was because he wanted to break them. But involving his father changed the rules. "If your dad comes, I have to pay him. And I can't afford it. You know the fall semester's tuition is due next week."

He looked away for a moment, then fixed her with the piercing stare he was so good at. "My dad won't charge for a consult. Especially not for a—"

He paused to search for the word. She didn't want him to find it.

"Thea," he said. "I don't get it."

"Huh?"

"You live in this house. It's a decent-sized house in an okay neighborhood, but you can't afford to fix it up. Yet you're going to school full-time. You don't seem to have a job, and you also don't have a husband earning money, but Jacob's carrying around the latest cell phone and that tablet Benji's obsessed with is top-of-the-line."

Thea didn't speak at first. Liam made a disgusted noise and ran his hand down his beard. "God, forget it. That was totally over the line. Sorry."

"No, I know..."

"Forget it." He came off the corner of the table where he'd been leaning.

"Liam," she said, making up her mind. "Do you remember what my last name is?"

"Donaghy? Isn't it the same as Jake's?"

"No. That's Jake's father's name. It's Fielding." She waited for him to make the connection.

Liam shrugged, shaking his head in confusion.

There was no reason not to tell him, except her embarrassment at the riches that kept her in school. "Fielding Paper?"

His look pinned her like a wolf with a deer. She rushed on. "When my dad was running the company, he set up trust funds that we came into when we were twenty-five. But by then, the company was in the toilet, and I thought the fund was empty. It wasn't. When I kicked out Gabriel—my ex—after Benji was born, I used it to buy this house and tried to keep the rest for the boys.

"But I was dying, answering phones for a bunch of scientists who don't need me, knowing I'd dreamed of better for myself, up until I had Jake. I was a shitty mom, and in the end the only way I could think of to change that was to use some of the rest of the money to go back to school. But"—she felt it was important he understand this—"I only take what I absolutely have to for school. The house is... I want to fix it up when I'm making my own money and not taking it from the boys."

"Wasn't the money left to *you*?"

"Yes, but they got a shitty deal for a father. Their legacy is in that trust fund. College. Except I've been taking the capital, and now there might not be enough for Jake to go without getting a bunch of loans."

She faced him. He was frowning at her. With her in her flip-flops and him in work boots, he stood two inches taller and so much broader Thea wanted to just sink into his arms and forget about all the decisions she had to make, all the insecurities and questions she had every day.

She went on. "The phone and tablet and anything else you see here that's worth anything are gifts, from my brother, usually."

"Company not in the toilet anymore, then."

"Kane nearly killed himself bringing it back, but no. So," she finished, trying to smile. "I'm a rich girl playing at being poor, if you want to see it that way. Or a poor girl too stubborn to take her own money."

He unfolded his arms, and she thought for a second he really might put them around her. "How long have you been alone?" he asked, his voice rough.

She laughed. Since her mother had died? Since Sam had gone off the rails? Since she'd realized Gabe was all blarney and no substance? Since she'd thrown him out the first time, after Benji was born? Since he'd left them all? Since just before Liam had somehow made his way into her life?

"I'm not alone," she said, "not really. Not like some single moms. My bosses are very understanding and give me all the flextime I ask for. I have a family who'd never let us starve. Most of my fights with Kane are me fending off his offers of help. My sister Cat would mother the crap out of all three of us if I let her—and she takes the boys once a month so I can have a weekend to myself. See," she said, one corner of her mouth lifting, "I use my nearest and dearest for just as long as it suits me, and then I tell them I don't need their help."

When had he gotten closer to her? Another couple of inches and her chest would brush his. The refrigerator door was behind her back, and Liam's body was no less unyielding in front of her. She struggled to keep focus. "Like you," she said. "I should have been paying you."

It didn't come out strongly enough, and when he replied, his own voice was low and intimate. "I don't mind," he said.

Thea closed her eyes. He was going to kiss her, and she couldn't drag herself out of the space he'd created for them. "Don't, Liam," she whispered. "I'm all out of trust."

He opened his mouth, a breath from hers...

And the front screen door banged and a voice said, "Phew! Thank God for a/c! Hey, is it broken? It's not making as much noise."

Liam stepped back, and the air-conditioning seemed to swirl around her skin, raising goose bumps along her arms. He took the tray of lemonade glasses from the counter next to her and walked into the living room with it. "'Cause it's fixed now," he said to Zahra.

Thea stayed in the kitchen for a moment more, trying to make her breath come out in the normal way, not these short gasps.

Chapter 6

That night, with their final paper looming, they spoke less and wrote more. Liam found that they asked him more questions tonight, which gave him something to do, since he'd finished his final paper two weeks ago. He hadn't told them that, though. If he admitted that, he'd have to admit that the only reason he'd come to their study group in the first place was to see more of Thea. Which was entirely pathetic.

A Fielding. She might as well have been a Rockefeller. What a laugh she must be having at the idea of him and her ever getting together. His dad did well, but he wasn't a fucking Fielding.

And to think he'd nearly kissed her.

Benji was in the room with them, as Thea had been unable to keep him distracted with a movie for more than a couple of weeks. Tonight he sat at Liam's feet. From Liam's position, he could just see the port-wine birthmark that spread down one cheek and one side of Benji's neck. The weight of the boy as he was lulled to sleep by the quiet tap of fingers on keyboards seemed a reproach to Liam. He'd gotten himself into this family. Benji had taken a shine to him, not that Liam had encouraged him. He liked kids, and Benji knew it. But while Liam wasn't about to tell Thea that the boys needed a father figure, at least one reason for Benji latching on to him was clear.

Liam winced and took a mouthful of beer from the glass Thea had poured for him. Thank God the class was nearly over. He could get out of the group and out of her life and not embarrass himself the way he had with Avery. Another woman who'd expected a different way of life than he could give her. At least this time, the idea of exploring any kind of relationship with Thea had all been in his stupid, naïve mind.

When Thea came down from carrying a sleeping Benji up to bed, Chloe was waiting for her with a full glass of red. "Sorry," she said, "but I'm going to talk about the elephant in the room. What happened with their dad?"

The others froze. "Chloe!" Zahra said.

Seth and David looked deeply uncomfortable. "You don't have to—" David began.

"I know," Thea said. "But you're my friends." Did her eyes cut to him, just for a second? "I don't want you to think I—" She shook off the thought, whatever it was. "He worked in construction when I was at college. I met him in a bar. He was off-the-boat Irish. That accent, you know?"

Chloe and Zahra sighed in agreement.

"Well, so I had Jake." Her mouth tightened. "And it turned out Gabe... wasn't the fatherly type."

"He dumped you?" Chloe breathed.

"Yes. And no. And then yes." Thea smiled. Liam couldn't tell if it was to throw them off the scent of how devastating that must have been for her and the boys or because she still had feelings for her ex. The idea made him want to growl again. "But don't get me wrong," she went on. "He loves his kids. He just doesn't know how to be a father to them."

"It's not fucking hard." Oh shit. Apparently, that was him talking. "You just show up."

The rest of them nodded. But Thea said, "Just showing up doesn't cut it in my book, I'm afraid. He'd show up, all right, when it suited him or when the guilt was too much or... I don't know why. He rarely explained himself, except to give abject and heartfelt apologies and promises that he then had to repeat six months later."

She froze for a second. "Whoa. Sorry. Debbie Downer here."

"It's okay, hon," Zahra said.

"Does he ever see them now?" Dammit. Liam couldn't keep his mouth shut. As if he didn't have enough reason to stay away from her, now he had the knowledge that she'd slummed it with another blue-collar worker for years and had no desire to repeat the experience.

"He went back to Ireland. Two years ago." She looked past Liam, through to the kitchen for some reason. "And it's a good thing he did, because if he hadn't, I wouldn't be here now. I'd be sitting by the phone, waiting for the next time he decided to grace us with his presence."

She still sounded bitter. Liam fought an insane macho urge to find the guy and punch him in the balls.

Thea shook her head. "All right, your turn," she told them. "You've heard my sob story, now let's hear yours."

"You already heard mine," Zahra said.

Seth and David also shook their heads. Nothing to tell, they said. A few dates, some girls. No great claps of thunder across a crowded room. "Once they see the state of my hands," Seth said, holding up fingers ingrained with grease, "they're off like a shot."

"It's a sad day when girls turn their noses up at a good man with a steady trade." Thea sighed.

Amen.

"Are *you* interested?" Seth asked her.

Thea smiled in apology. "Well, no, hon."

Seth threw up the offending hands. "I rest my case."

"But I'm not interested in anyone!" Thea tried to clarify.

"Mm-hmm," Zahra said.

She might have let you kiss her. She didn't say she didn't want you to. Just that she was out of trust. Her story backed that up.

Why was he torturing himself like this? She was a *Fielding.* End of story. End of crazy thoughts of trusting another woman. Before Avery had put him through the mill, Liam had been an optimistic person. It was what had gotten him through the apprenticeship. In his world, people did what they said they'd do. Avery's betrayal had disabused him of that fantasy, and he'd do well to remember it.

Chloe had met her wife, Stephanie, at art school. "I'd only gotten in by the skin of my teeth and a kick-ass interview, and Steph was genuinely talented. I was a goner the minute I saw her photographs."

"Wait," David said. "Stephanie Seton? That photographer?"

"Uh-huh. I know, I know, we don't look like a couple. She comes up to about here on me." Chloe indicated somewhere just below her chest.

Well, didn't that just put the cherry on the gold-plated freaking cake. "Wow," Liam said, sitting back in his chair and stretching out his jean-clad legs. "Seems we're in the company of greatness."

"Uh, married to greatness," Chloe pointed out.

"Or born to it," he said, nodding at Thea.

Her cheeks flushed as all eyes turned to her, and she glared at him. "But living far outside it, remember?" She waved her hand at the shabby paint and cracked plaster.

"What the hell are you talking about?" Chloe demanded, her wineglass paused on the way to her lips.

"She's a Fielding of Fielding Paper," Liam said.

"Oh, I know," Chloe said, taking her sip of wine, but the others stared at Thea as if they'd never seen her before.

"How did you know?" Thea asked.

"I know Kane. He and Steph are friends. Saw the resemblance as soon as I met you."

"Why didn't you tell me?"

Yeah, why didn't you tell us? I could have gotten myself out of this situation before the curl at the end of her hair started driving me crazy at night.

Chloe shrugged. "You never brought Kane up. I didn't know if you guys were on the outs or something." She looked around her. "Making it on your own kind of thing."

Thea laughed. "We're on the outs every other day. But we're family. We don't do that not-speaking thing."

"You're related to Kane Fielding?" Zahra said, who had a hand to her chest as if her heart were pounding. "Can you get me a photograph? For a friend, of course."

"Ew, Zahra," Thea complained. "That's my brother you're talking about. And he's married. With children."

They all looked at her like Liam probably had the other day. Assessing. Finding similarities. And differences.

Thea fake-grinned that giant Fielding smile he'd glimpsed at class last week. Now he knew where he'd seen it before. Her brother had been on the news a few years ago, and his cheesy grin had always annoyed Liam.

But on Thea...

Liam looked away. The others were still staring at her.

"Holy crap," Chloe breathed.

"Moving on!" Thea almost shouted.

"But how do you... why do you...?" Zahra stammered.

"Live like this?" Thea grimaced. "Life decisions. Stubborn pride. Gabe."

"Jesus." Liam didn't know why he was pissed, but tonight was apparently fuck-it night. "You don't live in a fucking tent, Thea. You have a great house and a pretty good life. Quit acting like you're on food stamps."

She blushed to the roots of her hair, and he hated himself. She'd told him her financial situation, and he'd just thrown that small amount of trust back at her.

"Damn, Liam," David said. Liam couldn't look at him.

Thea scowled through her blushes. "Happy now? Got that off your chest?"

He scrubbed at his beard. "Pretty much." *Asshole.*

"So, Liam," she said, her voice now suspiciously bright. "How's *your* love life?"

So that was her revenge. She was taking her pound of flesh, and it was going to hurt. But he deserved it.

Still, he tried to dodge the question. He folded his arms. "Nonexistent," he said shortly.

Her eyes turned almost black when she was pissed. "Aw," she teased. "Married to your work, are you?"

His brows lowered even farther. "Married to a coworker, yes," he said. He sounded as though his jaw had locked in place. "She slept with my mortgage rep. So I stopped being married to her. But one of us had to quit. I made it me."

♦

A profound silence blanketed the room. Even Chloe's hair was still. Thea watched the tautness of Liam's body, the thin line that was his lips. So much for any intimacy they'd developed over the last few weeks. Tonight he'd taken what she'd shared with him and chosen to read her as a trust fund baby playing at being poor. He seemed to have no emotion of his own except for snark and judgment. So she'd pushed back, because everything about him made her do that.

But here was the evidence of a Liam who felt and hurt and lived. They all could see it in the clipped, cold way he described it, in the hand that drew down his beard, and the slight pink that came into his cheeks.

"I'm sorry, Liam," she said.

He unfolded his arms. "Yeah, me too." He looked at her, and Thea's heart ran a little lap around her chest. He wasn't just saying that about himself, about what his ex had done to him. He was apologizing for what he'd just said about her.

He's been burned, too. That means he and I are definitely off-limits. "Okay," she said brightly, ignoring the disappointed jog her heart had settled into. "Enough sharing for one week. Who's going first with their lesson plan?"

Chapter 7

Liam drove up to the house in a Pat the Plumber van. Thea, peeking through the living room window, found herself missing the blue monster baby, but she supposed it couldn't carry all the supplies his father might need.

Pat McConnell got out of the passenger side and looked up at the house, his eyes narrowing. Thea found herself feeling guilty all over again for what needed doing on the exterior but drew herself up. No more apologizing, not even to the Famous Pat himself.

Pat said something to Liam as he came up alongside his father, and they walked up the path—the weedy, crooked path, but who cared, right?—and the three steps to the porch.

Thea was moving to the front door, but the window was open. She heard a voice, lower than Liam's and with the slight scratch of age, say, "This porch is a liability. Look at that railing."

"I know, Dad. They don't spend much time out here. I'll get to it."

I'll get to it. Class was over. Everyone was coming over tonight to celebrate. In a couple of weeks, the online technology class would begin. Was Liam still planning on coming by to work on her house? She'd thought that him knowing she was a Fielding meant she was beneath his notice, his help. She'd reconciled herself to this, mostly. It would be a shame not to see his brawny arms fixing stuff around her house, but it would also be a lot less complicated. Maybe she'd cool her jets herself, stop feeling so breathless around him, stop missing him when he wasn't here.

You are a glutton for punishment, she'd told herself four times this week. *Are you always going to go for the guys who don't think you're worth much?*

"You know you're mine, pet," Gabe would say when he was feeling vicious or Thea had tried, again, to be the one to close the door on their pathetic marriage. "I mean, who else would have you?" And then he'd slam out of the house and go drinking, and come back maudlin and contrite, swearing that he couldn't live without her and the boys. And Thea hated herself for loving him in the first place, and felt ugly and unkempt and nothing beyond a maker of meals and wiper of noses, and before she knew it, she'd be making him coffee the next morning. And a couple of months later, Jake would need money for a school trip and Gabe would be gone again.

The knock on the door shook her out of her memories. She opened it to find Pat filling the doorway. He was the same height as his son but had about forty pounds on him. His hair was white and he was clean-shaven, but his eyes were the same sharp blue as Liam's. He looked at her with the same skepticism as Liam had.

That look straightened her spine. Fuck 'em both. She was done explaining herself. "Mr. McConnell," she said, holding out her hand and lifting her chin. "I appreciate you coming out."

Pat shook hands, his own large, red hand swallowing hers. "My son told me your radiators were banging all winter."

"Yes. This is the first I've heard that that's not normal." She gave him a determined Fielding smile. "Come on through."

She led them into the kitchen and out through the back door. When she went to open the cellar door, Liam said, "I got it," and leaned across her to grasp the handle.

Chivalrous? Or assy? Before she could decide which, he and his father were halfway down the stairs.

Turning back to her, Liam said, "You don't have to come down."

"Good," she said, though she felt dismissed. "I still have to get ready for tonight."

As she climbed the back porch to the kitchen, she heard Pat say, "What's tonight? Hot date?"

"No."

If Liam had used that tone of voice with her, Thea would have known not to pursue the subject. But Pat didn't seem to have gotten the memo. She closed the kitchen door with a bang, but now she could hear him through the floorboards.

"'Cause she's pretty enough, I'll give you that."

"Dad. Can we focus on the boiler?"

Thea pulled open the oven door with excessive force and closed it again, hoping that they'd hear and lower their voices. She really did have food to make—proper food, not stuff she was reheating from the supermarket—and needed to stay in the kitchen. Jake had disappeared off with his friends, and Benji was at day camp. Despite the boys' general lack of noise during the day once their noses were stuck to their computer screens, the house was a gaping maw of silence without them. One where every sound from the basement carried.

It was curious to hear Liam defer to someone else's wisdom for a change. He asked questions; Pat explained. They referred back to projects they'd done together in the past, but mostly Liam listened and agreed. Pat was the expert now. Thea bridled a little at the way Pat spoke to him sometimes: impatient when Liam asked a question Pat thought meant he hadn't understood the explanation. Liam stuck up for himself at these moments but never brought out the sarcasm Thea was so familiar with.

"So," Pat said eventually. "What about all this damp?"

"Short of repointing the entire basement or replacing the walls, there's not much she can do about it."

"It's a shame," Pat said, "seeing these old houses go like this."

Thea paused in stirring her cookie batter. Waited for Liam to agree with him.

"She's not trying to 'let it go,' Dad. Her ex split, and she's had almost no help since then. The house had to come second. Or third."

Well, well, well. Thea was far too pleased to hear him defend her.

"Might have known you'd be on her side. What exactly is going on, anyway? You bringing her to July Fourth?"

"God, no!"

What the hell did that mean? The small smile that had been playing at the corners of her mouth fled. What, she wasn't good enough for his family?

Uh, Thea. You have your own July Fourth to go to, remember? Your own family? And you and Liam are barely even friends, let alone about to spend holidays together.

She shook herself and started stirring the batter again.

"Dad, believe me. She's too fancy for the likes of me."

"Are you kidding me?" There was a silence in which Pat was probably looking around at the damp basement.

"She's a Fielding. You know, the Fieldings?"

"Oh. That's where I've seen that smile before. We lost that job to Duke's. His house. Big pile out on Chestnut Hill."

"Exactly."

"What, so you're not good enough for a Fielding?"

"No, Dad… it's not that. Jeez, I'd've thought you'd get it, given Avery and all."

"Oh, she's one of those, is she?"

No, I'm not. She couldn't move, couldn't even shift her feet in case they heard her and realized she was there. *I would never cheat on Liam. On anyone.*

"Someone who looks down her nose at blue-collar guys? Yes."

Hey!

Liam's voice went on. "Someone who'd pretend everything was fine and then cheat on her husband? I don't think so."

There was a silence while Thea fumed. Then Pat said, "So my question to you is, what are you doing here? I haven't seen any bills come in for this address, for no Fielding."

"I'm just helping her out."

"For free? Nothing's free in this life, Liam."

"Yeah, you taught me that pretty good, Dad." She heard the clang of a tool hitting another tool. "Look, she's a student like me, she needed a hand, I helped her. End of story."

"Well, just see that it is. I don't want your mother upset again."

His mother? Liam was the one who got cheated on! Who had to quit a job he loved because of it!

Liam didn't answer his father. Thea tiptoed over to the cupboard to get the chocolate chips and tipped them into the batter. Her arm ached from stirring in the flour, and her whole body burned from the injustice of Liam saying she looked down on blue-collar workers. Where had he gotten that idea? Hadn't she had one in her life for fourteen years?

Okay, bad example. But Gabe's job wasn't his problem. It was his lack of one.

The cellar door banged down, and Thea started stabbing the chocolate chips into the batter with her wooden spoon. The men came into the kitchen, assiduously wiping their feet on the mat first.

"Can I wash my hands?" Pat asked, nodding to the bathroom door.

"Of course," she said, hoping her voice indicated she had not a care in the world.

He left the door open as he did so, so Thea couldn't even lay into Liam in a furious whisper, but she did glare at him hard enough that he raised an eyebrow. Then he looked down at his feet and back at her. The dawning horror on his face turned her scowl into a giggle. She could see him going back over the conversation he'd just had, and he obviously didn't like what he recalled.

Okay, you never heard anything good about yourself when you eavesdropped, but it had almost been worth it to see that unguarded expression on his face.

"It's not funny," he growled, which of course made her laugh more.

"What's not funny?" Pat asked, joining them.

"The state of that boiler," Liam covered.

"That's right," Pat agreed. He talked to Thea, marking off the problems on his fingers. "You need the whole thing drained and cleaned. It's probably so furred up by now that won't even help, but you should do it anyway. Then we're going to look at your radiators because they're probably not shimmed properly." He looked pointedly at the table she was working on, behind which the radiator was hidden. "How often do you refill the boiler?"

"When it needs it," she said, trying not to sound defensive.

Pat sighed. He wasn't improving her impression of contractors. Especially the older guys who considered it a waste of time to explain anything mechanical to a woman.

"An empty tank can be dangerous," Liam broke in. Was it her

imagination, or did he sound more diffident, more patient than she'd ever heard him? "You should check it every week in the winter, especially since you don't have an automatic feed."

Thea waited a beat, then said, "Okay." She'd have to ask him later what an automatic feed was. She imagined the furnace in *Home Alone*, chomping on Macaulay Culkin's cherubic little fingers.

"Is that for tonight?" Liam was looking into the mixing bowl.

"Mm-hmm."

"Looks good."

Okay, now he was just trying too hard.

"Yeah, well," Pat said. "Let's look at these rads. I gotta get back."

Thea picked up the bowl and Liam pulled out the table. "Knew it," Pat said at once. "It's level."

"Isn't it supposed to be?" Thea said.

"No. It has to drain. Can't drain if it's level. Liam, go get the shims."

Liam went to the front of the house. Without him, the silence quickly got awkward. Thea's brain couldn't think of a single thing to say that wouldn't reveal that she'd heard their conversation. So they just stood there, until Pat crouched down by the radiator again and started spinning the valve.

"This valve should be all the way on or all the way off," he said in that low growl that so resembled Liam's. "Halfway like this and the condensate can't drain."

"Oh." Thea flushed. "But it's the kitchen. It gets hot in the winter. And the living room is too cold."

"Lots of windows in the living room. Plus"–he looked into the offending room at the radiator, which was behind the couch–"no circulation."

Well, where the hell did he expect her to put the couch? That was the only long wall she had.

Thankfully, she was saved from answering by Liam coming back through the front door. Thea was so glad to see him, she almost forgot she was pissed at him. Funny how a person could be your biggest pain in the ass, until you met a bigger one.

Now she remembered that Pat had made Liam promise five years of his life to him, back when Liam had had no choice in the matter. So Liam's restraint today was admirable. Then again, Pat was also his boss. Had to be difficult.

The two men moved the couch, and Liam put a level on the radiator. Thea went back into the kitchen and stabbed at her dough some more. Their quiet voices came to her, but finally, thank God, she couldn't hear what they were saying.

By the time she'd got the cookies into the oven, cut up onions and mushrooms, and rolled out some filo dough, they were back. The smell of sautéing onions and mushrooms filled the room, and her stomach growled.

"That's all we can do for now," Pat said. "You should have the system drained and cleaned before winter."

He still sounded so damn pissed off. Like her entire existence was a burden to him. Well, screw that. "Thanks again for coming out. What do I owe you?"

Pat's eyes slid to Liam's.

"That's all right," Liam began. "It was just a—"

"You were here for about an hour, wouldn't you say?" Thea said to Pat, not looking at Liam. "That's, what, one-fifty? For two of you, three hundred?"

Pat looked slightly nonplussed. Thea reached behind her for the checkbook she'd gotten out on purpose.

"Thea," Liam began, but there was nothing he could say about it. She was going to have to transfer some money into her account pronto after they'd gone, but it was satisfying to hand the check over to Pat.

Then she started to write another check. "Thea," Liam warned.

"The faucet, the toilet, and the air conditioner, right?" she said airily. "Plus the time you took to teach me the tiling. Appreciate that, by the way."

Pat seemed to find his voice. "This is too much, uh, miss—ma'am, uh, Ms. Fielding. We'd charge two hundred, max, for what we did today."

She loved hearing him stammer. He'd obviously expected her to make big eyes at Liam and not pay anyone anything for today. But she'd warned Liam when he'd made the suggestion. And now she had even more to prove.

Liam's face was thunderous. "Okay, then," she said, "give the other hundred to Liam and I'll write this one for another two. Okay?" She'd already done it, ripped off the check, and thrust it out to Liam.

His arms were folded, as usual, but he couldn't ignore her outstretched hand. He took the check as though it carried smallpox.

"Good!" she piped, brushing between the two of them to open the front door. "So I'll see you later, Liam? With the others? Celebrating the end of class?"

Liam let his dad out of the door first, but he stopped before he walked out. "Goddammit, Thea," he said in as low a growl as she'd ever heard from him.

"I'm glad we're all square," she said, equally low, with a giant fake smile on her face. "I'd hate to feel obligated to you or anything."

He couldn't say anything else; his father was waiting at the van. "We're not done," he said, jabbing a finger at her, and walked down the stairs, remembering not to touch the railing.

Thea let go of the door handle she'd been holding in a death grip and sank onto the couch. Five hundred dollars. She'd just given him five hundred dollars because she was pissed. Not that she didn't owe it to him, but if she'd been thinking straight, she could have maybe paid off what she owed him in installments.

But it wasn't about the money, was it? And logic didn't come into this... dynamic she and Liam had gotten themselves into.

She collapsed back into the cushions and took a deep breath to try to stop her racing heart. This was how she'd felt after yelling at Gabe, sometimes. Justified but still feeling as though she'd lost.

Another deep breath. In through the nose, out through the—

"Shit! The cookies!"

Chapter 8

Liam contemplated skipping the party altogether. Half the time he was so ticked at her he was blinded by it. Handing him her check like she was giving him a knighthood. That pissy look on her regal face.

You didn't think it was regal until you found out who she was.

What did that say about him?

Wait a minute, I'm not the one at fault here. I was just trying to be nice. She threw it back in my face, along with that goddamn check.

So don't go to the party. You never have to see her again, right? This was all a big lie anyway, remember?

But he liked the others. He needed to fix a date with Zahra to visit the kids in her neighborhood. He'd been thinking of pulling David aside to ask about the best way to save the money he needed to start school again next year. He figured David could be trusted not to tell the others. He didn't feel like getting that knowing look from Chloe again.

So, yeah, he'd go. He changed into a collared shirt, Chloe having made it very clear it was a party tonight, not a study group, and a nicer pair of jeans Avery had bought him when she was busy "fixing" him. He hadn't realized that was what she was doing at the time, of course. And he was frugal enough that he wasn't going to throw out a two-hundred-dollar pair of jeans. Besides, he got more respect at school when he wore labels the kids recognized. Same with the decent pair of brown suede oxfords. He stopped the truck at the liquor store and picked up some wine and beer, then at the restaurant where he ordered a couple dozen sliders to go, and drove to Thea's house.

The sun was lowering in the sky, but it was still light out when he arrived. Still, the lights were on in Thea's living room, and as he cut his engine, the sound of music blasted out of the window. He could see someone small dancing in the middle of the room.

"Hi, Mr. McConnell!" Benji called when he walked in the door. "Chloe's teaching me the jitterbug!"

Chloe was holding both of Benji's hands, and their feet were moving at impossible speeds while an old-time piano played out of the TV. On the set, Jerry Lewis was flinging himself around a dance floor with a platinum blonde in a sparkly silver dress. Seth and David were on the couch with their feet lifted to give Chloe and Benji more room, and Zahra was over in the entrance to the kitchen, laughing and keeping her drink out of the way of the action.

Liam was quite dazed, and it was a second before he found Thea. This was because she was crouched down by the TV, facing the shelf of books and DVDs beside it. "I know I have it," she was saying. "Just wait, Ben-ben, you can dance the Charleston next."

The song ended, Jerry Lewis collapsed onto the floor in a tuxedo-ed heap, and Thea said, "Ah-ha!" before turning around with a DVD in her hand and noticing him.

Her hair was down again, cascading over her shoulders and chest and onto her crouched knees. Her eyes looked huge, looking up at him like that, and she was in a red dress—God help him, a *red dress*—that floated over her frame. A gold bar sat at her throat, above a hole in the fabric, which from her position gave him a view he immediately had to look away from.

She was trying to kill him. She was actually trying to kill him.

His throat got stuck or something. There might have been a silence. Only when Chloe said, "Hello, Thea. Hello, Liam. My, don't you look hot. Want to kick everyone else out and—?" did Thea break position and stand up with a yelp of "Children! Children in the room!"

The dress almost reached her knees and floated around the rest of her in a way that should have helped him but only hinted all the more at what it covered. At least the hole at her neck was in its proper place now. Her cheeks almost matched the dress.

Liam was holding the box with his contribution to the dinner. It was Zahra who took it from him, saying in a kind voice, like one you'd use on an invalid, "That smells so good. I'm starving."

He followed her into the kitchen, blinded, stupid, but the mundane act of putting the sliders on a serving plate gave him some breathing room so he could go back into the living room with some idea of not acting like a horny teenager.

David also helped him out by immediately pouncing on him and demanding he show him and Seth the truck. After twenty minutes of standing out in the street, beer in hand, staring down into the engine of the Chevy, Liam finally felt like he'd regained his equilibrium.

This was as good a time as any to bring up the money.

"You weren't married long," David said, frowning, when he told him about his tight funds. Liam could see him getting into his accountant role. "Was the divorce that expensive?"

"She stretched out the separation agreement negotiations. Wanted half my house." Liam's jaw hurt from getting the words out. "I bought it when it was a piece of shit, and I brought it back before she and I got married. I gave her any of the furniture she wanted, but I was damned if she was getting my house too."

"Must have been hard to persuade the judge."

"It didn't get that far. Just a few months of a pissing contest back and forth between our lawyers. Me quitting my job was part of the compromise. She wanted to see me suffer one way or another."

"Nice lady."

"Yeah. In the end." Liam looked determinedly at the Chevy's hood, not wanting to see sympathy in their eyes. "Still, I got my house and the mortgage that goes along with it." The mortgage, which always made him wince nowadays, thanks to the broker who'd given it to him—and taken his wife in exchange. He'd actually been relieved when the bank sold it to some huge, faceless company. "And my new job is a big pay cut, so..." Time for confessions. "I'm not going back to school yet."

The twins stared at him. Waited.

He hooked a hand behind his neck. "I could afford only this one class. Like I said to Zahra, I wanted to make sure I had the language immersion theory down before I start in the fall. But I'm not taking any more classes."

"So why did you—?" Seth began, but David nudged him and he fell silent.

"Let me ask you a question," David said. "Do you own this truck outright?"

"Uh-huh."

"Any other student debt?"

"No." His dad had been true to his word on that. Unless you counted the debt of obligation Pat continued to cash in on.

"And you fixed up your house? You know what the value is now?"

Liam told him.

"Well, then, I hate to break it to you, but you should borrow the money and get into the fall program as quick as you can."

"What?"

David snorted a laugh. "Welcome to the twenty-first century, Mr. Retro." He nodded at the truck. "You put a lot of equity into your house when you renovated it, and your mortgage is half of what the house is worth. You can get a home equity line of credit so you only borrow what you end up spending on school. Or you can get a regular ole student loan."

"I thought you couldn't get loans for graduate school."

"Who told you that?"

Liam ran his hand down his beard. "My dad, probably. Mr. Retro, Senior." Pat didn't believe in debt. Liam didn't realize how much he'd assimilated his father's beliefs.

"Debt is great when you don't borrow more than you can pay back," David said. "This is an investment in your career. You know how much more you'll make as a principal, I assume? Well, so the thirty thousand you spend now will make you more than a hundred thousand a year. And since I assume you're gonna be studying part-time, you'd better get on it."

Liam pondered his words. They gave him hope, which he'd learned was a tricky emotion. He'd been waiting ten years to get this degree, to move forward into the career he really wanted. Avery's destruction of their marriage had pushed that idea back at least five years, or so he'd believed. If he listened to David, he could have his master's in three.

Going back to work for his dad had been a blow, he could admit it. He'd figured that even when he started the new job, he'd have to work on the weekends for his father to save enough money to get back to school. If he followed David's advice, he could concentrate on doing what he loved.

He felt as though he could straighten his spine for the first time since he'd found Avery in bed with that slick bastard. "Right," he said. "Thanks, David. I'll look into it."

"Cool," Seth said. "I'm out of beer. And what was it you brought to eat?"

Back inside Thea's house, Benji was dancing to the punk part of the *Silver Linings Playbook* dance while the women clapped along. The men went into the kitchen and brought out the food, and although Liam noticed real hard that Thea was sitting nowhere near him, he was buoyant enough about his own future now that he almost didn't care. They fell into easy conversation, and time passed. Benji went reluctantly to bed but rallied when Chloe offered to read him a story.

A short while after she'd come back downstairs, the front door slammed back into the wall, and Jake burst through it as if an entire squad of cops were after him.

He stopped short when he saw them all, his eyes wide. He was sweating and breathing hard; he'd obviously been running for a while, and Liam could decode the guilty look on his face from a hundred paces.

"Oh," Jake said.

"What the hell, Jake?" Thea asked. "Who's after you?"

"No one," he said—lied, Liam could tell, although the street beyond seemed quiet. "I just—we had a race."

"Well, I hope you won," Seth said.

"Uh, yeah, I did."

"So if it's a race, where are the rest of your friends?" Thea said, her voice chilly.

"Umm..." Jake looked around him frantically, as if the answer would appear in front of him. At last he settled on, "They gave up."

Thea folded her arms and glared at him. "You trying to kid a kidder, Jacob? Where the hell have you been?"

"Nowhere. I mean, in town, and we raced. Like I said. I need a shower." Jake got this out in staccato bursts and walked past Liam and Seth into the kitchen. The smell of cigarettes that followed him filled the room.

Time to dust off his teacher voice. Liam got up and followed him. "Jacob," he said.

Jake paused; Liam was banking on the teacher voice acting as an automatic stop, at least until Jake remembered he wasn't his teacher anymore.

Jake came back down the step, not meeting his eyes. "Yeah?"

"How did the job hunt go?"

"Huh?"

Liam knew he'd been expecting to be given a hard time for the cigarettes. The job hunt question threw him off guard, which was what Liam wanted.

"You know, the job hunt? That thing you've been out with your friends doing for the last week?"

Jake's eyes stayed lowered, and he put his hand to his neck to hide his face more. "Oh, well, you know..."

"So what are you going to do with your summer?" This had been bothering Liam for a while, and tonight he felt strong enough to bring it up. "Mooch off your mother?"

Now Jake glared at him. His words were as icy as his eyes. "I don't mooch off my mother."

Good. At least the boy had some pride. "I'm glad to hear it. So you have another plan for where you're going to look?"

"Why are you riding me about this? You're not my coach anymore."

Okay, he'd remembered. "Because a healthy fifteen-year-old should be working his summers."

Jake rolled his eyes. "Oh, like you did, and look at you now."

"Yes, Jacob." Liam didn't let him get away with that. He came closer so that Jake couldn't ignore him. "I have a vocation I love. I found it by going to school, but I also found it by doing jobs I didn't like as much."

"But you've quit teaching." Jake seemed way more angry about that than Liam thought he should, but then again, who knew what the rumor mill at his old school had been churning out about his breakup with Avery?

"I left Central. I didn't quit teaching. I have a new job starting in the fall, in the city. I will never quit teaching."

Jake looked up at him. *Whoops.* Might have been continuing an old conversation with his dad, there—or with himself—instead of focusing on what Jake needed now.

Jake seemed to shy away from the dangerous waters of an adult's emotions, for which Liam was grateful. "Okay, okay," he said, his eyes sliding away again. "I'll get a job."

"All right." Liam folded his arms. "I'll be checking in with your mom to make sure you do."

The teenage snark reared again; it was fascinating how hard it fought with the general respect Jake had been brought up to show to his elders. "Super," he said, and booked it up the stairs before Liam could say anything else.

◆

In the living room, Thea said to the others, "You don't have to tell me. I'm a terrible mother." She looked at Zahra. "I bet none of the parents at your kids' school don't know where their kids are all day."

Zahra held up her hands. "You're not a terrible mother, Thea. Of course you're not. We live in a safe town. You have to trust your kids sooner or later."

The memory of that cigarette smell was going to choke her. "But if he's too dumb not to smoke, who knows what else he's been persuaded to do?"

"I smoke," Seth said. They all looked at him.

"Yeah." David sighed heavily. "Dumbass."

"I'm just saying," Seth said. "It happens. Doesn't mean I'm a delinquent."

"I've never seen you smoke," Chloe accused.

"My brother used to smoke," Thea said, à propos of nothing. "He just did it to tick off my sister."

"That's an even worse reason," David said.

"Well, he always said that was it. I think a little teenage rebellion and a fat dose of grief had something to do with it."

Chloe nodded. She was old enough to remember the story in the papers about Thea's father dying in an explosion at one of his paper mills. It was the defining event of Thea and her siblings' lives. It had killed her mother as well, only two years later, and the official diagnosis had been breast cancer. If she'd still been alive, there was no way Thea would have let things get so out of hand with Gabriel.

"That's why Jake's doing it."

Liam had come back into the room without her noticing. His deep voice made them all jump. Thank God he was wearing a shirt that actually covered his muscles today; he'd looked too good already when he'd walked in, in that blue shirt that matched his eyes, the beat-up jeans, shoes in the perfect shade of suede, his beard and hair perfectly groomed. She was still pissed at him, but for those first few seconds, she'd completely forgotten why.

Now he seemed to look right through her and her kids with those blue eyes, and she knew he was right, damn him. Jake *was* grieving. He missed Gabe as if he were dead, which to all intents and purposes in the last two years, he had been.

The rush of memory of her own father's death and her mother's soon after, when she was only a couple of years older than Jake, pushed against her chest, and tears pricked the back of her eyes. She took a deep breath, afraid that she was going to melt down in front of everyone. Tonight she'd told herself she was not going to ask him for a single thing more. And that included counseling. Once a teacher, always a damn teacher. Well, he wasn't going to go all sniffer dog on her and her kids.

"Thanks, Dr. Phil." Sarcasm. Yes. That she could handle.

He scowled at her and folded his arms, his mouth that thin line she'd gotten so used to. "You know I'm right."

"You always are, aren't you?"

"You know, it's getting late," Zahra said. "Sorry, guys, but if you want a ride, we'll have to go."

Thea had killed the mood with her snark. Or Liam had killed it by getting serious. Either way, the awkward was rolling off everyone. Now she felt like shit again.

Zahra, who'd told them she drank only at weddings and funerals, was the designated driver, so Chloe, Seth, and David had been the ones making most of the holes in the drink.

"You need a ride, Liam? I can fit all of you in the minivan," Zahra said.

"I'm good," Liam said, not taking his eyes off Thea.

"Yeah, for real," Seth said, who was definitely looking cross-eyed. "You've had, what? One point five beers? You really know how to party, dude."

"You guys go ahead," he said. "Zahra, I'll see you Sunday." But he didn't look at her.

"Okay," she replied, uncertainty in her voice. "Thea? You want us to hang out a little longer?"

"Of course she doesn't," Chloe said, hefting Zahra's enormous bag from the floor and pressing it to her chest.

Thea was damned if she was going to blink first. If he had something to say, she was ready for him. "I'm fine. Got a couple of things to clear up with Mr. McConnell, here."

"Is that what they're calling it nowadays?" Chloe asked. Zahra poked her on their way out of the door.

Liam and Thea stayed in the middle of the room, eyes locked on each other, until the last threads of sound from Zahra's engine had died away. Then Liam opened his mouth, but Thea got there first.

"What the hell is your problem?" she said, furious but trying to keep her voice down.

"My problem? What about *your* problem?" He reached into his back pocket. "What the hell was this all about?"

He had the check she'd written him. "Payment, Liam. For services rendered."

"I told you I don't want your money."

"That was before you found out I'm a spoiled rich kid playing at being poor."

"That's not what I—"

"Yuh, Liam, that's exactly what you think."

"It is *not*. And what about you, huh? You've been looking down your nose at me since the minute you met me."

"I have *not*! You're the one who was scowling at me every time I walked into that classroom. I didn't *ask* you to fix my house, especially not for free, and now that I finally pay you, you get mad at me!"

She might have been able to hear his back teeth grinding together. "I—don't—want—your—money," he reiterated. "I was trying to help. Like a friend." He spat out the word.

"What friend? You don't even like me!"

"You don't like *me*!"

"That's 'cause you're always so damn cranky!"

"And you take people's generous gestures and throw them back in their faces!"

"I told you about my family in confidence, and you crapped all over it in front of everyone!"

"I didn't—" He paused. Seemed to lose a lot of the energy that was keeping him fighting. "I'm sorry about that. I just—hadn't expected it. That you were..."

Thea eased back as well. "What difference does it make?" she said, her voice softer. "Except that now you know I do have some money and I could pay you, so I did."

"The difference is..." He took a step closer to her, and his expression changed, his eyes not glaring anymore but sympathetic.

"The difference is that you don't need me, and I kinda wanted you to."

She hadn't expected that answer, and the low rumble with which he admitted it sent all her hibernating girl parts to dancing. Her breathing quickened. She could feel her skin more clearly, the light touch of her dress's hem against her knees and her neck, along her arms.

Her silence made him look away for the first time, rubbing the back of his neck with one hand. "Yeah," he said, with a small laugh, "your basic macho bullshit."

"I don't want to need anyone," she heard herself saying. "Ever again. Not you, not anyone." The fabric of her dress was in her clenched hands. When had she done that?

"I get that, Thea," he said. He was closer now. "And I still can't stay away."

The cool breeze trickling from the air conditioner made goose bumps rise up on her forearms. At least she thought that was what it was. Not his shirt that now brushed her arm or the warmth of him or the way his voice got richer, lower when he said her name.

She focused on the shirt button at his neck. If she looked up at him, she would meet his eyes. Maybe he wanted to kiss her. Maybe she could just lean in, a little. Maybe his arms would go around her and she could stop trying to do this all by herself for once in her life. He had so many answers; she wouldn't have to find them for herself for once.

He put out a hand and picked up a lock of her hair, letting it fall through his fingers, the ends curling around his forearm. Thea's girl parts went into the rumba, roused by the scent of him so close, the light rasp of his shirt on her skin. She bet his beard would be soft against her cheek.

She wanted to touch the spaces below his lower lip where the hair didn't grow. If she just pressed her finger against them, what would it feel like? Would he take a hold of her hand and press a kiss onto her palm, letting her feel his beard scratch on her skin the way his shirt touched her arm?

"Thea," he said.

"I'm complicated," she blurted out. *Smooth.*

"I know. I just got divorced."

"Yeah."

"I don't need this."

"Neither do I."

"Okay, then," he said, "as long as that's clear." And somehow, in one move, he was gathering her hair up behind her and his beard was tickling her chin and *thank God* he was kissing her.

Chapter 9

Thea let her head fall back and gave herself up to his mouth, which coaxed hers open. His tongue found hers, and she reached up her own hand to hold his head to her while the kiss went deeper and deeper. She was dimly aware that he was holding her up with one strong arm behind her back, but all she could take in was the nearness of him, the wetness of this kiss. *Thank God,* this kiss, the relief of being this close to him after so many weeks of teasing, so many years of being alone.

She moaned a little, and he broke away from her mouth to rain small kisses along her cheek, her temple, her hair.

"Dammit, Thea." He groaned into her hair.

"I know," she breathed, running her hands through his hair, feeling his breath warm hers. He smelled of wood shavings and peat, of safety and home.

But she wasn't supposed to be thinking these things. She was never going to rely on a man again. *Right?* So she should break away. *Now.*

He kissed her again, turning so that he sat on the couch and she sat on his lap. Tucked into him like this, she could reach his neck and jawline and press his head into the back of the couch and kiss him more deeply.

Okay, after this kiss.

Or this one.

Some time passed. Thea's whole body was waking up to him, though he kept his hands to her shoulders, back, and face. His rough fingertips on her cheek sent heat directly to her core, and she strained against him, loving his strength surrounding her.

Eventually, it was Liam who pulled away, dropping kisses on her as he did so, then taking her hands in his and kissing her palms. His beard was abrasive against her sensitive skin, and he left her only wanting more, more, more of him, not only in her bed but in her life. And that was a very dangerous road to go down.

"T," he whispered against her palm.

"Mm-hmm," she said. Or might have moaned.

"Quit beating yourself up. Your kids are great. You're doing great." He was wrapping her hair around his wrist again, letting the strands capture him and then freeing himself again and again.

She closed her eyes and fit her head under his chin. "How do I help Jake?"

He was silent for a moment while she listened to his heart beat steadily in his big chest. Then he said, "Have him come work for me."

That made her back up. "Seriously?"

He gave that white slash of a grin. "Sure. Let him see how the other half lives."

That ticked her off, a little. "Do I have to remind you that his dad is a carpenter? Was, maybe. Who knows what he's doing now."

"I'm kidding." She loved how he was looking at her now; the heat from their kisses was still softening his lips, but there was also a deeper warmth that made her trust his motives. "A couple of days with me and he'll figure out pretty quick how he wants to spend the rest of his life."

She frowned. "You won't torture him, will you? I think he's scared enough of you as it is."

"I'll treat him exactly as I was treated when I was an apprentice."

She paused. "That's what I'm afraid of."

He laughed. "No torturing, I promise. Just hard work. And a paycheck. And being too busy to think about what he doesn't have in his life. Because what he does have is pretty great."

She smiled at him, then sobered. "Don't let your dad make you feel small."

He raised an eyebrow. "Is that what I do?"

"It sounded like it." She put her hand on his chest. "You did everything he asked of you, and you still do. It's okay that you want to do something for yourself now."

"He thinks I've betrayed him. I'm his only child, and I don't want to continue the family business."

"It's not betrayal. That's not how it works. Don't let him let you believe that."

Finally, finally, she pressed her finger to one of the spaces under his lip. The gesture seemed more intimate than all the kissing they'd done so far. Liam sat very still while she ran her fingers over his face, feeling where his beard began and ended, until she could—and later did—recall every inch in her sleep.

The next time he took her hands in his, she knew the evening was ending. "I have to go," he said.

"You sure do." She grinned. "I've got kids sleeping upstairs. What were you thinking?"

"I haven't thought straight since I met you." He smiled back.

"Ditto."

She extricated herself with a heavy heart from his embrace and they stood. With the change in position came real life and the responsibilities that went with it. Thea's face fell. "I can't date you," she said at once. "The boys."

He nodded. "I know. We said this was going to be complicated, right?"

"Not complicated. Impossible." Dammit. It had been so nice to rely on him for a few minutes.

"Not impossible. We just have to go slow." He was still holding her hands, and he shook them a little. "Trust me."

"How can you be so positive? This has disaster written all over it."

One corner of his mouth quirked up. "Believe it or not, before about six months ago, I was considered an optimist. I've tried it the other way, and I still couldn't convince myself to stay away from you. So, yeah, Thea. We'll figure it out." He kissed her again, a gentle, chaste kiss, a squeeze of her hands, and he let go. "Have Jake ready, eight o'clock Monday morning. I'll give him an hour extra to sleep, since it's his first day."

He left her in the middle of the room, her whole body tingling. She'd never been so terrified or so exhilarated in her life.

Chapter 10

As promised, Liam arrived at Thea's house just before eight o'clock the following Monday. And as promised, apart from a quick text to confirm that he was coming, Liam hadn't tried to see her again. So to say that he was keen for her to open the door so he could get a good look at her for the first time in almost a week was an understatement.

He'd never seen her in work clothes before. She wasn't in a power suit or anything, just a pair of slim black pants that made her legs go on forever and a pale-blue blouse that tied to one side of her neck. Right where he'd nuzzled her last week. He had trouble taking his eyes off the spot long enough to meet hers.

"Hi," he said.

"Hi," she answered, and the welcome in her eyes made him itch to snake an arm around her waist and pull her closer. He'd been the perfect gentleman last Wednesday and had spent every night since dreaming about being everything but.

"Hi, Mr. McConnell!" piped a voice from behind her. And in a second, Benji was between the two of them, beaming up at him with Thea's eyes. "Are you really taking Jake to work with you today?"

"That's right."

"Can I come too? Mom said I couldn't, but I can, can't I?"

Liam met Thea's eyes for a second. She grimaced. He crouched down to Benji's level. "I'm sorry, Benji," he said, inwardly cringing as the kid's face fell. "Smaller kids aren't allowed on site. There are a lot of holes and bare electrics and things you could hurt yourself on."

"I'll be careful!"

"Yeah, I know you would. But people can hurt themselves anyway. And your mom wouldn't like it much if I brought you back extra-crispy from an electric shock. But I tell you what." Benji looked at him with so much hope, it made Liam's heart ache. How much had he already inserted himself into their lives? What if things didn't work out with Thea?

Still, he was here now. And he knew he'd always be there for these boys, if they'd let him. "The siding on the house? By the air conditioner?" Benji nodded. "Next week sometime, will you help me replace it? The air con leaked on it, and it's all rotten."

Benji was beaming again, a mini-Fielding smile. "Do I get to use the nail gun?"

He didn't have to look at Thea to know the horror on her face. "Better. You get to use the drill and the electric screwdriver. It's got twenty-one clutch settings."

Benji's eyes were huge. It didn't matter that he didn't have a clue what a clutch was. It mattered that he thought Liam thought he knew. "Okay," he said.

"Great," Thea said. She'd put on a pair of ballet flats and had her purse in one hand and Benji's backpack in the other. Her hair was back in a ponytail again, and Liam missed the silk of it against his wrist. "We have to go get the bus for day camp, and I have to get to work. Jake'll be down in a second. You good?"

"Yeah."

"There's coffee in the pot, a couple of muffins, and I made Jake a sandwich." She was walking and talking, throwing the last few words over her shoulder as she hustled Benji into her car.

"I want Liam to drive me!" he heard the boy say as she buckled him in.

"Nuh-uh. That blue monster baby probably wouldn't make it up the street."

Blue monster baby? Liam was offended, but then he looked at his pride and joy. It kinda fit. "I'm right here," he called. "And so is my truck. And she can hear you."

Thea giggled and closed the door on Benji's echoing laugh. "Bye," she said, getting into the driver's seat.

"Thea," he said. She rolled down the window. "Thanks. For trusting me."

A moment of stillness from her, in which he could take in how beautiful she was. "Thank *you*," she said. "Good luck. And please, don't bring out cranky Liam today."

Before he could answer, she was backing up and out of the bumpy driveway.

Liam went inside. The house was messier than he was used to seeing it, with clothes hanging on chairs, several pairs of sneakers at the door, and a half-eaten banana flopping on the coffee table. He appreciated anew how much work Thea had to do by herself. She must have needed a lot of time off work to clean up before they had their study group here every week.

"Jacob?" he called. No answer. Liam picked up the banana, brought it into the kitchen, and began to clean up the mess left over from breakfast. The coffee smelled good, so he poured himself a cup, even though he had his own in a thermos in the truck.

"Holy crap." Her coffee was amazing. Now he really might be falling in love with her.

"Jacob!" he yelled again, harsher this time. That wasn't a road he was going down yet. There was optimistic, and there was foolhardy.

"All right, all right," a morose voice said from the top of the stairs. Jake came down wearing a pair of skinny jeans that sure as hell weren't going to let him squat down to remove a wax ring or snake a drain. His hair was in those black spikes again. He must have gotten up early to fix them.

"It's not a fashion show, Jacob," Liam reminded him. "You're going to get some crap on your pants—possibly literally."

"Oh, God, really? Gross."

"Yeah, well. Luckily for you, I came prepared." Liam reached for the bag he'd brought in and gave it to Jake, who pulled out a pair of Pat the Plumber overalls as if they were a tutu and high heels.

"I really have to wear this?"

"You'll thank me later. Go put them on now while I finish up here. Put shorts on under. It's going to get hot today. And be quick about it. Our first appointment's in thirty minutes."

He put the kitchen to rights as best he could, went out to his car to replace his coffee with Thea's heavenly brew, and changed into his own overalls in the bathroom.

Jake schlumped down the stairs again, looking older and more professional in his overalls, and they left the house. Jake at least remembered to lock it on his way out.

They swung by Liam's father's office to pick up a van, then went to a house with a leaking showerhead a couple of towns over. Liam was methodical in his instructions to Jake, explaining tools and pressure and exactly why he was doing what he was doing. Jake was almost silent, but he looked as though he was listening.

On the way to the next scheduled call, Liam's cell phone rang. It was Laurie, the dispatcher. "I've got an emergency," she said when he put it on speaker. "You're in Needham?"

"Yep."

"I got sewage coming up in a first-floor bathtub. Looks like a blocked line."

"Awesome." Liam looked at Jake, whose face had paled at the word *sewage*. "We'll be right there."

"You got the new kid with you?"

"Uh-huh."

"Great. Trial by fire, huh?"

Well, it would certainly teach Jake to look for his own job next time. "What's the address?" Laurie gave it to him, and he hung up and made a left turn.

"Bet you're glad I gave you the overalls now, huh?" Liam grinned.

Jake still looked pale. "Why would it come up in the bathtub? That's so gross."

"When the block is farther down the drain, the water goes wherever it can go. And brings whatever it likes with it."

"So when she said sewage, she really meant..."

"Raw shit, yeah."

Jake went from white to green. Liam had to laugh.

He got out of the van at the house, a well-loved 1960s cape with an extension to the side he'd bet his bottom dollar hadn't been permitted properly, and directed Jake to get the power auger. He picked up the case with the inspection camera in it and knocked on the door.

The bathroom the homeowner directed him to already stank, and sure enough, the evidence was sitting morosely in the bottom of the bathtub. On further questioning, she confessed that the sinks and tubs all over the house had been draining slowly for weeks. As Jake wheeled the auger to the front door, Liam bit his tongue on the folly of people ignoring obvious problems until there was an emergency and met him outside.

The cleanout drain plug was halfway down the yard. This was not going to be fun. "All right," he said to Jake. "Gloves and glasses, second shelf down, right-hand side." Jake went and came back, and they suited up. Liam took a wrench and approached the plug. "Better not stand too close," he told Jake, which was pretty nice of him, he thought.

Sure enough, a good twist of the wrench and the plug popped out as if it had been waiting for Liam all its life. And out of the drain spewed everything that hadn't been able to drain down to the town sewer. Liam jumped back—looked like everything reached a good two feet high there—and then looked around at Jake.

"Oh God," the boy was saying. "Oh Jesus." And he added the contents of his stomach to the debris.

"Pretty cool, huh?" Liam grinned.

Jake carefully sat down and ran a shaky hand over his mouth, keeping his eyes averted from the mess. "You're sick."

"No, *you're* sick. Go get some water. There's nothing to do here but wait for the backup to settle down. Then we'll snake it."

When the pressure had released, Liam got some bags and began to clear up the godawful contents of the pipe. Jake didn't come back for a while. *Mission accomplished.* Jake'd be lugging buckets of spackle at the home improvement store by Thursday.

Liam checked the plug at the street and found that it had been knocked over, by a lawnmower probably, and had cracked and fallen into itself, creating the blockage. He went back to the van to get PVC pipe and a new plug to replace it, and found Jake sitting on the back fender, still shaky and green.

"All right, Jake," he said, "the worst of it's over. Just some digging and PVC and solvent. Come on."

They were carrying some supplies to the street cleanout when another Pat the Plumber van pulled up. Later, Liam swore he knew it was his father before the van had even rounded the corner.

"How's it going?" Pat said, walking over to them. "Broken cleanout?" Then he said, "This the new guy?" before he got a hard look at Jake.

When Laurie had asked the date of birth when they put Jake on the payroll, Liam had said, "I'll get back to you on that," because he knew what Pat would say.

Which was what he did say when he saw Jake's pallid face and spiked hair. "What?" Pat exclaimed. "He's just a kid!"

"He's fifteen. Same age I was."

"He's—but he's—" Right now, Jake did look young, unsure, and scared as the older man's voice rose. "Who the hell *are* you?"

Jake seemed to hope Liam would answer for him, but Liam didn't.

"Jake Donaghy, sir."

Pat dismissed him easily, turning his rising ire on Liam. "Where did you pick him up? Since when do we give summer jobs to teenagers? I don't have room for them. I need my apprentices doing these jobs, and you know it."

"He needed a summer job. Duane and Javier have plenty of work. I could use the help."

"If you need help, you ask *me* for a helper! You don't go find your own!"

Pat was turning red, and Liam was sure his own cheeks were following suit. He'd wanted a quiet day today, a day to get Jake in and out and ready to go find his own job before Pat realized he was involved. Typical that Pat would choose today to check up on him.

"Where did you find him?" Pat said again. "One of your students? Sorry," he added with a relish Liam hated him for, "*ex*-students?"

"Actually, yes." No need to mention Thea, whom Pat had taken such a dislike to.

But Jake, choosing this exact moment to get pedantic, said, "You were never my teacher. And I didn't get to varsity when you were coaching."

Shit. "Yeah, Jake, I know, but—"

Pat suddenly turned his sharp blue gaze on Jake. "So what are you doing here?"

Jake swallowed. "Umm... like he said. He's been coming to the house for study group. My mom must have told him—"

"Wait." Pat put a hand up, almost in Jake's face, cutting him off as he looked back at Liam. "This has to do with that Fielding woman, doesn't it?"

Liam was now wound so tight, he could feel the wrench in his hand cutting into his palm. "You don't have to talk about her like—"

"Goddammit!" Pat yelled.

"Jesus, Dad, the client—"

"Don't give me that bullshit!" Pat shouted at full volume. "I see the whole goddamn thing now! Your spoiled little rich kid here was too lazy to get a job, so you thought you'd scare him straight by bringing him here and showing him the shittiest job we do!"

"No, Dad—"

"You've got no respect at all!" Pat came up close to him, jabbing his finger in Liam's chest, spittle landing on his face. "No respect for me, no respect for the job that paid for your goddamn college and every stitch of clothing you ever had on your ungrateful back, no respect for the men you work with. I'm fucking sick of it!"

Liam opened his mouth, but Pat was in full flood. Pat had been pissed with him before and was known for yelling before he thought, but Liam had never seen him this angry.

Pat picked up the pipe they'd brought from the van and threw it at Liam, who only just caught it.

"Get out." Pat went back to the street cleanout, picked up Liam's bag, and swung it at him, letting go of it so that Liam had to drop the pipe to catch it with both hands. "Get the fuck off my jobsite. You're fired, and so is your little friend. Put my van back, get in that stupid truck of yours, and get out."

"You've always wanted this," Liam answered, standing his ground. "You've wanted to say this since the first day I told you I didn't want to be like you." He could feel his own voice rising, his own control ebbing away. He fought to keep his voice even. "Your precious ego is still bruised, and instead of dealing with the son you got, you keep on wishing for the one you'll never have."

He took the tool bag in one hand, put the other on Jake's shoulder so he spun around to face the van, and marched him away. Out of the corner of his eye, he saw the homeowner standing on her front doorstep, her mouth open. *Great.*

Pat either didn't notice her or didn't care. "A real son would respect his father!" he shouted after them. Liam closed his eyes momentarily, then opened Jake's door. Jake got in in silence, and they peeled away from the curb, burning a little rubber on the way.

Liam had been driving for four minutes, his mind teeming, Jake still mute beside him, when he said, "Damn it," and turned the van around.

"Where are we—?" Jake began, but apparently the look on Liam's face silenced him again.

When they pulled back up to the house, Pat beside it, the ground around the cleanout plug now partly dug out, Jake looked nervously at Liam again. Liam didn't look at him; he got out of the van and strode over to his father. He heard the door slam behind him, telling him Jake was following.

Pat looked up in surprise, then his eyes narrowed.

"You're right," Liam said.

Pat wasn't expecting that. "What?"

"You're right. I brought Jake out here to teach him a lesson. It was disrespectful to the job. When we got the call about the overflow, I should have taken him home."

It was Pat's turn to stand in silence. His mouth moved a couple of times, but Liam took advantage of the stunned expression on his face.

"I don't want to do this job, as I've told you many times. But I do appreciate that I know how to do it. And that you've given me extra work whenever I've needed it. I appreciate that you're a man of your word, and when I'd finished my apprenticeship, you paid for college even though you were disappointed I still wanted to go. I've thanked you for that, often, but I don't think you hear it." He ran his hand down his beard. "Thanks for the work you've given me this summer. I needed it, and you were there."

Pat just stood there, his shovel forgotten at his side. With his mouth slack and his white hair sitting any old way on his head, Liam was suddenly struck by how old his father was getting. Not far from retirement age, but he had no one to take over the business.

Still, if it was a choice between pleasing his dad and teaching for the rest of his life, there was no contest. "Come on, Jake," Liam said.

"Wait," Jake said, putting on the brakes as Liam began to walk to the car. "Mr. McConnell?"

"Yes?" they both said.

Jake was looking at Pat. "I want to stay."

Pat stared at him for a second, then snorted. "Yeah, right." He began to dig at the hole he'd made.

"I do," Jake insisted. And a look very much like his mother's came into his face, a stubborn look that said no obstacle was going to get in their way. Liam stayed quiet and let him finish.

"I didn't want to come, yeah," Jake went on. "And I'm sorry about the..." He waved at the lawn. "But I'm here now, and I learned something this morning, and I want to finish the job, and I promise I won't puke again."

Liam was sure his face registered as much surprise as Pat's, but for him there was something else, something he had no right to feel: pride. Jake was a good kid who dealt with adversity better than Liam would have believed. Talking to Pat McConnell after seeing him in psycho mode was a brave thing to do.

When Pat still didn't react, Jake put out his hand for the shovel. Pat gave it to him. Jake straddled the hole and began widening it with a lot more vigor than Pat had probably been using, rage-induced energy aside.

Pat watched him for a second and then said, "Liam, start snaking the line from the house to here; make sure we don't have tree roots or something to deal with on top of all this."

And just like that, they were hired again.

♦

Later that afternoon, when the lawn was cleaned up and the pipes replaced and Pat had gone off in his own van, Liam took Jake out for a burger.

Jake ate three. "You really want to do this again tomorrow?" Liam asked. A teenager's hunger still amazed him, especially after what they'd waded through today.

Jake stopped mid-chew and tried to swallow. "Jeez, you only have to nod!" Liam laughed.

Jake did so and then finished his baseball-sized mouthful. "You think your dad'll let me back?"

"He liked you," Liam said. "Couldn't you tell?"

"No."

"Well, he ordered you around and called you a Muppet when you stripped those threads. I'd say that's a ringing endorsement."

Jake took five French fries and eyed them. "Sorry I got you in trouble," he mumbled before shoving them into his mouth.

Liam stretched out his legs and put his hands behind his head. "You didn't. I did. And it was all stuff that needed to be said. In a way, I should thank you."

Jake concentrated on eating for another few minutes. Then he said, "Mr. McConnell? Why did he call Mom 'that Fielding woman'? Why doesn't he like her?"

"Preconceived ideas, Jake." Liam picked up the rest of his burger, but he must have been getting old or something because it just didn't look as good to him as it used to. "Preconceived ideas." Pat wasn't the only one who had those.

Before he took him home, Liam said, "And if I'm going to be your boss, you'd probably better call me Liam."

Jake looked scandalized. "Oh, no… I don't think I could."

Liam shrugged. "Like you said, I'm not your teacher. My dad stays Mr. McConnell, though, right?"

"Of course." Jake got in Liam's truck, which they'd exchanged the van for. "Is he going to be on the job with us a lot?"

Liam laughed hard for the first time at the apprehension in Jake's voice. "At first, probably. He'll want to catch us screwing up. But he'll back off eventually." Liam turned the key in the special way he'd agreed with his truck. "Like just before you go back to school." He grinned as the engine roared.

Chapter 11

Thea came home with Benji to find Liam and Jake playing a video game. The dynamic of teacher and student seemed to have changed utterly; Jake was yelling at Liam to "Get him! Get him! No, with the blue gem!" and Liam was yelling back, "All right, all right, I don't know how to—" and Jake said, "Hit A and green and—aw, crap. You suck at this."

"Jacob!" Thea gasped, but Liam grinned in a way that squeezed her insides and threw the controller down onto the couch beside him.

"I'll have you know I was playing video games when you were in diapers," he said.

"Yeah." Jake snorted. "I can tell. Haven't played much since then, huh?"

Liam scrubbed his hand through his hair and looked up at her. "Nope. Hi."

This was all way too easy. Benji was thrilled to see him and immediately asked him if he'd play a game with him. Jake was more relaxed than she'd seen him around adults in months; his spikes were wilting and he didn't even notice. Thea clutched her purse to her stomach and tried to regain some equilibrium.

"You didn't have to stay," she said to Liam.

"I asked him to," Jake said.

"Is that okay?" said Liam.

More than okay. Way too okay. "Sure. I don't want to put you out more than we already have."

"He's not put out," Benji said. "Can he stay for dinner?"

Thea's throat tightened at the easy question. "I can't," Liam, thank God, told him. "Sorry, bud. Maybe Jake'll play a game with you."

He was calling him Jake, she noticed, rather than the formal, teacher-ish Jacob he'd been insisting on all these weeks. "I guess today went well," she said.

"Uh-huh," Liam said, his eyes sliding over to meet Jake's.

"Yeah," Jake said, and if she was a suspicious person–and face it, around Jake she was–she'd have thought he looked a little shifty. "It was good. But I'm starving, Mom. What's for dinner?"

Liam stood up. "I'll go now. See you tomorrow, Jake. Seven o'clock, okay?"

Jake groaned but nodded. Thea was still at the door, and when Liam joined her, the area suddenly seemed much too small. Jake was taking out the game card and putting in another one he and Benji could play, and she was left with Liam standing very close to her, giving her that hard blue stare that was never far from her thoughts these days.

He reached around her to open the screen door, still holding her gaze. "You all right?" he asked, his eyes crinkling at the corners, the smile he gave her warming her, showing her that he remembered the last time they'd been this close.

She nodded. "Was it really okay today?"

His smile widened. "It was really okay today. How are the scientists?"

"Great. They didn't need me, as usual. I read five chapters of the textbook for our next class."

He smelled so good, of soap and grass and not at all what he might have been dealing with in his job today. His jeans were the perfect amount of beat-up, his T-shirt showing off those biceps again. What wouldn't she give to be able to sink her teeth into one of those puppies?

She blushed and her eyes widened, and he smiled even bigger. "I'll see you tomorrow."

Oh, yeah, right. She was in the way. She stepped back, holding the screen door open with her back, and Liam went through. "Bye, Jake. Bye, Benji," he called. And as they called their goodbyes back, their eyes glued to the screen, he took one of Thea's hands and brought it to his mouth, pressed a kiss into her palm, and closed her hand over it with both of his. That kiss was regret that he couldn't do more, and a promise that at the next available opportunity he would.

"Goodbye, T," he said so that only she could hear, then stepped off her porch.

♦

Four days later, Thea was in an almost constant state of sexual anticipation. She'd seen him every day that week, eight times, total. Eight minutes, ten max. And every time, he only had to look at her with those eyes and she'd melted.

On Tuesday, Jake had been a minute late downstairs. Liam had used the time to his advantage, kissing Thea so hard she had to escape into the living room to fix her lipstick when they heard Jake's footsteps. It had been a risk, and hell, she wanted him to risk it again so *bad.*

On Wednesday, Jake was on time. Liam followed him out of the front door, having only time to run his hand down Thea's back, caressing her spine and, yeah, copping a quick feel of her butt before they were gone. Thea spent so much time recovering from that, she woke Benji up late and they had to race to the bus for camp.

On Thursday, she found herself silently willing Jake to be late again. And thank the sweet gods of lust, he was. This time Thea backed Liam into the refrigerator, knocking off three magnets and a self-portrait of Benji while she grabbed Liam's hair in both hands and pulled him down to her mouth.

They barely spoke, spent only seconds with each other, and didn't text or call each other all week. She wanted to, because there was no study group that week and she was disappointed not to have a full evening to ogle him. But what could she say? *Please come ten minutes early tomorrow so I can start something we won't be able to finish?*

So those eight minutes were a precious memory she kept to herself. More than any other time in their fledgling relationship, Thea clung to those stolen moments, and the softening of his eyes when he looked at her.

Now it was July Fourth, and she would not see Liam. She tried to relish her lie-in and enjoy not waking the boys up until almost lunchtime. She tried not to think about how much more fun this lie-in would be if Liam were there.

After a leisurely bath and a quiet cup of coffee on the front porch, she made spinach salad and spinach dip and thought about Liam. Then she got the boys up, fed them, and thought about Liam. Sam called for their pre-family-ordeal conversation, during which Thea did not bring up Liam, but she thought about him. Then she drove with the boys to Kane's house. And thought about Liam.

Perhaps it was just that Liam was the first man she'd had any interest in, apart from Gabe, in fifteen years. Perhaps this was the first extended time she'd spent with a man apart from Gabe. Perhaps she was finally seeing the end of her years-long mission to become a teacher, and she had some small leisure to look around her. These were all reasons she was mooning over Liam so much.

Also, could be that ass in those jeans.

Kane's house was a colonial on Chestnut Hill, with enough bedrooms that Thea kept losing count, enough bathrooms that they talked about them by color, a giant conservatory where Ellen grew lemons, and a pool in the backyard big enough for their whole family and several friends.

Thea understood that, as president of Fielding Paper, Kane needed a place where he could entertain clients and staff, and that the extra bedrooms helped when Ellen's family came to visit from England. But after her own tiny house, she was always a little dazed when she followed the boys into the pristine backyard.

Her family was just where she expected them: Kane and his best friend, Carl, were arguing at the grill. Antonio, Cat's husband, was in the pool with his sons and Cat, who was in the shallow end, holding Kane's baby daughter and watching his four-year-old swim in floaties. Ellen's best friend, Penny, who was married to Carl, was sitting in a lounge chair, her toddler children in a fenced-off area of grass next to her while she nursed a baby.

Even half-covered with a towel, Penny looked exquisite, the sun shining off her platinum blond curls, a fifties-style bikini and mules, for crying out loud, completing the look. Cat was wet and bedraggled and hefting a twenty-pound baby and yet looked like she'd just stepped out of a photo shoot. Kane was the Greek god over there at the grill, the gray that two daughters had put in his hair detracting not even a little bit from his chiseled cheekbones. Carl was dark-skinned and stocky, with big brown eyes and broad shoulders. Antonio was smaller than all of them, but he had those beautiful Italian black curls and a smile that welcomed the world.

Thank God Sam's not here, Thea thought, though she didn't mean it. *My ego couldn't take another one of the beautiful people.*

Right on cue, Ellen and Megan, Thea's youngest sister, came out of the kitchen onto the patio, carrying a plate of shish kebabs and corn on the cob. Thea sighed, straightened her old cover-up, and went over to them.

Megan squealed and dropped the plate of corn on the nearest surface before pulling Thea, spinach dip and all, into a hug. "So good to see you!" she said. "You look great!"

"You are so going to heaven," Thea said, patting her cheek. She planned on spending the afternoon in the pool, so she'd worn no makeup and her hair was back in her usual ponytail. Her swimsuit was just a boring black one-piece, but it fit, and the cover-up was a turquoise she'd always loved, so if she could just stop comparing herself to her perfect siblings and their spouses, she would be feeling quite pleased with herself today.

And Liam kissed you a whole bunch. You've got that going for you.

"Phew! You look hot," Ellen said, hugging her. "Scorcher of a day, isn't it? Is that my spinach dip?" She handed Kane the kebabs and grabbed the container. "I don't know how I lived before your spinach dip." She sighed, fluttering her eyelashes. Ellen had no makeup on either, but unlike Thea, her skin was flawless and glowed with health. Thea had office-lights-pale skin.

Jake and Benji had already dumped their towels and cannonballed their cousins in the deep end of the pool. The noise level doubled. Peppy summer music came out of the speakers on the patio, and jugs of iced tea and Pimm's cup were sitting in ice. Ellen had been a party planner before she stayed home with the kids, and it showed.

"Pimms?" she asked Thea, already pouring her a drink while Kane and Carl waved their tongs at her from the grill.

"Of course," Thea said. "You've trained me well." Then she turned to Megan and added in a stage whisper, "Then get me a Corona, two limes, for the love of Pete."

Thea followed them into the cool kitchen, which was huge but welcoming with its cream cabinets and soft beige countertops. It was a lot to take in, but Thea didn't begrudge Kane one inch of its custom tilework. He'd worked hard for it; without him, she wouldn't have a house, so he could do whatever he liked with his.

Also, she knew that Ellen had actually reined him in on some of his ideas for the house. "You know how many fridges he was planning?" she'd once complained. "Five! And not just a couple of little wine fridges under the counter, oh no. One on each floor, one in the garage, and one on the patio." They'd compromised on three, and although Thea still couldn't figure out what they did with them all, there was no denying that the Fieldings were never out of ice.

Thea put her drink down and found a bowl for her salad, and they settled into the comfortable routine they'd fallen into over the years. When everyone was called to the long farmhouse table on the patio, sheltered by a trellis and grapevine that Kane said he regretted planting because it dropped leaves and overripe grapes into everything, Thea sat back for a moment and closed her eyes. It wasn't a bad life, all in all.

She opened them again. Wow. What a difference a year made. This time last year, Gabe had been gone only ten months and she still alternately railed at the thought of him and missed him with all the hurt of a rejected nineteen-year-old.

Things were different now. She looked at Kane and Ellen, teasing each other about how well-cooked the burgers were, and at Cat and Antonio, who'd been married since the Flood. Carl and Penny looked pooped but content, as they had ever since their son had been born. Thea had grown up knowing Carl, but she'd never seen him the way he was with Penny and his baby. He was so happy it was indecent to look at.

What was different this year was that for the first time, Thea wondered if she might be able to find that kind of contentment with... someone. She wasn't going to say Liam, because he was new and scary and, God help her, young. She was afraid to ask how young. But maybe, one day, she might find herself ready to trust someone again. Maybe there were good guys out there.

And maybe those good guys had beards that could give her rugburn in all the right places if she let him.

"What are you smiling about?" Cat asked, ever alert to her family's moods.

"It's a nice day," Thea said, smiling more.

"Yeah," Cat said slowly. "It is." But she didn't look convinced.

"I'm going in the pool. Benji! Don't rattle the gate. And finish your peas."

"They're cold!"

"They're supposed to be cold. It's a salad."

"Gross."

"Fine. Have the spinach salad instead."

"Urgh!" He ate the pea salad. Once he figured out there was bacon in it, he was much more amenable.

"Take Johnny?" Penny asked next to her, and Thea held out her hands. The baby was a gorgeous little boy with gold skin and blue eyes, which were closed now as he slept. Thea let his weight sink into her and felt the rare contentment expand in her chest. Yeah. Things could be a lot worse.

She might have dozed off. The next thing she heard was a shriek from the house. She and the baby jerked awake. Someone had put a blanket under his butt so that he wouldn't roll off her lap. Cat, probably. But there was some new crisis coming from inside the house.

"Kane!" Ellen was yelling. "Quick! It's frigging Niagara Falls!"

Kane, who had obviously been in the pool, ran past Thea, dripping wet. She heard more raised voices, and her curiosity got the better of her. Hefting Johnny more tightly in her arms, she followed the sounds.

Everyone except Megan, who stayed with the other small kids, flocked into the kitchen and through it to the hallway that led to the main staircase. In the middle of it, between the butler's pantry and the dining room (seating for twenty), water was pouring through a recessed light fixture and onto the two-hundred-year-old floor tiles.

"Make it stop!" Ellen cried.

"Hon," Kane said, sounding just as stressed. "How the hell do I make it stop? How the hell did it get in the light fixture anyway?"

"You could turn off the main water line," came another voice.

They all turned as one to face Jake. Under so much attention, he blushed. "I mean, it's a leak somewhere that's finding the path of least resistance. So first of all, we should—"

"*How*?" interrupted Kane.

"Jesus, Kane, tell me why we bought this ancient pile again?" Ellen snapped. "It's in the basement!"

They all moved off, Jake, Ellen, and Kane running, the others seemingly attached to them by long strings, following behind, too riveted to do anything else.

At the top of the basement stairs, the rest of them waited while the voices carried from downstairs. "Jake, do you know what it looks like?" Kane asked.

"I know what it looks like!" Ellen retorted, but then Jake said, "Here it is," and she said, "Oh. I thought it was that one."

Then Jake said, "Okay, it's off."

The others looked back down the hallway. The water was less of a deluge now, and more of a light rain shower. By the time Jake, Kane, and Ellen had come upstairs, it had stopped. "Jacob," Kane said, "You're a genius."

Jake was flushing again. "Now I should see if I can find what's leaking." He grinned at his uncle. "And hope it isn't a drain stack."

But after a few minutes of looking, Jake couldn't find the source of the leak. Everyone else except Thea and Benji, who'd been mopping up the mess with towels, had gone back out to the pool.

"We can't call a plumber!" Ellen exclaimed. "It's a holiday!"

"We can't be without water all weekend either, hon," Kane pointed out.

Jake looked at his mother. "Liam might come."

Kane said, "Who's Liam?" at the same time Thea said, "Oh, I don't know, Jake."

"Who's Liam?" Ellen repeated.

"Mom's... friend," Jake said. Thea closed her eyes at the pause. Now it was going to hit the fan. "And my boss." He added that with a pride that almost outweighed her dread at the next question.

"Your 'friend'?" It was Cat, of course, leaping on every nuance, every detail of Thea's life that she dared not inform Cat about.

"Yes," she said in what she hoped was a robust voice, though she could feel her cheeks burning. "A student I'm at school with. But we can't call him, Jake. He—"

"Wait a minute." Cat wasn't done. "How is he a student in a teaching program *and* a plumber *and* Jake's boss?"

"He was a teacher at my school," Jake said. "Before that, he was a plumber. He gave me a job, helping him out. Learning." He looked at his mother. "I bet he'd help."

Cat folded her arms and glared at Thea in a way that reminded her of early Liam. "Would he, T? Would he help if *you* asked him?"

"It's July Fourth," Thea said weakly, still looking at Jake.

"Yeah," Jake conceded. "But..." He pointed up at the bubbles of water still clinging to the ceiling above them.

"Do you have his number?" Of course, she did too, but she wasn't about to get her phone out and confirm it to her siblings.

Jake looked at her scornfully. "We both do, Mom." Yeah, she was no good at subterfuge.

Thea paused, with Johnny still in her arms, an ineffective shield against them all. It was too soon. Too soon to bring that part of her life into this. She would have liked another few weeks, perhaps months, before inflicting her family and their knowing smiles on him.

"All right," she sighed. "I guess you can ask." Jake made to turn and run out to where he'd dumped his stuff by the pool. "Jake! Ask him if he knows anyone who'd come. Don't ask him directly." Jake turned away again. "Make sure he doesn't feel obligated!" she called after him.

They all trooped back out to the patio, where Carl took Johnny from her.

"Want to tell me something?" Cat asked.

"Nope." And Thea stripped off her cover-up and dived into the pool. The water soothed her burning cheeks as she swam laps, letting the rush of water over her ears block out the sound of Cat's silent disapproval.

When she finally resurfaced, everyone was pretty much in the same position they'd been earlier that day. Carl and Penny were beginning to pack up their things.

"Can you quit swimming long enough to say goodbye?" Penny asked from the sidelines. "We promised my parents we'd visit, and we've still got a bit of a drive."

Thea climbed out and gingerly hugged Penny, not wanting to get her wet. Then she helped them fold up the playpen and gather towels and burp cloths and bottles from all the corners of the yard. The family each got their hugs in turn, and Thea, carrying one of the diaper bags, followed Carl and Penny out to the circular driveway and their car.

A big baby-blue truck pulled up as they were clipping the children into their seats. Thea's heart rate doubled. She couldn't help but look down at herself, at her wet swimsuit and flip-flops and nothing else. She might as well have been naked.

"What the hell?" Penny said.

"That's his—"

"Liam?" Penny interrupted, not looking at Thea.

Chapter 12

Penny met Liam as he got out of the truck.

Thea had been so embarrassed at her lack of clothing, she couldn't look at him, but now she looked up, and all her girl parts fired at once. He was in a pair of board shorts and a UV T-shirt that clung to his chest like a second skin. Thea forgot how to breathe.

She thought he looked over at her, but then he kissed Penny's cheek. "Hey," he said. "What are you doing here?"

"What are *you* doing here?" Penny replied, her eyes wide and round. "Oh. Wait. You're Thea's Liam?"

Kill me now. There were pillars and bushes and the like in front of the house, but none she could easily run and hide behind. She closed her eyes, and when she opened them again, Liam had her with those blue eyes of his, his mouth quirked up on one side. "I guess so," he said, and everything in her clenched again.

"Jake's Liam," she tried, but no one was listening. Carl introduced himself and went in the back to let Kane know that Liam had arrived.

"I didn't know you were back to being a plumber," Penny was saying.

"Just for the summer," Liam said.

"So how did you meet Thea?"

"At college. I'm taking some classes."

Did he take his eyes off her once during this exchange? Could he see her chest rising and falling in these stupid quick jerks?

"You had a baby?" he said to Penny.

"Yeah! Johnny. Wanna see?"

How does she know him? What was it like to be that easy around him?

Liam obediently went around to the open car door where the baby was sleeping in his car seat. "Cute," he said.

Thea finally found her voice. "How do you know each other?" she burst out.

"We're cousins," Penny said, and for one heart-stopping moment, Thea thought that meant she and Liam were cousins too. Carl had been a fixture in their lives for so long, the word *family* included him and all his connections. Then she mentally slapped herself.

"Well, second cousins once removed or something," Penny clarified. "There are a lot of us." She grinned up at Liam. "Liam got all the redheaded Irish stepchild genes."

He grinned back. "You never know," he teased. "If anyone could remember your original hair color, it might be red too."

She winked and fluffed her platinum curls. "You'll never know."

Kane came down the path from the backyard then, and Penny kissed Liam again, waved at Thea, and got in her car.

"Hi. Kane Fielding."

"Liam McConnell." They shook hands. Kane was taller than Liam, but Liam was broader.

"I really appreciate you coming out. I think Jake saved us from permanent damage, but we have no idea where the leak's coming from."

Thea stood there like a deer in headlights, waiting for the moment when they would walk past her. As he did, Liam said, "Hello, Thea."

He shouldn't have done that. Right there, for everyone to hear, was every kiss he'd given her that week. The timbre of his voice was a glowing neon sign—even Kane looked around at it, frowning at Thea.

She didn't trust herself to follow him into the house, so she went around back and found her cover-up. The boys were playing soccer on the grass behind the pool. Cat and Megan were entertaining Kane and Ellen's daughter while Ellen spooned something into the baby's mouth.

Thea got herself a beer and sat on the other side of the pool, watching the boys. It was a pathetic attempt to keep Cat away, and it failed, because she just got into the pool with Libby and fired questions at Thea from there.

"So?" she began.

"Hey, isn't it time to call Sam?" Thea said, looking up at the sky as if Sam would appear from there and rescue her.

"Oh, yeah, I'd love to see what Sam thinks of this. Does *she* know about him?"

"Cat, there's nothing to know."

"So why did you go bright red when Jake brought him up?"

"'Cause I knew what you guys would say. Seriously, can we call Sam?"

"Come on, T. Spill. What's the big deal if it's no big deal?"

"She's got a point," Megan added.

"Thanks a bunch. You just wait till it's your turn."

"It'll never be my turn." Megan smiled. "Better get it over with now. Rip the Band-Aid off, so to speak."

"Fine. He's in a study group I'm in. He fixed a couple of things around the house. We fight a lot. That's it. Okay?"

Megan laughed and Cat scowled. "So not okay," Megan said. "You fight a lot? That's passion right there."

"Shut up, Meg."

"Yeah, Meg, shut up," Cat said. "This is serious, T. Did you get that paperwork in like I told you?"

"Yes."

"How long ago?"

"Three months." Actually, it was six weeks, but Thea wasn't about to tell her that.

"Look." Cat did that thing where she jumped from bitchy mother to caring sister in a blink. She put her hand out to cover Thea's. "You look better. Less tired, less... hopeless. If this guy's done that for you, I'll love him to the end of time. But first"–she gripped Thea's hand hard–"you have to sort out your little abandonment problem."

"Jeez, Cat," Megan said, "it's been two years. You think you could give her your royal approval to move on, maybe?"

"I wanted her to move on fifteen years ago," Cat said. Thea rolled her eyes. They would never forgive her for Gabe.

"I'm not 'moving on,'" she said, pulling her hand away. "There's nothing to tell. Liam's just"–*hot as hell, and my fingers are constantly itching to touch his beard and his hair and wrap themselves around his bicep and*—"really, truly, being a friend right now."

"Giving Jake a job?"

"What about me?" Jake had heard his name. She hoped he hadn't heard the rest of the conversation.

"Liam's here," Thea said.

"Why didn't you tell me?" he said, dropped the soccer ball, and ran into the house, closely followed by Benji. His cousins looked after him in surprise.

"So they're fans of Liam, too?" Cat said slyly.

"Please, stop," Thea begged. "I'm well aware that things could get very complicated. Which is why I'm telling you not to make a big deal out of it. Especially in front of the boys."

Her sisters seemed to accept this and fell silent. Ellen brought the baby back into the pool, and there was peace for a few minutes.

Then Kane brought Liam out to the patio. "At least have a glass of iced tea," he said. "I feel bad taking you away from your family."

"It's not a problem," Liam said. He lasered in on Thea right away. Her cover-up helped her return his gaze with some courage this time.

"Oh, do have a glass before you go," Ellen said, stepping out of the pool like Aphrodite from her shell. Megan, in a gold and black bikini, was lounging like Elizabeth Taylor as Cleopatra, and Cat, even after twenty years of marriage and two teenage sons, was striking with her dark hair and strong jaw.

Yet, among all her beautiful family, Liam was looking at *her*. And Thea was smiling at him; she couldn't help it.

"Okay, thanks," Liam said to Ellen, accepting the glass of iced tea.

"It's not a leak," Kane told her.

"How is that possible?"

"It was your drain pan under the air conditioner in the attic," Liam said. "The pipe must have gotten blocked and it overflowed. There's a safety shutoff on the units nowadays that stops the unit from running when the tray fills up. But yours..." He paused.

"Is ancient. Dammit." Ellen thumped her thigh. "I knew we should have done the mechanics first." She mock-scowled at Kane. "You and your heated wet bar."

"Yeah, complain when it's winter and you've got fifty guests and ten feet of snow outside," he retorted.

"It's lasted a long time," Liam said. "You should have the HVAC guys come in as soon as possible to look at it, though. You might be able to get away with just adding the shutoff valve."

Ellen sighed. "So we called you away from your family for nothing."

"It's fine," he said, his eyes flicking to Thea and back. "It was a big crowd; I won't be missed."

"The water's back on," Kane said to Ellen.

Jake, for some reason, scowled. "You did good," Liam said, catching it. "Always the correct first move. The leak stopped because the pan was empty, but you had the right idea."

"And he knew where the shutoff was when we didn't," Kane added, ruffling Jake's hair. Jake, predictably, ducked out from under him and put a hand to his head, flattening his pool-styled curls. "So Jake's working for you for the rest of the summer?"

"Until about mid-August, yeah. I'm starting a new teaching job around then. If he still wants to come." Liam smiled at Jake.

"Yeah, I do," Jake said. "Apart from when we go to the Cape, right?"

"Right," Kane said.

"When's that, Jake?" Liam asked.

Jake looked at Kane. "In two weeks," Kane answered for him. "For a week."

"Is that okay?" Jake asked.

"Sure. I'll try and survive without you for a whole week." Liam put down his empty glass. "Thanks, Mrs. Fielding."

"Oh God. Ellen, please." She came up, putting the baby on her other hip, and shook his hand. "Any friend of Thea's is a friend of ours."

"Well, thanks, I appreciate that."

Kane, accompanied by Benji, who was prancing around Liam's legs, walked him to the path that led to the front of the house. "You sure you won't let me pay you for your time?" Thea heard him say as they turned the corner.

She made a movement, as if she had any chance of getting in front of Kane and forestalling that conversation, but she stayed where she was.

"What's the matter, Mom?" Jake asked. "You hardly spoke to him. You didn't even say thank you."

"Oh." She unstuck her throat. "You're right. I'll say thank you on Monday."

Jake shook his head. "I thought going to school was supposed to make you smarter."

"Hey, Mom!" Benji was back, running through the gate. "Liam says he can pick me up from the bus!"

"What?"

Now it was Benji who looked at her like she was crazy. And maybe she was. This afternoon had been surreal. There wasn't one part of it she could hold on to, ever since Ellen's first scream from the flooded hallway. "The bus, Mom! So I don't have to go to aftercare! And he and Jake'll take me to the park every day, or we can stay home and play video games!"

"Oh, Benji," she began, finally moving her stiff legs toward him. Liam and Kane appeared again at the gate.

"Really, Mom, he said it was fine!" Benji ran up to her, pulling her hand to make her go faster. "It's perfect! Then you don't have to spend the money on aftercare"—Thea cringed—"and Jakey isn't home alone!"

Liam had a look on his face like he'd been caught doing something he knew was wrong. "Benji, Liam and I have to talk about it," Thea said. "Go on back and swim some more."

"Why do you have to—?"

"Go on, Ben." She put on her no-questions voice, and Benji obeyed.

"This isn't a good idea," she hissed at Liam.

"I didn't suggest it," he said quickly. "It kind of... snowballed."

"I don't want him to get—"

"Thea," he said, and she clenched her fists against the longing that his use of her name created in her. "I'm sorry, but I think that horse has bolted."

She closed her eyes and sagged against the frame of the gate.

"What horse?" Kane said. She'd forgotten he was behind Liam.

"Never mind," she said. "Okay, look."

"No, you look." Liam put his hand on her arm. Just a light touch, only enough to keep her in his sights, but he might as well have kissed her. That touch was more intimate and told Kane everything she'd been hiding from the others. "I'm here, okay? I'm not going anywhere."

"You can't say that," she said weakly. "You don't know—"

"You're right, I don't. But I know enough to know I'm not going anywhere."

Tears came into her eyes. It wasn't just that he was brave enough to say it and not care who was listening, but it was the sincerity in his voice and the words themselves that he must have known she'd been wanting to hear for fifteen years. If they fell apart now, more than the boys' hearts would be broken.

Her mom brain kicked in. "I'll have to get the form filled out for the bus to release him to you. Can you come at six o'clock on Monday night so they can meet you?"

"Sure."

"All right, then. Thank you." She hoped her eyes said it the way she meant it.

"You're welcome, T," he said. "See you in a couple days."

And then his hand was gone, and Kane was walking beside him to the blue monster baby.

Chapter 13

He shouldn't have come. His father would have taken his place. He would love to get his hands on this house, and this would have been the perfect opportunity to ingratiate himself with the Fieldings. Old house, ancient plumbing, deep pockets. Every contractor's dream. But no. Liam couldn't resist the chance to see her again, among her family. And Jake had asked for him; if he hadn't come, Jake might have taken it personally.

He'd been plenty punished for his lack of restraint. First, there was Thea waiting for him but not waiting for him on the driveway. Her swimsuit was black and simple and gave him no chance. A deep V held together with a silver bar that he swore still had droplets of water on it. Her hair was up and wet, and her legs went on for—God, forever. He was surprised he could even talk to Penny in coherent sentences.

That was the next revelation: how Penny could be here. Penny, whom he'd known his whole life. If Penny was mixed up with the Fieldings, that made them... more human, less aloof. More difficult to stereotype as rich kids with trust funds.

The house was just what he'd expected, but it was also messy and lived-in, and the furniture outside the public spaces looked like his. Kane had been warm and friendly, throwing him that Fielding smile—which was a little freaky on a guy, now that he was used to seeing it on Thea—and had laughed at his own lack of home improvement skills. He and his wife weren't in one of those marriages Liam had seen so often during his apprenticeship: the husband and wife moving in different spheres, the marriage merely for show and to get a tax break. Liam had seen the way Kane looked at Ellen and she at him, even when she was pretending to be mad at him.

No wonder Thea shrank into herself a little around these guys.

Liam could bet they judged her decisions worse than she did herself and reinforced her bowed shoulders and apologetic stance. He wanted to take her home right now, strip off that damp swimsuit, and show her just how important she really was.

And then there were the boys. Jake, looking to him for approval. Benji, thrilled to see him, telling him how far down he could swim now, that he'd been playing soccer with the big kids, that he was going horseback riding at camp this week and had Liam ever been on a horse?

Then Benji had said, "Hey, since you're home early with Jake every day, can I hang out with you guys?" And his brown eyes had formed perfect circles, and he'd said, "Oh! You could pick me up off the bus!" and Liam couldn't think of a quick enough reason to say no. The worst part was, he didn't want to.

It was one thing to have a classroom full of teenagers rely on you for their education and, sometimes, validation. It was quite another to have an almost-six-year-old look at you with absolute trust, put his hand in yours and smile and hum as you walked, just because your presence made him feel safe.

He was too far in already. And who knew? Thea had what he'd said he wanted when he married Avery. A home, kids, a regular life. What his parents had had. That was all Liam had ever asked for. Maybe he could convince Thea to try again for that too.

"You should know," Kane said as Liam opened the truck's door, "I punched out her last boyfriend, and if I hear you've done anything like what he did, I can do it again."

Liam laughed, but Kane was serious. No five-hundred-watt Fielding smile here. He used his advantage in height to loom over Liam. Liam wasn't intimidated, but he respected Kane's concern for his sister. "Must be hard, three sisters."

"Four. And only one of 'em's had a guy in her life I remotely like."

"I'll remember that." Respect or no respect, Liam wasn't about to make promises to Kane he hadn't yet made to Thea. "Good to meet you," he said and held out his hand.

Kane was surprised but shook hands. "You too. I think."

Liam figured it was a start.

♦

On Monday morning, Jake had clattered his way down the stairs the second he heard Liam come through the front door. So Thea had no time alone with Liam. They arranged to meet that night at the church parking lot where the camp bus dropped Benji off, and she had to be content with that.

The blue monster baby was growling in the parking lot when she arrived, Liam leaning against the side. All he needed was a Stetson and a sheepdog to be an old Coke ad.

"Hi," she said, stopping a few feet away. It seemed safest.

"Hey, T."

Did he see her shiver? Did he see that she was in an almost constant state of sexual arousal, a position she hadn't been in since her college days?

"Is Jake with you?"

"Nope. He wanted me to drop him home. So get over here."

They had maybe two minutes till the bus came. Plenty of time. But there were other parents here, all sitting in their cars, engines running, ready to be entertained by the sight of poor Thea Fielding making out in public with her cowboy—er, plumber... er, teacher—oh, whatever the hell he was.

So she got closer but stayed a respectable two feet away, leaning on his warm truck like he was. They stood there, watching the road and the church, listening to the birds and the car radios, in a silence which was somehow more intimate than if they'd found something to talk about.

"So," he finally said. "You're going to the Cape in a couple weeks?"

"No, not me. Just the boys. We have school, remember? I'll go down for a few days in between classes, but the boys have so much fun there, and my brother and sister are sweet to take them."

"So... you'll be alone for a week?"

"Oh shit, Liam." She hugged her stomach, which had done a backflip. "I don't know if I'm ready for that tone in your voice."

We're ready! said her thighs.

"Okay." He turned to face her, still leaning on the truck, his hands in his jeans pockets. "You're running this show, T."

Now her heart was leaping like a jackrabbit. "Thanks," she whispered.

"Anytime." He slid one hand along the curve of the truck to hold her elbow where no one else could see it. "Anytime, anyplace, anywhere," he added, grinning.

She did shiver then, a full-body shudder he couldn't fail to see. "You're a mean man," she said.

"Uh-huh," he said, looking at her lips.

"Quit it. Oh, thank God, the bus."

Benji was happy to greet Liam, and Thea filled out the form the counselor gave her to allow Liam to pick him up by himself.

"Can we go to the park now?" Benji asked Liam when he was done dancing around him.

"Not today, bud. It's late, remember?" Thea said. "We have to get dinner."

"Can't Liam have dinner with us?" Benji said. "Mommm. You always say no!"

"I can't, bud." Liam crouched down next to him. "But I'll see you tomorrow, and we'll go to the park, okay?"

"Okay," Benji said slowly, trying on a pout. Liam just laughed and patted him on the shoulder.

Liam straightened up and suddenly seemed to fill her vision. "I'll see you tomorrow," he said–promised.

"Yeah," she said, tucking that nonexistent piece of hair behind her ear. She was going to be dead by tomorrow.

◆

The next two weeks were heaven and agony for Liam. He began arriving five minutes early and opening the front door quietly so that he could catch Thea for one kiss and refill his coffee mug before Jake came down the stairs. Each kiss was a drink in the desert and left him just as thirsty. The reminder of her, in the taste of her coffee that he drank throughout the morning, was a poor substitute.

Jake was a good reward for abstinence, though. He learned quickly and well, asked sensible questions, and never pretended he knew something when he didn't. Liam felt a pang that he would never have him in his AP history class, but this was pretty good too. The day he let Jake use the propane torch to solder a joint, the boy's face lit up as though he'd been given a quad bike.

And Benji. Liam had known he'd fall in love with him easily. The boy was a typical five-year-old, in all the best ways. He was dirty; he didn't want to brush his teeth; he hated vegetables. He was crazy about power tools. One evening at the park, he got in an argument with another kid who called him a dickhead and he called the kid an asshole, and Liam and the other boy's mom had to exchange chagrined apologies. The next day Benji and the boy spent an hour racing each other up and down the spider gym.

Benji would bring him cool rocks or bugs or decapitated toys he'd found in the sandbox. He'd require Liam's participation, his admiration, and when it was time to go, he'd take Liam's hand and look both ways before crossing the street. After a week or so, Liam gave in to instinct and dropped a kiss on the boy's head when he said goodbye. His reward was Benji's arms around his waist for a brief hug before he ran in to give his rocks to his mother.

He observed Jake more closely, because Jake was older and had further to go to trust again than his brother. But he loved Benji with all his heart, and the idea of being his dad rolled around in his head and wouldn't let go.

Class started up again, an online class this time that they could have completed in the comfort of their own home. But the group wanted to meet up, and Thea again offered her house. In the balmy July evenings, they carried the kitchen table outside and sat around with beers, talking more than studying.

Yeah, Liam joined them. Even though he didn't need to take this class. Even though he had gone to the college and asked about taking up his place after all. Even though he'd been to the bank and figured out loans and interest rates, and his faceless mortgage company had sent paperwork, and a Realtor friend of Seth's had appraised his house at more than double what he'd borrowed to fix it, and he was on his way to having financing in place to pay his fall tuition. Even with all that, he wasn't about to miss an excuse to see more of Thea.

He thanked David for his advice in their first meeting that week. "That's great," David said. "I'm glad it worked out." He nodded at Thea, who was deep in conversation with Chloe and Zahra at the table. The men were across the lawn behind her house. Audrey was stalking butterflies between them in the drowsy July heat. "You told Thea you're only here for her yet?"

Liam hated that telltale flush his skin often let him down with. "Let me admit that to myself first," he said with a wry grin.

"Better get on it," Seth said. "I still think she might take me, even with my greasy hands."

Their banter was desultory; it was too hot tonight. Even his pride and joy, the truck, was feeling the heat; her air conditioner was a mere trickle these days. He was going to have to go to a mechanic about that one day, but he didn't know who he could—

"Oh my God," Liam exclaimed. "The heat's turned me stupid. Will you take a look at the truck? Her a/c is on the fritz."

So the men went around to the front of the house and didn't come back for an hour, except for beer refills for David, who was the only one not driving. Seth didn't do anything to the truck then and there, of course, but it took them an hour to discuss what he *would* do.

"Did you have the refugees at your garage yet?" Liam asked.

"Yeah!" Seth said. "Not just refugees, or at least, not recent ones. Zahra got the youth group at her mosque to come, and several of the fathers came too. I pulled out an old Lincoln we had in the back, and the kids were all over it. With the older engine, we did the simple things like oil changes, filters, batteries, that kind of thing. I think they enjoyed it. I think they just enjoyed doing something outside of their neighborhood, to be honest. Something different."

Liam nodded. "They were happy to talk to me, too, when Zahra took me over there the other week. They schooled me on African history, I can tell you. I spend half my free time these days boning up on it so I don't look like a doofus once school starts."

"But they'll learn US history with you, won't they?"

"Yes, but if I don't create a frame of reference, I may as well be reading them a Dickens novel. Some of them know World War II because they were still colonized then, but Korea? Vietnam? What do they care about them?"

"Have you talked to Zahra about it?"

"Not yet."

"Well, she's right inside. You know, the one sitting next to the one you can't take your eyes off?" David smirked.

They ambled back inside, and Liam cornered Zahra. There was so much to learn about the community he was about to enter, and he was beginning to realize he had only a month or so left to learn it.

That night, buoyed by the knowledge that he'd see Thea first thing in the morning, Liam didn't hang around when the others had left. But he went ten minutes early the next day, and the kissing became so intense he almost had her bra off before he remembered where he was.

"We can't do that again," she whispered, breathless, when they'd come to their senses after hearing Jake's door close. She ran into the bathroom just in time, leaving Liam to drive off with an image of her untucked, silky blouse and her newly released, oh-so-tempting breasts pressing against it.

He was dying here, and the boys were still eight days from going on vacation.

At their next group meeting, they all sat on the back patio again. Thea wore a floaty pale-green top that hinted at her breasts the way her work blouse had, and shorts that were shorter than anything he'd yet seen her in, apart from that damn swimsuit. Liam died all over again when he saw her, then picked himself up, held himself in, and acted normal, as he had for two weeks, or three hundred and thirty-six hours. Or Twenty. Thousand. Minutes.

At some point in the evening, Thea went back inside to bring out ice pops for them all. Oh, and look at that, Liam's beer needed a refill.

The screen door banged behind him, and he was, finally, alone with her in the kitchen. The boys were upstairs, Benji a lot more tired these days now that Liam was hanging with him so much. Thea was at the freezer. She turned from pulling out a tray of ice and Liam was there to take the tray from her hand and open her fingers with his. With her hand still stretched out toward the counter, he pressed a kiss onto her palm, which was cool and hot at the same time. He let his tongue touch the center of her hand just a little bit, and Thea's legs buckled.

Liam's arm was around her before she could drop an inch. "Everyone..."

"Is outside," he said, tickling her skin with his breath. Now that he had her, he took his time, dropping kisses onto the pad of skin below her thumb, her wrist, the veins visible under her skin on the inside of her forearm, and up to the crook of her elbow, where he indulged himself in another swirl of his tongue against that cool-hot skin and got a moan from her for his trouble.

"Liam," she breathed. "You're killing me."

"I don't know how that's possible," he said, brushing his beard against her skin, "because I died of wanting you about a week ago."

Her waist was under his other hand, and it was slim and soft against his arm, but he kept it there, knowing he had time to make love to only this one arm before they were found. He kept on his journey up toward her shoulder, the ruffle of the blouse now tickling his cheek, leaving small wells of moisture where his tongue tasted the salt on her—

"Jesus," a voice said behind them. "Get a room. Seriously. I'm begging you."

It was Chloe. Thea dropped her arm and tried to shy away from him, but Liam held her waist more tightly. They were two consenting, unattached adults, and there was no need to keep this from their friends.

"About time you two got it on," Chloe said, putting a hand on her hip. "You could cut the sexual tension in this house with a knife."

"Shh!" Thea said and pointed upward. It was still possible that Jake would hear them, though Liam knew he spent most of his time with his headphones on so his mother wouldn't know what movies he was watching. Liam, who'd grown up an only child in a quiet house where his mother knew most of what he was doing, approved.

"So," Chloe said. "Where are we at?"

Thea spluttered and Liam said, "We love you, Chloe, but it's none of your business."

"Ooh, Thea. Note how easily he says, 'I love you.' This one's a keeper."

"Chloe!" That was Thea.

Chloe put up her hands. "I'm just pointing it out. Now, someone promised me ice pops."

Thea reached behind her and wrenched Liam's hand from her waist; at least that was what it felt like. But still. Now they had two more days and then, *then*, the boys would be at the Cape and Thea would *please God* call the shot he'd been waiting for.

Chapter 14

Thea: **You're going to murder me.**

Liam: **Why? If I'm going to sharpen the ax, I'd like to know I had a good reason.**

Thea: **The boys just left. I'm knackered, as Ellen would say. I need to go to bed for three days.**

Liam: **Sounds good to me.**

Thea: **Alone.**

Liam: **Where's that whetstone?**

Thea: **I'm sorry. I'm no good at this.**

Liam: **Me either.**

Thea: **I don't know how to... be a modern**

She deleted the word. She sounded like someone out of the 1920s. *I'm a thoroughly modern woman. Look, my dress barely reaches past my calves.*

But there was still the issue that she had never properly dated and Liam probably had, several times, before he met his ex-wife. She was in her own immersion class, but the language she was learning was the contemporary way to flirt, to tease, to make love.

Thea clutched her hair in her hands. Look, see? She'd texted several sentences to him and hadn't used an emoji once. She was a dirty old woman, and Liam was going to notice as soon as she took her clothes off.

She still didn't know how old he was, and now she was too afraid to ask. He was younger than thirty-one, but how much younger? If she added four years of college to five years of apprenticeship, the number still came out too low for her peace of mind. So the big question was, how long had he been teaching?

No, the big question is, how long are you going to torture the poor man?

She deleted the whole sentence.

***Thea*: I have a question.**

***Liam*: Fire away.**

***Thea*: When you were in college, did you play Quidditch?**

◆

On Sunday, Liam caught up with some old college friends who were in the campus fields for a pickup game of Quidditch. It was just the silly, intense, sweaty, complicated exercise he needed to take his mind off Thea. When the game ended, he walked back to his bag with the rest of his team, laughing and recalling bludger hits—Liam was a beater—and promising to do it all over again soon.

He drank the rest of his water and threw his broomstick in the back of his truck, thinking of nothing but how badly he needed a shower. Halfway to his house, his phone, buried in his bag, buzzed. Instantly, he reorganized his priorities. He pulled over and dug through the bag.

Four texts. "Goddammit," he muttered. It would take too long to reply to them all; he would just call her.

"There you are," she said. She sounded quiet.

"I'm sorry, I was playing—soccer."

"Oh, okay. Well, if you're not doing anything else today..."

"I'm not. Believe me, I'm not."

"Then come over. I'll make lunch."

Honey, you are *lunch,* he wanted to say, but that would sound like he was only going to her house for one thing. Which he wasn't. Was he?

Then he smelled himself. "Let me take a shower. I'll be..." He calculated the time. Crap. "An hour."

He shaved ten minutes off that time, though it meant he showed up almost completely empty-handed. Thea opened the door looking fresh and young and beautiful, her dark eyes huge and a shy smile on her face. "Hey," she said.

He walked in and put his arm around her waist at once. "I just want you to know," he said, lifting her up so her legs automatically went around his waist. "This is *not* a booty call." And he kissed her.

She didn't care what it was. She'd spent three days in delicious and terrified anticipation of what would happen when she finally broke her own embargo, and now he was here, and his hands were under her butt, his strong arms easily holding her so her head was above his so she could delve deep into his mouth, holding his head to maneuver the kiss however she liked.

Liam lifted his head and looked at her. His eyes were a clear, uncomplicated blue against the tan of his skin. This close, she could see the few freckles that dusted his nose and cheeks and count every one of the hairs in his beard.

He was hesitating, the beautiful, sweet man. She brushed her lips across his as he'd done to her neck, before taking them in a kiss he was happy to lean into, his face filling her vision. His beard was soft and held a very faint scent of whatever it was he put on it.

Warmth and a sense of the end of a long wait went into her side of the kiss, feeling his rough, wavy hair under her hand, the smoothness of his lips next to the hair of his beard, his hands holding her firm while he moved his lips over hers. It was so right, she couldn't believe how long she'd waited to do this.

He raised his head at last, just a little. He lowered her until her feet touched the ground. One hand cradled her head; the other hand flattened out over her collarbone. He smiled as if Christmas had come again. "I'm crazy about you, T," he murmured.

She blinked tears out of her eyes before she'd even realized she was crying. "What are those for?" he asked, gently wiping them from under her eyes.

She shook her head a second time. "Just happy," she said, beaming it back to him.

Liam picked her up like she weighed nothing and placed her

gently on the couch cushions, making sure she was comfortable and no clothes were twisted under her before kissing her again.

Thea pulled him down on top of her, the weight of him making her laugh and groan.

"Too heavy?" he said, immediately getting up onto his elbows.

"No." She got both her arms around his chest and pulled him close. "No," she breathed again. "Never."

He'd given her so much these last few weeks. She was happy to take all his weight.

He backed up long enough to put a hand on her waist, spanning it and slowly lifting her T-shirt, watching her eyes the entire time, until he was cupping one breast and Thea shivered, closed her eyes, and arched her back toward him. He slid her bra to one side and took her nipple into his mouth. Thea cried out. The contrast of his cool, wet tongue and the abrasion of his beard set her blood on fire.

She'd waited long enough. Before he could pay any attention to her other breast, she had his zipper undone and was awkwardly shoving his jeans and shorts down his legs. "Thea." He laughed, struggling to help her but with his hand tangled in her shirt. "Wait, I want to–"

"Later. Just for now... please, Liam."

She had him between her legs now, her knees lifting and parting without conscious thought. He was hot and hard against her roving hands, and when he gasped and backed away from her, she knew she'd won. She put her legs back down so he could remove her own jeans, but both of them were still partially dressed when she pulled his mouth back to hers. She ran her tongue along his lips, then plunged deep into his mouth, making him groan and his hands tighten on her hips. She held his head still so she could play with his mouth and tongue while he massaged her, pressing and releasing her skin so that their moans mingled.

It wasn't long before he broke away from her lips and put one hand out to the floor beside him. After a second or two, Thea realized he was looking for something. "What?" she asked, looking over at the coffee table.

"My backpack," he said, his voice cracking with the effort of concentrating.

"Now?"

He looked back at her, a slight flush coming into his cheeks. "It's got a condom in it, T."

"Oh." Thea blushed herself. "Well," she went on, trying to recover. "You do come ready for anything, don't you?"

His eyes bored into hers. "I've been ready for this for two months."

"Oh." It was a sigh of pleasure, relief, longing. She didn't move, and he tried to move as little of his body off her as possible, finally finding his backpack behind the arm of the couch. He had the condom on in seconds, and his blissful weight was on her, and then he kissed his way down her exposed skin, leaving a line of open-mouthed kisses along her belly, to her hip, to her thigh and closer, so that she was shouting his name and pulling his hair and her nails dug into one bicep.

"Okay, okay," he said, smiling that heart-melting smile up at her.

"I'm going to kill you!" She pulled any part of him she could reach. Liam finally consented to move back up her body, settling onto one elbow above her. His smile gone, he watched her carefully as he entered her. Thea tried to be embarrassed about this, but she felt only beautiful and sexy and desirable, and she closed her eyes again and arched her breasts closer to him, knowing that it would turn him on even more.

He began to move inside her. "Oh shit, why don't we do this all the time?" Thea said and gripped his thighs with hers, her feet still caught up in her jeans and his. Liam laughed and kissed her and used the hand that wasn't supporting him to play with her breast, putting his thumb in her mouth to moisten it and running it over her nipple.

This, combined with his steady strokes, turned her to white fire. Thea felt herself melting, falling, with an anticipation that built with exquisite force until she crashed, then crashed again, crying out against his mouth, tears coming back into her eyes and a laugh following right after.

In one smooth maneuver, Liam had moved her off the couch, the coffee table pushed out of the way so he could press her hard into the floor. Thea helplessly welcomed him, angling so he could thrust deeper and deeper, until he buried his face in her neck and yelled her name, and Thea held him to her until they'd both stopped shaking and their sweat had dried on them and she realized they were still half-clothed and she still, in fact, had not seen Liam naked.

Chapter 15

"Liam!" she exclaimed.

"What?" The panic in her voice made him raise his head and look around—was someone looking at them through the windows?

"How old are you?"

"Oh, for Pete's sake." He dropped his head back onto her shoulder. "You scared me."

"Seriously. I need to know this."

He knew that. He wasn't sure why he was reticent about telling her, unless it was that she would make a bigger deal out of it than it was. He'd hate to lose her over a pedantic thing like age.

"How old are *you*?" he countered, buying time.

She shifted his head off her shoulder so she could frown at him. "I'm old. That's my point."

"For God's sake, T. You are not old."

"I'm thirty-five. There. I said it."

"Wow. Okay, that's it." He pretended to get up. "I'm outta here."

"Come on, Liam," she begged. He saw that she was genuinely worried.

"Haven't you figured out yet that I like old things?" He waved toward the window, where the blue monster baby—dammit, now he was calling her that—slept.

Thea punched him. "Ow," he said, rubbing his ribs. "Jeez, I'll have to remember not to get the old lady angry."

"Liam!" she warned.

"This is ridiculous."

"Oh shit, you're like, twenty-five, aren't you? That's why you won't—"

"I'm thirty, T. Okay? The math doesn't even work out that I could be twenty-five."

"Oh. Thirty." She lay back, and he watched her take it in, her eyes on the ceiling. "I couldn't figure it out. When I first met you, you seemed young, and the way you dress and your beard—"

"A beard makes me twenty-five?"

"I've been out of the loop for a long time." She sighed, her breasts rising and falling in a most distracting way.

She thought about it some more while Liam went through a hundred scenarios where she put the brakes on this whole thing and he was left out in the blue monster baby, flayed to the bone.

"Okay," she said, and flipped on top of him and began kissing him again. "You gonna get those pants all the way off or what?"

◆

Since the idea of being apart was laughable, Liam brought a change of clothes to her house and left for work from there in the morning. In the evening, he came home before her, showered off his work from the day, and made her dinner.

When she got home on Tuesday evening, Liam was screwing nails or nailing screws or whatever it was, into her deck, and he was cranky.

"You don't have to do that." She remembered his comment to his father.

"You need new boards," he said in the grumpy way he had when he talked about her house. "Here and here. And the rot's creeping up this pillar. And that one—"

"Okay!" She covered her ears. "There's no point in telling me about it when there's nothing I can do about it."

"It's only a couple of feet of wood and some screws."

"And a saw and a miter box and a bunch of screws and any possible clue of what the hell I'm doing."

He turned away and drove another screw into the floor. With his back to her, he said, "I have a saw. It wouldn't take long. I'll show you how to do it, and you can do the rest of them. Borrow the saw."

Thea paused. "That's very nice of you," she hedged. "But—" She didn't want him to work on her house anymore. It smacked of some kind of exchange she didn't want to look too hard into. Of payment for services rendered or something.

He shrugged. "Don't want Benji falling through a rotten board."

Ooh, the guilt-trip-inducing sonofa–plumber. There was nothing she could say against that. Thea leaned on one of the pillars. Which moved a tiny bit. She jumped away and nearly tripped over his toolbox. Liam turned around, giving that white slash of a smile again, and she found herself melting.

"Fine," she said, trying to regain some dignity, though her feet were splayed on either side of the toolbox and she had grasped the doorframe so her top half was leaning toward it at a bizarre angle.

Liam laughed out loud. Thea had to grin back at him. He put down the hammer and went to her, his strong arm around her waist easily straightening her as he held her to him. "Hi," he said right next to her lips. "Did you have a good day at work?"

"Are you still talking? Or are you going to kiss me?"

Liam obeyed, and Thea let him take most of her weight, the thrill of being encircled, protected in his arms still new and enough to turn her legs to mush.

"Babe," he murmured, running a path of kisses from the corner of her mouth to her ear, "I'm starving."

She thought back on their nights–and afternoons–together, on the well of need she had for him that wasn't nearly tapped. "Me too," she breathed.

"No, I mean, I'm really starving." He backed up and gave her that white slash of a smile. "I worked through lunch today."

"Oh." She got her feet under her properly. "Okay."

He turned back to his hammering, and she went inside to change, make a pitcher of iced tea, and assemble a towering plate of sandwiches. If Jake could eat his way through two or three rounds, she figured Liam would need twice as much.

They sat together on the porch floor, Liam with his back against the house, chewing methodically through everything she handed him.

But it wasn't the action of feeding him that was sending a lethargic heat through her limbs. She sat across from him—"Don't lean too hard against that railing," he said with his mouth full—her legs alongside his, her denim shirt unbuttoned over a white tank top and red capris. His legs were in jeans, as always. Just once she wished he'd wear shorts again, like he had at Kane's. His dark-green T-shirt with the Pat the Plumber logo on it showed off his arms.

Liam held her eyes with his. Such a blue. The kind of clear blue she could fall into. He took a drink from the glass she'd given him, and Thea couldn't look away. *Just one little drop of sweat... going down his neck... that's all I ask.*

He'd finished drinking, and she was still staring. She might have blinked slowly at him. She didn't mean to, but her lips were parting of their own accord, and she found herself pressing her leg against his. And, oh dear, here she was, crawling over to him, taking his head between her hands and planting a good, hard, iced-tea-sweetened kiss on those lips.

"I'm never going to get a thing done with you around," he said a few minutes later. She was tucked on his lap, arms around his neck. The porch had become its own world, a moment in time before something happened that could break her or wake her up.

"You've been getting something done." She smirked and wiggled in his lap.

"Quit it!" He laughed but put his hands on her hips and pressed her down on him harder. Thea gasped and arched her neck. "For God's sake, T," he groaned. "Let me finish this while I still have the light."

She pouted and got off his lap.

"Don't look at me like that," he said. "We've got all night."

We've got all night. What a promise. What a dream. Thea slumped back and hit the railing, which wobbled.

Liam grabbed her arm and pulled her back. "Dammit, don't lean on that railing!"

♦

The next evening, Thea went to his house after work. She brought a spare toothbrush and he made love to her on the old scrub pine kitchen table he used as an island.

"You're not kidding about liking old things," she'd said when she first walked up the stairs to his apartment. The rooms had wide-plank flooring stained a rich dark brown, and the thickest molding and trim she'd ever seen framing the walls. The kitchen had no fitted cabinets; instead, Liam had taken old hutches and consoles, painted them the same color, and laid countertop only where he had to. The kitchen table was the main work surface.

"That's true," he'd said, and then proceeded to show her just what kind of work the table was good for.

They curled up on his couch and watched old movies Thea could quote by heart. Seeing James Dean brooding his way through the heartland was much more entertaining now that she could tease Liam about his cranky mood when she'd first met him.

"Why'd you have to scowl at me every time I walked in a room?" she complained.

Liam laced her fingers with his. "Because my plan for the summer didn't include falling for a hot mama the first day I walked into class."

Falling for her. Of course she was head over heels for him, too, but she couldn't tell him that yet. Maybe when the boys were home and they were still finding their way through this and he was still prepared to be involved in her messy, overscheduled life. Maybe then she'd tell him.

They had seven days. Seven blissful days, split between his home and hers, where they told each other about themselves, supported each other, and gave each other the hope they needed to try again.

◆

On Sunday afternoon, by mutual agreement, Liam cleared out anything he'd left at her house, and Thea reluctantly said goodbye.

"I'll see you in the morning," he reminded her. "Picking up Jake at seven, remember?"

"Yeah," she said. This was only the beginning.

The boys were tan and happy and tired. They'd been sailing and surfing and eaten their body weight in ice cream, and they were not interested in coming with her to the grocery store.

But their mood quickly descending into real-life misery didn't even bother her. She took them into the cookie aisle and said, "Have at it," and they cheered up. Jake even got a six-pack of Coke and she didn't care.

"Why are you so happy?" Jake said suspiciously.

"'Cause I got away from my awful children for a whole week," she answered, putting one arm around his bony shoulders and giving Benji a noogie with the other.

"Can we have ice cream for dinner?" Benji asked at once.

"Nice try. But you only have to have one bite of your veggies tonight."

"Woo-hoo!"

They parked the car in front of the house as usual, and while the boys got the bags out of the back of the van, Thea opened the front door and walked through to the back to call for Audrey.

Only someone was standing on the back porch.

He unfolded himself from one of the plastic lawn chairs that lived there, wearing a coat that was too warm for the weather and a large backpack by his feet.

"Hullo, pet," he said.

She was in the open back door, the boys spilling in behind her, dumping shopping bags any old way on the counter.

Benji saw him first. "Dad!" he shouted and barreled past Thea to fling himself into Gabriel's arms.

Chapter 16

It was a good thing Benji was occupying his father's space and conversation because Thea had lost all ability to speak. She stood in the doorway where she'd stopped. The cool air from the air conditioner blew past her legs. The food in the grocery bags shifted and slumped to its side. *I hope that's not the eggs,* she thought faintly.

"I knew you'd come back!" Benji was yelling, and Thea couldn't tell if he was laughing or crying. "Jake said you wouldn't, but I knew you would!"

Jake. Thea unfroze long enough to turn her head to the left, where Jake looked as paralyzed as she felt. He still held two bags of groceries.

He looked at her. His eyes held years of hurt and disappointment and anger and fear and—worst of all—love. She wanted to shield him from so much, and she couldn't do it.

She went back into the house, the screen door slamming behind her, and took the bags from him. Under Benji's piping voice, she said, "If you want to scoot, you can. You can deal with him later."

Jake frowned but let her take the bags. "Just come home, okay?" she said to his retreating back as he pushed through the kitchen and out the front door.

Now she had no one to shield her. Not that that was Jake's job. But she'd come to rely on him to be her partner in the last two years—too much, she knew. But how else could she have survived?

And it was the fault of the man standing on the back porch.

Gabe was still standing out on the porch, Benji clinging to him. "Sure, and haven't you grown!" he was saying.

"Uncle Antonio says I'll be as tall as him any minute!" Benji sang.

"You're almost as tall as me!" Gabe bent over his son to hug him, a long body hug that brought a lump to Thea's throat.

Gabe's hair was longer, curlier. The black was speckled with gray—she saw it more clearly with his head bent over Benji. There seemed to be more of him... but perhaps that was because she hadn't seen him in so long. A memory of the last time she'd slept with him, the exact weight of him as he'd pressed her into the mattress, made her wince.

He broke the hug, then crouched down to Benji's level. "Do you still play with your Legos, Ben?"

"'Course!" Benji's brown eyes, which he'd inherited from her, were the shape of his father's, and the two of them were peas in a pod when they looked at each other.

"What's the latest thing you've made? Will you show me?"

"Okay!" Benji went to clatter up the stairs but halted within a few feet. "You're staying, right?"

Gabe's eyes flickered to Thea and back to him. "I'm not leaving, I promise you."

Thea folded her arms, but Benji grinned and ran upstairs.

Being alone with him again took her breath away. He was still on the porch, looking at her through the screen. Even in the shadows, his Cillian Murphy eyes filled her. He was older, heavier at the jaw, but she felt that heaviness all through him—in his heart, piercing his soul.

"T," he said.

Thea to you, she wanted to say but couldn't get any words out.

"T," he said again. "I'm so, so sorry."

Thea looked up at the ceiling. His voice was rough and low, as heavy as the rest of him. She hated and loved it at the same time.

"I've regretted leaving you every single day." She still looked at the ceiling but shook her head incredulously. "It's true. I've loved you for fifteen years, T, and the boys are my life."

"*Your life?*" she burst out, unable to stand it anymore. "*Your life?* Then I suppose you were dead when you walked onto that airplane and left *your sons* without a father!"

"I was dead for years before that," he said. "Every time I let you down. Every time you looked at me, the way you are now. I know I was never good enough for you."

"*Don't. You. Dare* give me that 'it's not you, it's me' bullshit!" Her voice was tight with emotion, with some final effort not to scream at him, with Benji about to come down. She took a shaky breath, pressed her hands onto the sturdy, cool surface of the kitchen table, and leaned over them, cutting off her view of him.

"What do you want, Gabriel?" she asked, hoping she sounded as cold as she felt.

"I want you back," he said simply. "All of you."

She laughed, a jagged sound that made him flinch. "Are you *fucking* kidding me?"

That was loud. Benji ran down the stairs, a Lego airplane in each hand, and heard her. "No!" he shouted. He ran up to his father and stood in front of him, his small arms ludicrously outstretched as if to protect him. "Don't yell at him! You'll make him leave again!"

She couldn't take this. This much hurt piled on hurt. She dropped her head into one hand.

"Ben," Gabe said, crouching down and taking one of Benji's outstretched hands to spin him around. "Your mam didn't make me leave. I did it all by myself. And I feel terrible about it. But don't blame your mam, okay?"

"She shouts," Benji said, his initial joy at seeing his father now outweighed by all that had happened since the last time they'd been together. "All the time."

"That's my fault, kiddo, not hers. I'll explain it to you another time." He looked up at Thea, who saw it through her fingers but didn't take her hand away. Her heart throbbed in her chest, and if she didn't get away from him soon, she was going to break into pieces.

"Ben," he said gently, wiping away the tears on Benji's cheeks with one thumb. "I'm staying with your cousin Sean. You remember him? I'm staying right there, just a ten-minute drive from you."

"We don't see them anymore." Benji sniffed. He sounded suspicious of their continuing existence.

"I bet," said Gabe. "But that's where I am. I'm going to go now, 'cause I see you've got some food to put away and dinner to make and such—"

"Mom! Can he stay for—?"

"No, I have to go. But if it's all right with your mam, I'll come back tomorrow, same time."

Thea took her hand away from her face long enough to nod, but she still didn't look at Gabe. "All right," he said. "We'll have a proper chat then, and you can show me your Legos."

"Okay." The uncertainty in Benji's voice brought Thea's hand back up to her face.

"I promise," Gabe said. "You'll see. Tomorrow. Oh, and I have a new mobile number. Here." He pulled a piece of paper out of his pocket on which he'd already written the number. Benji took it and looked a little more hopeful. "Call me anytime you like between now and then, okay? Anytime." He hugged Benji to him again like he was planning to absorb him. "I love you, Ben."

Benji was still staring at the number. Gabe stood up and looked at Thea. "Thanks, T. I'll be back tomorrow."

Whatever, she wanted to say. Goddammit, he'd taken her back to that nineteen-year-old again. The screen door shut. Benji ran to her purse, which lay among the bags of food she'd forgotten about, and found her phone. He dialed Gabe's number and waited.

She heard Gabe's chuckle when he picked up. "I'm not even at the end of the road, Ben."

"Just checking." Benji held the phone so tightly to his ear then that Thea didn't hear what Gabe said next, but Benji seemed satisfied and the call wasn't long.

"Put away the groceries," she said when he started to move back toward the stairs.

"Mommm," he said, as if the appearance of his father was reason enough to eschew all chores.

"Come on. And I'll make dinner." She turned away from him and put her hand to her chest. *Be normal. Breathe in, breathe out. Don't think about how much Benji might prefer to be with him than you.* "I haven't forgotten that I said you only have to have two bites of your veggies tonight."

That news spread a grin over Benji's face almost as big as the one

Gabe had created. He turned back and reached into a bag, as usual somehow figuring out which one had the cookies and snacks in it before any of the rest. Thea turned on the stove, the oven, got out pans, spread fries over a tray, poured water to boil, and generally tried to act as normal and un-shouty as possible.

When dinner was nearly ready, she texted Jake but wasn't surprised when he texted back that he was an hour away.

You want me to pick you up? she texted.

No. I want to walk. Be back by ten.

And now she would have to spend the rest of the evening worrying about his reaction, coaching him on what she wanted him to believe about his father, and riding the fine line between truth and putting a rift between the two that Jake would eventually blame her for, the way Benji did.

♦

Thea didn't sleep that night. At least Jake was home at a reasonable hour, though she hated the pensive look on his face when he'd come in. But was that worse than the devotion on Benji's when he looked at his father? Just what did Gabe really want? He couldn't possibly expect her to just let him back into their lives, could he? After more than fifteen years of promises and disappointment?

But what if he's changed?

What if it's better for the boys that he stays?

That thought made her flip onto her other side and grab her pillow in fear and uncertainty.

On this side she'd think of Liam. Liam, who had made everything so clear just a few hours ago. A man with whom she might be able to build a relationship carefully, mindfully. Plus, a man who made her thighs quiver. And who could fix a leaking faucet. A man who would be a helpmeet in life, not a burden. A man who might have loved and respected her kids and given them a father figure they could look up to.

It had been possible. But now? She felt as limp as that twenty-year-old girl, eight months pregnant and seeing her life mapped out before her in the hopeless look in her partner's eyes. School seemed like something someone else did. And Liam? How had she thought she would get to have that life without consequences?

When Jake had come in, he'd looked so pale, despite his tan, his eyes so wounded, that she'd told him he didn't have to go to work in the morning. "Tell Liam... tell him we're all sick, we ate some bad shrimp."

Lying to Liam did make her feel sick to her stomach. But she couldn't even form the words in her mind to tell him what had happened. It was much easier to send an email to her bosses and leave a message at the camp that she and Benji were going to stay home too.

Liam texted her. **Sorry you're sick. Anything I can do?**

You can stop reminding me of what I had.

No. Don't come over. I'm green, she wrote after much deliberation.

He texted back, but she didn't reply. When he called the next morning, she didn't answer.

Benji was up early, Jake late, as usual. It was eleven thirty before she heard him thump down the stairs. Unable to settle on anything else, Thea was watching an old movie while Benji slumped against her, playing on his tablet. Unlike the brooding bad boy movies she'd watched with Liam, she buried herself in a world of shiny dresses and 1950s manners that had always soothed her when Gabe had been around.

The whole day, she felt that she was in suspended animation, waiting for him to come back that afternoon, waiting for whatever the rest of her life was going to bring.

Jake came into the living room, a huge bowl of cereal and milk in his hand. He'd hardly spoken to her last night, but she had to prepare him for this afternoon.

"Hi, babe," she said. Jake lifted his chin in response, as his mouth was obscenely full.

Thea hoped he'd come and sit with her, but he was on tenterhooks just as much as she was and seemed to prefer to stand. The haunted look in his eyes reminded her, as he did so often, of Gabriel, and she sighed. However this turned out, a lot of damage had been done to Jake that she wasn't going to be able to fix.

"So…" she began, "your father's coming—"

"Don't call him that." Some Cheerios fell out of his mouth as he spat the words.

"Don't be mean to him!" Benji shouted from next to her. "He's come back! Don't be mean or he'll leave again."

"Shut up, doofus. You don't know a thing about it."

"Stop it, Jake—"

"*You're* a doofus!"

"Benji, stop. Both of you." She loved them both so much. She wished she could make everything easy for them. But life, and her life especially, didn't work that way.

She started again. "He's coming over this afternoon, and I want you to hear him out." Jake rolled his eyes. "Jacob, he is your father, and he has the right to ask for ten minutes of your time."

Jake snorted, shoveled more cereal into his mouth, and mumbled, "What does he know about being a father?"

She shook her head, going for honesty. "I don't know, honey. But last night he said he was sorry and… that he wants to stay."

"Not here!" Jake said at once. "Mom!"

"No, of course not here," she said. "I'm not that crazy."

Jake snorted. "You've been alone a long time, Mom. Maybe—"

"Okay! Thank you! Not appropriate!" She tried to calm the blush that heated her cheeks. It wasn't the memory of Gabe that brought it.

If she pushed Gabe away and continued with Liam, Benji might never forgive her. But if she allowed Gabe back in and he let them down again, the boys might pay for it for the rest of their lives.

"Suffice it to say," she said, still trying for a calm voice, "that I would like to hear him out. And I would like you to hear him out.

If he wants a relationship with you, Jake, that can only be a good thing."

"Bullshit."

"Dammit, Jake!" she barked in her old tone. "Language!"

"Mom!"

"Dammit!" Benji said.

Shit. I suck at mothering.

"Okay, okay. Just be back here by five o'clock, all right?"

Jake drank the last of the milk from his bowl and went back into the kitchen for a refill. "All right?" she called.

"Fine," he called back, his voice dead. He had no hope that Gabe would be better now.

It was only stupid Thea's stupid heart that still betrayed her sometimes, reverting back to those years when she couldn't throw him out, couldn't keep away from him when the kids went to Cat's for the weekend. When he'd looked at her and she'd felt like Superwoman.

That was what really scared her. Not that Benji and Jake would believe that he'd changed, but that she would.

Chapter 17

For this appointment, at least, Gabe kept his word. Since it was dinnertime and Thea couldn't see herself sitting across the table from him while the kids ate, she cooked for all of them. Jake scowled when he saw the small kitchen table set for four. "We're feeding him now?"

"What do you want me to do, Jake?" She sighed. "It's dinnertime. We have to eat. He'll be here."

"I'm not hungry."

Thea raised an eyebrow. Jake's stomach growled. It did that a lot; he'd gained two inches in height this year.

"Fine," he said and slouched off. All the progress he'd made in the last few weeks, the confidence he'd gained in working with Liam, had disappeared. His hair was spiky and angry again, his eyes sliding away from hers whenever she looked at him. She didn't know what he'd done the night before, but the local news website had said someone had cut through the fence on the town baseball field. A pointless, petty act of vandalism she couldn't believe her son would be involved with. Unfortunately, she could believe it of the friends he'd started hanging out with last year. Friends whose arms she'd probably sent him straight into last night.

Thea fidgeted over whether to put out wineglasses. If she did, it would look as if she were welcoming Gabe to a party. If she didn't... well, she wanted—needed—the wine, and she couldn't exactly drink without offering him some. So the wineglasses came out. But she used the oldest napkins she owned. *So there, Gabriel.*

He knocked on the door at exactly six o'clock. Even if she hadn't been suspicious of his every move, Thea could have bet he'd stood on the corner of the street until he could arrive at the time he'd said. Still, better than not showing up at all, which she'd half dreaded and half hoped he'd do.

He'd brought flowers. "Gabe, what am I supposed to do with those?" Really? Romantic gestures *now*, after the flood that had gone under their bridge?

"A little water usually does the trick," he said with a smile. "They're for you, pet. Just because."

She took them. They were from the local florist, not the supermarket as they might have been two years ago. Custom-arranged roses and camellias were interspersed with daisies and elderflowers; the effect was of refinement with a hint of meadow.

"They're lovely," she had to admit. Gabe beamed. She let him in and through to the kitchen, which was suddenly laughably small.

She'd never noticed before that he was too big for the place. He was about her height, but perhaps it was that he seemed bigger now than then.

The stairs shook before he'd even made it through the doorway, and Benji was throwing himself at his father. "You came!"

"I promised I would," Gabe said solemnly. "I've got a lot of promises to make up to you, my lad."

Benji hugged him and sighed happily. Thea wished she could be that easily pleased.

"Jake!" she called. "Come down, please!" Her tone said that the "please" was merely a formality.

The thump on the stairs preceded him. Jake got to the bottom step without looking at his father and seemed set to continue to ignore him as he turned and sat at the table.

"Hello, Jakey," Gabe said.

Jake snorted and folded his arms. *Like Liam*, she thought with a pang.

She wanted Jake to have a relationship with his father. Of course she did. But right now she was also feeling all the things Jake was feeling and was jealous that he could express them when she had to be the grown-up.

It's worse for him. This is his father. He only gets one of those.

"Jake," she said with as much patience and love as she could. "Please give your father a chance to... to talk."

Gabe gently set Benji down. "You still sit in the same seat, Ben?" he said. Benji nodded and went to it. Gabe sat down next to Jake; Thea stayed on her feet, leaning back against the counter, a wooden spoon dripping gravy onto her shorts.

"Jacob," Gabe began. "I know leaving you was unforgiveable. I don't have a lot I can say to defend myself. I was... I think I went mad, son, I really do. I... didn't know how to be a father–your mother said it often enough, and she was right–"

"Yes, you do!" Benji broke in. There were tears in his voice. "You do know! Tell him he knows, Jake!"

"It's all right, Ben," his father said. "He can say whatever he likes to me."

Jake finally looked up. The two men were so alike, it brought a lump to Thea's throat. Jake's hair stuck up all over and Gabe's curled over his collar, but their eyes were exactly the same.

"You can say whatever you want to me," Gabe repeated, not backing down from Jake's stare. "I'm back to stay, and I love you, and I'll do whatever it takes to make you see it."

"That's such bullshit!" Jake shouted, going from zero to code red in a fraction of a second. He stood up from the table, knocking it sideways and tipping the wineglasses over. Thea's broke. She didn't make a move to pick it up.

"I can say whatever I want?" Jake went on, leaning over his father, who looked calmly at him, though there were pink spots in his cheeks and his eyes were bright. "Fine. What kind of father leaves his kids like that? Without even saying goodbye?"

"I wrote a–no, you're right."

"Damn fucking right I'm right!" Jake shouted.

"Don't, Jake!" Benji cried.

"Shut up, Benji," Jake snapped, pointing a finger at him but not taking his eyes off Gabriel. "He was *three years old*. You left him just when he was starting to really understand what a father is for! You know who taught him to throw? Me!" Jake used the finger to jab at his own chest. "You know who read to him when Mom was working to get enough money to feed us because you didn't? Me.

Who babysat him after school because she couldn't afford aftercare? Me."

Now his hand was twisted into a fist, and he shook it at Gabe. "That's what you deserve to get punched out for. What you did to him. You want to apologize to someone? Do it to him. I don't fucking need you. You're wasting your breath. I'm fine. Apologize to the son who fucking gives a shit whether you're around or not."

Gabe didn't back away from the fist or the spittle that landed on him with Jake's words or the fury and hurt in Jake's eyes. Benji was crying now. "Ben," Gabe said, still looking at Jake. "It's okay. I want him to say this, okay? I'm not leaving. Ever again. Mother of God, I swear it."

Thea thought numbly that he was, too, leaving, and within the next few minutes if she could arrange it, but she couldn't move or speak. This was for Jake and Benji, not her.

Jake continued to glare at him. Gabe held his gaze. "I am sorry," he said slowly, deliberately. "If you knew how badly I've missed you, Jacob... all of you. You're a young man now, and you were a boy then... and I missed it all."

"You chose that!" Jake shouted again, but he was fighting to keep his anger.

"I know. I did. I regret it so much, son, I tell you. And I wanted to come back. But I... was too ashamed."

"And now you're not?" Thea said. Oh, look at that, she could speak after all.

He finally broke Jake's gaze to look up at her. "I've sorted myself out now. I'm qualified now. I have a real job, and I'm staying."

Thea wanted to fold her arms as well, as protection against the plea in his eyes. But she kept a tight grip on the wooden spoon and said, "A real job?"

He nodded. "I'm a cost estimator. Once I... got my head sorted out and really sat down to think about what I could do to get back here, I realized that most of my work experience–"

Thea snorted. She couldn't help it.

Gabe acknowledged the slam. "When I had it," he agreed, "but

I was working on costs all the time. I took more classes, and my cousin took me on at his company so I could learn the rest. Then I called up Sean and begged him to take me back."

Sean, the cousin Ben remembered, had gained his green card years ago and was a successful contractor. He'd been the source of most of Gabe's jobs but had had his own generosity rewarded by Gabe's late starts and mysterious disappearances.

"Sean is a saint," Thea said, which they'd both said often back then.

"Sure and he is," Gabe said. "But this time I came with money, and he's given me the tiniest little piece of the company." He put his finger and thumb about a millimeter apart. "I'm here. I'm invested. I'm not going away."

"You're not staying *here*," she said.

"I know, pet," he said. Thea wanted to find a patronizing tone in him, but there was nothing. No self-pity, no excuses, no slick storyline to persuade her. Just those light blue-gray eyes she'd once believed could see to her very core.

"All I'm asking," he said, eyes widening, "is for the chance to talk. And maybe a cup of tea and a bite to eat?"

Thea turned her back on him and pulled the kettle to the front of the stove. She'd remembered that he drank tea at any hour of the day or night and despised microwaved water. So she'd dutifully taken the kettle out of the back of a cupboard where she'd thrown it after he'd left, and washed the dust off it, ready for just this request.

Jake scowled when it became clear his father really was staying for dinner, but he was too hungry to leave the room, and they were soon eating the baked ziti she'd made. It was comfort food for her and the boys, and Gabe also loved it. He ate about half a loaf of Italian bread with it and slathered Benji's slice with so much butter, Benji's eyes widened.

Thea thought fleetingly of kneeling down in the cramped bathroom space, getting told off by Liam for putting too much adhesive on the back of the tile. *I should have jumped him then.*

"I can swim to the pontoon now!" Benji was saying about his day camp.

"I'll bet you're a fish," Gabe said, which made Benji preen. "Have you been playing much basketball?" he asked Jake.

Jake scowled. Again. "Nope," he said. "I quit." He said it with such relish that Thea knew, if she hadn't already guessed, that this was precisely the reason he'd left the team.

"Ah, no, Jakey, really?"

"And it's not Jakey, Da... Dad. Jakey was a kid you left the country to get away from." Jake dropped his fork with a clatter and looked down and away from all of them, furious with himself for showing that he did, after all, care.

"Ah, Jacob, you've got the right of it there." Gabe dared to put a hand on Jake's forearm. Jake didn't remove it, but he didn't lift his head either. "But I wasn't trying to get away from *you*." He leaned back. His eyes met Thea's, and he gave her the potato famine look she had to steel herself against. "I think I was running away from me."

Jake threw off his arm, and Thea said, with a twist of sarcasm, "'It's not you, it's me.'"

Gabe laughed at his own words, and Thea did too, hearing the very words she'd used on Gabe. "I know what it sounds like."

He held Thea's eyes, and a tumbling rush of emotions poured over her, feelings she thought she was immune to hope and pain and faith and disappointment and, worst of all, an echo of love.

"If any of you," Gabe said, but he was talking to her, "have any thought in your heads that you did anything to make me the biggest eejit on the continent, you shouldn't. If it takes me the rest of my life to tell you I've changed, I'll do it. Swear on the Holy Bible, I will."

He'd used that phrase endless times before, and Thea was grateful for the reminder. "Finish your dinner," she said. "You can get to the swearing and promising later."

Gabe looked disappointed, then repentant. Thea began getting mad at him again, which was tiring. She'd forgotten her wine.

"Jake," Gabe began again. "What are you doing with your summer?"

Jake shrugged. "Hanging out." So he wasn't going to mention his job.

"Who with? Anyone from the team?"

Thea tried not to look as though she was listening. She was curious who Jake hung out with on his long absences from home too. It was one of those things she'd been meaning to follow up with him on, but she'd been too busy to do it.

"No." Jake took a gigantic bite of bread, so his next words were muffled.

"Who?" Thea said, forgetting herself.

Jake swallowed like a crane forcing down a toad. "Just some friends."

"Zachary Benedetto?"

Jake looked surprised that she'd heard him with all the bread in his mouth, but Thea had at least a few Mom tricks at her disposal.

"You're still hanging out with him?" she insisted.

Jake set his jaw and nodded.

"Who's Zachary Benedetto?" Gabe said.

"He's notorious, is what he is. More money than Croesus and no attempt to be responsible. I heard he and his lackeys carved up the swings in the playground. Tell me you didn't say Zachary Benedetto, Jacob."

"He's not that bad," he said, not meeting her eyes.

"Were you with him when he cut through that fence last night? That was him, right?"

"He didn't cut through the fence."

Jake was hiding something, but Thea could only deal with one family crisis at a time, and Gabe was it tonight. "We'll talk about this later," she promised Jake.

"Can't wait," he said and picked up the serving spoon to bring a huge scoop of ziti to his mouth.

"God, Jake!" Thea protested.

"Show your mother a little respect!" Gabriel said. The boys forgot what they were talking about and stared at him.

"*You* show my mother some respect!" Jake yelled. "Jesus Christ!"

He said that because he knew Gabe hated it. Then he threw the spoon back into the tray of ziti, splashing blood-red pasta sauce droplets over them all.

"Jake, language," Thea said.

"What? You're such a hypocrite, Mom!" Jake was in full flow now, and Thea pictured the violence with which he'd shove himself away from the table and out the door—apparently, to see Zachary "Career Criminal" Benedetto. "You're the one who got the call from school 'cause Benji said *goddammit* to the cafeteria people!"

Shit. This was not how she wanted the conversation to go. She didn't want Gabe to see her with any weaknesses. "Yes, thank you, Jake. You can go now."

Just as she'd imagined, Jake clattered his way out the door, giving Gabe one more triumphant look as he went.

"Is that how he talks to you now?"

"He's fifteen, Gabe, and no, it usually isn't. Something upset him more than usual tonight. I wonder what."

Benji was sitting at his end of the table, eyes wide. Gabe turned to him, eyes twinkling. "You gonna storm out of here as well, son?"

"No, Dad." Benji's voice was uncertain, but when Gabe grinned at him, he gained confidence. "Da," he said, "can I show you my Octopus game?"

"Sure, Ben. If you've finished your dinner."

"I'm done!" He wasn't, but Thea was too happy to have the minutes to herself to argue.

They disappeared upstairs, and she began to clear the plates and her broken glass. How strange to clear up four plates instead of three. If she squinted, she could imagine that this was normal, that Gabe had come home after a regular day of work, that she'd fought with Jake about some normal teenage thing, and Gabe was now spending his usual piece of quality time with Benji before bed.

But that wasn't how it was. This was *her* house; these were *her* kids; this was *her* schedule, *her* little piece of life she'd managed to carve out of the wreckage he had left. Gabe didn't belong here.

Except that Benji thought he did.

Gabe put Benji to bed as well. By that time, the kitchen was cleaner than it had ever been and Thea was on her second glass of wine. Big glasses.

She was sitting in the living room when he came down. "His lights are out, but he wants you to say good night," he said.

"I know," she snapped. That anyone but she could put her younger son to bed was ludicrous. But Benji hadn't even thought to ask her to come until after Gabe had done all the fun stuff. She went up to him in a bad mood, but the sight of him all snuggled in his Star Wars sheets and comforter, his Darth Vader nightlight gleaming through the darkness—how the hell that made him feel safer, she had no idea—took away her crankiness.

"Good night, big guy," she said, enveloping him in her arms.

"You smell like wine." His voice was buried in her hair.

"You smell like ice cream." She nuzzled his neck. "Love you, Benji boy."

"'Ou too."

As always, he waited until she was almost out of the door before speaking again. "Mommy?"

Uh-oh, it was a Mommy question. When it was Mom, he wasn't as bothered about the answer. "Yeah, babe."

"Can Dad come back tomorrow?"

Thea sighed and went back into the room, closing the door. She sat on the edge of the bed, leaned over her son, and said, "Benji, I don't know how long your dad is going to be here."

"He said for always he's going to be here!" A dark head on his pillow, his eyes were wide, half-fearful, half-trusting.

"And I really want that to be true. I'll promise you this, Benji: I'm going to make sure your father stays in your life from now on. Whether he's in this country or not."

"He *is*!"

"Yes." For now, anyway. "He loves you, big guy. Don't doubt that, okay? We'll help him find ways to show it."

She wasn't going to swear to more than that. She kissed Benji again and told him to close his eyes. He did. The rush of painful, exhilarating love that often came over her when she looked at him was more powerful today because the source of so much of his pain was waiting for her downstairs. She stroked his cheek that had the birthmark, smiled at him, and left.

Her steps felt as heavy as Jake's as she walked down the stairs. *Where's that glass of wine?* In the living room, with Gabe.

He was on the couch, looking relaxed; one arm was on the back of the couch and the other held another glass of wine. Hers was on the coffee table.

She could sit next to him, though he took up a fair amount of space and the couch was hardly bigger than a love seat. She could sit in one of the armchairs, but then she'd have to look at him, and she didn't want to. The sun had sunk behind the trees, and the room was dim enough that he'd turned on a couple of lamps, one of which he sat under.

"Will you sit for a glass of wine before I go?" he said.

If she sat on the couch, she could look in front of her, not at his eyes, illuminated as they were by the lamplight. She squeezed herself into her corner, throwing cushions from behind her into the chair across the room.

There were a few moments of silence. Thea held her wineglass to her, a paltry protection from him.

"Does Benji fall asleep fast?" he said.

"Pretty fast." Then her eyes narrowed and, breaking her own rule, she looked at him. Scowled at him, really. "Why? What do you think is going to happen?"

"Nothing!" He held up both hands. "Jaysus, Thea, nothing, of course. I just want to talk. Or, I want you to talk."

She snorted in disbelief. "Oh no, you don't."

"I do, pet. I deserve it; I know I do. And if you don't tell me all of it, we can't get beyond it."

"God, Gabe! Have you been to a therapist or something?"

"Well..." He looked abashed. "You know when I... got home–"

"When you abandoned us, you mean?" She couldn't help it. Her voice was harsh and cold and she was glad of it.

"Yes." He lowered his head. "Yes, that. So when I got home, you know I didn't have any money—"

"Neither did I, Gabriel."

He was still looking at his lap and paused before saying, "I'm sorry. I'll keep saying it for the rest of my life if there's any chance you'll believe me at the end of it."

She took a gulp of her wine. "Don't believe you yet. Did believe you. For thirteen years, I believed you, Gabe." With the wine and her anger coursing through her, it was easier to look at him. "It was a very bad habit; it hurt me and the kids and I've broken it now."

His eyes were the color of gray clouds. "T, all I'm asking is—"

"Don't call me T." She was being petty, but she was so afraid that if he kept talking, he'd somehow make her believe him again.

"Okay, I'm sorry. I'm just going to tell you what happened, and you can believe it or not, whatever you like. So I wasn't home more than a few days before I realized what a mistake I'd made. I missed you and the boys so bad, I'd bust into tears if I saw a family on the telly. Couldn't go out, couldn't go down to the pub, or see my cousins, or anything."

"God forbid," she muttered.

"I'd fucked up, T—Thea. And I tried to ignore it like I'd done all those other times. I knew I'd never get you back this time, and I wanted to not care about that."

"Not care that you left two *children* over here?" she spat.

"I know." God help her, there were tears in his eyes now. "I was mad, T, really mad. Away with the fairies, for real. And, you know, you don't live in America for fifteen years without someone telling you how much a shrink has helped them. But since I didn't have any money and I couldn't ask my mam or anyone, I... had to Google it instead."

She didn't want to think about the changes he had to have made to get to that point—if he'd actually done any of this—so she said, "How is your dear old mam anyway?"

Gabe's mother, Sheena, hated Thea. Hated everything about her, from her age to her religion to her pregnancy to her nationality to her taste in baby names. Gabe was an only child, and Thea learned too late that his mother had no desire to relinquish her ironclad control of him. Gabe had had enough principle to stay with Thea—or maybe he really had loved her, though she'd doubted it over the years—but he never stuck up for her in front of his mother, and the one trip she'd made to the States, after Jake's birth, had been a disaster.

Gabe seemed to be picking his words carefully. "She didn't want me to come."

"I bet. I'm curious, Gabe: does she care at all that she has grandchildren?"

He winced and brushed a nonexistent speck off his knee. "It doesn't matter," he said in a low voice. "It doesn't matter what she cares or doesn't care about. My kids are *my* kids, and I'm back to get them—to be with them."

"Get them?" She stood up in a rush—too much of a rush for the alcohol in her brain. She swayed.

"I don't mean—" He had stood as well. He gripped her arm, steadying her. "Are you all right?"

"Get off me," she said through a fog that was threatening to overtake her.

Get them.

"T, it was a bad choice of words. I'm not taking them anywhere. Sit down, pet, come on."

Her legs went out from under her, and she did as he asked. Gabe sat next to her, a lot closer than he had been. "Get away from me," she whispered.

"I will," he said, "as soon as you're all right."

His hand was still on her arm, his leg now resting alongside hers. Thea put her hand to her head. The third glass of wine had been a bad idea.

"I'm telling you the truth, T," he went on. He came into focus, his eyes as clear and honest as the day she'd met him. If only all the time in between hadn't happened, she could be so happy right now.

His voice was low and intimate, now that he was closer. "I love you, T. I've loved you from that first day we met in that crummy bar, with your sister flipping her hair at me and you trying to fade into the woodwork, and there was no one like us in the world and there's never been anyone but me for you and there never will be."

The tears seemed to have been waiting for these words, and she could no more stop them than she could shut out all the hope he'd given her all those years ago. They poured down her cheeks, and she collapsed back into the couch, not bothering to hide them. "God, Gabe, listen to you," she said through them. "You said all that all the time, and you *left me*, Gabe. You left me and the kids *alone*, and I am so *tired*, Gabe. I'm so *fucking tired*."

"I know, pet. I'm sorry." He leaned back with her; it was as natural as breathing to turn her face into his chest. "I'm so sorry," he said.

And Thea cried as she hadn't in months, sobbed and railed and sometimes punched him in the chest with fists weak with exhaustion, and Gabe just put his arms around her and stroked her back and repeated, over and over as if it they were magic words that would heal her, "That's it, pet."

And that was how Liam found them.

Chapter 18

His step on the porch stairs didn't rouse Thea, but his knock on the screen door, abruptly halted as he saw through it to her in Gabe's arms, sure did. She opened her raw, swollen eyes, swiveled her head toward him, then shot out of Gabe's embrace as if she'd been greased.

She would never forget the look in Liam's eyes. In the moment before he could shutter his feelings behind pressed-together lips and a dead blue stare, his eyes and mouth opened in shock and hurt. There was no question who Gabriel was; he looked exactly like Jake.

"Liam," she said, extricating herself as best she could from the couch. He'd already taken a step back from the door.

"Who the fuck is that?" Gabe said, his sharp voice a clear contrast to the gentle tones of a minute ago.

"Oh God. Liam," she said again, racing to the door, reaching for him. He took another step back, a step he didn't seem conscious of. His eyes hadn't left hers, but each step was a negation of everything they'd built over the summer, everything she'd thought they could become.

"It's not—" she began but stopped herself. *It's not what it looks like.* Wasn't that the worst cliché? It almost always was what it looked like, and was Thea even sure that this time was different? Gabe's soft words and huge eyes had put her under some kind of spell.

Liam stumbled down the first step as Thea opened the screen door. He caught himself on the stair rail, dragged his hand down it another step, and then quickly pulled it off, staring at his hand that had, no doubt, gotten a splinter.

"Shit," she said. "I'm sorry, Liam—"

That made him pause in his examination of his hand. That hand that had caressed her neck so gently only two days ago. She put her own hand to her neck just remembering it.

Did he remember that too? In the light from the porch, his blue eyes were icy, which meant he did. Or he didn't. "I bet you are," he said. His eyes flicked past her for a moment, and then he turned around and left the porch.

"Who *is* that?" Gabe said again from behind her. He put a hand on the small of her back, possibly from habit but also probably because he wanted to claim her. Liam got into the blue monster baby and broke the sleepy summer night with its engine rev. In seconds, he was out of sight.

The spell had broken. Now Thea remembered other words Gabe had whispered to her, words that had kept her from believing she could have a life without him in it. Gabe had always been so good at feeding her the kind of story that got her to do what he wanted, whether they were a sob story or tiny needles of abuse sinking by degrees into her heart. Tonight was no different.

"Get out, Gabriel," she said, not bothering to turn around. Her voice sounded as dead as Liam's eyes had looked. "Go away. No, you can't have us back. All that bullshit about googling your therapy. Just to suck me back in, I bet. Fuck the hell off. Get out of my house and leave my kids alone. We never needed you, and we don't now."

"T–"

"And *stop* calling me T." She turned around then, the anger that had left surging through her. "My family and the people I love call me that, and you are neither of those things. Get out."

"Thea–"

"*Get out!*" She was screaming like a fishwife, and she didn't care. "*Get lost! I don't need you! Get lost!*"

"All right, all right. Jaysus." He went down the steps. On the lowest one he looked back at her. "So was he your boyfriend?"

She counted the words on the middle fingers of each hand. "Get. Lost."

"*Mommm!*" She'd woken Benji with her screaming. Gabe looked up at the bedroom window above the porch.

Gabe looked back at her, and in the yellow porch light she thought she saw triumph. "I'm coming back, Thea," he said. "I told you; I'm not leaving ever again."

He blew a kiss to the window above her and walked down the street.

She heard the window rattling and rushed back into the house and up the stairs before Benji broke the thing trying to get to his father.

He was hysterical, worse than she'd just been. "You sent him away! I hate you! You told him to leave!"

"Shhh. Shhh." She tried to corral his flailing limbs, taking a few hits to her arms. "He'll be back. I was mad, but he knows you want him back."

"He won't! He'll go back to Ireland again!"

"He says he won't go back again." She pressed Benji's hot, wet face to her cheek. "He says he loves you, loves you both. He says he's staying. I'll call him tomorrow and ask him to come back to see you."

"Will you?" He gulped and looked up at her, his dark eyes shimmering in his nightlight's dim glare.

Poor kid. He didn't know who to trust anymore. That was what Gabe had taught him, that grown-ups couldn't be trusted, even those who swore they loved you. It was a lesson Thea had still not learned. And now she'd taught it to Liam.

"Well, I'm your mother. Have I ever lied to you? I don't mean about the little things. About the big things?" He looked down, unable to deny it. "I swear on your BB-8 that I will call your da tomorrow and ask him to come back." She said it past the lump that had appeared in her throat.

He looked over at the two-foot-high robot that sat in pride of place in the corner of the room. It was his most treasured possession, and she'd heard him talk to it like it was a friend. "On BB-8?" he said uncertainly.

She nodded. "I take BB-8 very seriously. I'm serious."

Goddammit.

♦

Liam wished hard that there was gravel on the road, so that when his truck peeled away from the curb, the gravel would flare up behind him, make a satisfying grinding noise, and convey a tiny amount of the fury overtaking him. He stamped on the gas and put as much distance between himself and Thea Fielding as his engine and the stop signs would allow.

He hadn't felt this exposed, this vulnerable, in months, and he hated it. He gritted his teeth against it. *You swore. You swore you'd never put yourself out there like that again.* And here he was, like a freaking idiot, surprised because a woman turned out to be faithless.

Thirty-six hours. That was all it had taken for her to turn those big brown eyes away from him and onto her ex. His day had begun with concern and ended in a sick panic when she hadn't answered any of his texts or his calls. Was she really sick? Or did she regret their week together?

He stopped at a traffic light and rubbed his hands over his face. The splinter in his palm stabbed him again.

She'd giggled when his beard had tickled her thigh. *Dammit. Stop thinking about it. It wasn't anything.*

Of course he'd gone to check on her. He was used to thinking about her, to worrying about her and those kids in that beat-up house. He'd thought of her as alone and needing him.

Turned out, not so much.

He smacked the steering wheel hard, driving the splinter in deeper. Then he did it again before turning onto the highway to his own town. The burn helped take away some of what was wrapping around his heart.

When he was nearly home, his phone rang. His stupid heart leaped up, but it was his father. There was no question of not answering. "Hi, Dad."

"You busy tomorrow?" No preamble. No, *how's it going?* No understanding that now that they were almost into August, Liam was going to have to start setting up his classroom and preparing lesson plans.

But some nice manual labor might be just what he needed. Think about water pressure and couplings and compression rings and not about Thea's breasts under his hands...

"No. What do you need?"

"Got a new build going up in Wareham. Can you do the estimate?"

Liam was surprised. This task involved a lot of trust on his father's part. If Liam estimated too high, they'd lose the bid. Too low, and they'd find themselves on the hook for the rest. "What kind of build?"

"Multifamily. Sean O'Brien's the CM."

Sean was a friend, but a businessman. He'd chosen other plumbers as often as Liam's father. The bid would have to be impressive.

"Sure, I can go." He pulled into his driveway.

"Bring your lad," Pat said. And that was when Liam remembered Jake.

Liam dropped his keys and phone on the table near the front door as he walked through the living room and into the bedroom he'd once shared with Avery. He'd stripped the place of anything feminine the day he'd kicked her out, and that weekend had painted the walls above the plate rails a navy blue that set off the white paneling and reflected his style much more than hers. He didn't have the money to fix the rest of the house how he liked yet, but at least this floor was how he liked it. It had still been months before he'd been able to walk in there and not see her with her mortgage broker, legs in the air, howling. Yes, she'd been howling. He didn't think the sound would ever leave him.

And now, a palimpsest laid over that memory, was Thea, tucked into her ex-whatever-he-was's chest, his proprietary arms around her, head lowered to hers. As they had done for years before Liam the dumbass showed up and now could continue doing when Liam had finished extricating himself from her life.

His phone rang from the living room. With heavy steps, he went out to look at it. It was Thea. This was how far he'd deluded himself about her, right up until he'd told her he was crazy about her. He winced even now as he remembered it, as the phone kept ringing.

He hadn't programmed her name into his phone, because why should he? She wasn't a permanent part of his life, no one whose number he needed to keep track of. Yet he remembered every digit of that number, could recall it in his sleep.

He stared at the phone. There was nothing she could say to him. He didn't want to hear her apologize, give him the sob story. *He's my children's father. He wants us back.* Yeah, Liam knew the drill. *He can give me something you can't.*

He folded his arms and watched the phone until the call went to voicemail. Then he went to the kitchen, a galley setup open to the living room, and got a beer out of the refrigerator. Drank it, walked out through his bedroom to the back deck and threw the empty bottle at the back wall at the end of the small yard, where it shattered with a satisfying crash. Then he went back in and did it all again.

♦

Jake came home at ten o'clock. Thea was sitting on the edge of the couch in the living room, waiting for him, a cup of tea at her side.

He stopped as soon as he got in the room. "So?" he said.

Thea couldn't bear the tension in his shoulders. She got up to hug him. It was a measure of how bad things had gotten that Jake let her. She almost wished he'd duck away, but no, she was able to put her arms around his thin, vulnerable back and squeeze as much strength and stability as she could into him.

He did, at last, pull away. "He's gone?"

"Yes."

Jake relaxed one iota. He put a hand to the back of his neck. She thought two things on top of each other: one, that Liam did that too, and two, that Jake's knuckles were bleeding.

"Jake! What did you do to your hand?"

He looked at his hand, the dark-red streaks along it. "I punched a wall."

"Jesus. Come on. Let me clean it." He let her lead him by the hand to the kitchen, where she ran the water hot and pulled out peroxide and gauze. "Looks like the wall won."

"Yeah. Felt good though."

"Jacob." What was she supposed to say to that? As she wiped away the blood and grit, she decided on the truth. "Feels good to deal with a pain you made for yourself, doesn't it?"

His eyes flew up to hers, his mouth open.

She'd decided he wasn't old enough to tell; too much information was a dangerous thing for a teenager. But he was a young man and hurting and feeling like no one understood what he was going through.

"When your grandma and grandpa died," she said, "I got very depressed. It was a pain so deep, I wanted to disappear into it. My brother and sisters seemed to be moving on—well, Aunt Sam found her own unhealthy way to deal with it, but the others... I was at college by myself and I felt... invisible." She got out the bacitracin and smeared some onto the cuts on his knuckles. "Do you know what cutting is?"

He nodded, still staring at her with his mouth open.

"Well, I did that a few times. It felt like... like this." She shook his hand. "It hurt, but I could control it, and I couldn't control anything else."

She turned her arm over and ran her hand over the faint scars inside her forearm.

"Mom," Jake said, his voice low.

"They're faint because I found out pretty quick that it didn't help in the end. I was just putting more pain out there. And I knew I was important to people, and if I went any further, I'd be creating pain for them as bad as what I was feeling."

And, she didn't say, *your father made me feel visible again.*

She picked up a Band-Aid and began covering his knuckles. "I'm not going to—"

"Good. Because we can't be without you, Benji and me." She finished the last knuckle and put her arm around his shoulders, touching her head to his spiky one.

"I know," he mumbled.

"And I don't just mean 'cause you're a cheap babysitter," she added, which brought a reluctant smile. "You want some hot chocolate?"

Summer or winter, it was their standard nighttime comfort food, like the baked ziti had been earlier. "Sure," he said.

They didn't speak again until Jake had taken a few sips of his hot chocolate. "So did he say anything else?" he said, taking a lot of interest in his spoon.

"Not really. The same thing he said to you."

"Do you believe him?"

"Not yet."

"So you might?"

"If it means he comes into your life more and does the right thing by you and Benji, then I'll be happy."

"Not *your* life?"

"No. Well, except for when he comes to see you."

Jake seemed to be holding something back. Finally, digging the handle of his spoon into the table, he said, "What about Liam?"

The question she couldn't answer. The name that sent a spike of dread into her stomach. His face through the screen door. The hurt. Worse, the resignation. He'd expected her to cheat on him, and to his eyes, she had.

And as she'd predicted, it was a whole lot worse because he now had a relationship with her kids, and any time he now gave them would mean he'd have to continue to talk to her. Which she could bet the last dime of her trust fund he didn't want to do.

"What do *you* want to do about Liam?" she hedged.

"I'm not the one dating him, Mom."

"Oh." She suddenly found her own spoon fascinating. "You figured that out, huh?"

"It wasn't hard." He scowled into his mug. "So are you going to keep dating him?"

The look on his face. The ice in his eyes. She couldn't tell Jake about that. "It's complicated," was all she could say.

"So you *are* going to take Dad back." Jake shoved his mug away.

"Dammit, Mom. Liam was good for you—for us. I guess now I have to stop working for him, too. Did you dump him already? Why did you—?"

"*Jake!*" Thea put her hand on his. "I am *not* taking back your dad. Liam... Liam knows we lied to him about today and that your dad's back. If you want to keep working for him, then maybe you should call him."

"Is he pissed?"

"Not at you, hon." That was as far as she could go. Even that was probably too much.

"Why don't *you* call him? Tell him what you told me?"

"Look, Jake. I don't want you to worry about Liam and me. I think he'll still be happy to have you work for him"—she crossed her fingers under the table—"but this is something you have to ask him."

Jake, like most teenagers, looked very sure that this was something he would much prefer Thea do for him, but he stood and pulled his phone out of his back pocket. Thea held her breath. Liam wouldn't take it out on Jake, would he?

Chapter 19

Liam was sitting on his couch, watching a medieval fantasy show he'd lost the thread of years ago, his head aching without the consolation of being drunk, when his phone rang.

He almost didn't look at it. She'd called three times already tonight. The phone was next to him on the couch, and if he hadn't noticed out of the corner of his eye that there was something different about the screen, he would have remained determined to keep his focus on the TV. But he did look down and saw Jake's profile picture.

Even then he let it go through another ring before he picked up. God, his head hurt. "Hello, Jake," he said.

"Hi." How did the kid feel about his dad being home? Had they all spent the day in family bliss, reliving the good old days, laughing at the trick they'd played on Liam? Was Jake thrilled to have his dad back and ready to drop Liam like a worthless gem in the video game they'd played?

Jake was silent for a moment. "What can I do for you?" Liam prompted. He wanted to get the call over with.

"Oh, um. I was just wondering. Do you still need me on the job?"

Liam leaned forward and scrubbed at his face. "It's fine, Jake," he said, his voice heavy. He was exhausted. "You don't have to work for me anymore if you don't want to."

"But I do!" Jake's voice came out with such force, it squeaked on the last word. "I really do!"

Liam felt an altogether unreasonable relief, even joy. "Okay, then. Good," he said, not wanting to sound too enthusiastic and scare the kid off. "I'll see you at seven o'clock tomorrow, okay?"

"Okay," Jake said on a breath. "Hey, Liam?"

Uh-oh. "Yes?" he said warily.

"Will you talk to my mom?"

He heard a noise in the background; she was there with Jake. Maybe in the kitchen, sitting with cookies, the coffee machine on the counter ready to switch on in the morning. She always made extra for him now. The familiarity, the comfort of it made his heart thick with pain.

What was he supposed to say to Jake? "Later," he chose. "It's past my bedtime." Jake began to say something, but Liam said, "I'll see you tomorrow, Jake," and hung up.

◆

At two o'clock in the morning, he felt just punch-drunk enough to listen to the voicemails. Sleep was a joke. He heard his third-floor tenants moving around, students whose idea of day and night seemed to be reversed. Liam didn't mind: he liked the company, and he liked the income.

"Liam," her voice said. The rush of... whatever he'd felt for her came back to him with that one word. She'd gone from a cold, clipped, sarcastic use of his name to breathing it into his mouth when he'd entered her. *Shit.* Maybe he couldn't listen to this.

"Please, please see me," she went on. "Everything I have to say sounds ridiculous, I know, so I have to say it to your face so you'll know I... oh, crap, now I sound like him. But I'm telling the truth, Liam. He's not back the way you think. He showed up on Sunday night and... and he's the kids' father..." Liam closed his eyes and rubbed a hand over his beard. "And I was just telling him how pissed I was—am—at him..."

By cuddling him?

"And it just all... overcame me. Plus, I was drunk a little bit. And I want to remind you that I wasn't at all drunk this week, with you. So please—oh God, I know you won't, and I don't blame you, but this is not like your wife. I sent him away, and I need to talk to you because... because it's important to me what you think of me. So if you can, please, call me."

Another message went on as if she hadn't hung up and redialed.

"And I know he's a total bullshitter, Liam, and you're not, and I do know the difference."

Another: "But if he's here for the kids, then I can't make him stay out of our lives, and I don't know what that means but I need to talk to you about it."

Another: "Forget it. I'm sorry. I'm asking the impossible. I know you can't do this, and I don't blame you. You said before you didn't do complicated and I am extra-complicated and it just got worse so... Thank you, Liam, for making me feel..." Ah, shit, she was crying. "Human again."

Liam dug his nails into the splinter in his hand, which he'd been halfheartedly trying to get out all night. Then, before he could think too much about it, he'd dialed her number.

She picked up at once, said his name with tears in her voice. "I said forget it, but don't, please don't, you don't know what—"

"What do you want to do about Benji?" he interrupted. Sticking to business might just help him hold it together.

"Oh." Pulling her explanation up short made it hard for her to switch gears. "I—I don't—"

"I'll pick him up. If he won't be—" He wanted to say *confused*, but he was kidding himself that he'd had any time to become a father figure to either Jake or Benji. Benji's *own father* was in town, like Santa after an endless twenty-four days of December. And was that what Liam had been going for, in spending those extra hours with the kids? If so, he'd been kidding himself for a long time. "If he isn't getting picked up already," he finished.

"No, he isn't," she said. "If you could pick him up tomorrow, that would help to give him a sense of normalcy in all this. But after that... well, we'll see."

Perhaps his father would pick him up after that. Liam burned with jealousy he hadn't earned. "Right," he said. "I'll be at your house at seven tomorrow then, for Jake."

"God, Liam, I—"

"What?" *Crap.* He hadn't meant to put that much emotion into the word. He should cut this off before he made a fool of himself. "It's no big deal, Thea," he said, pleased that his voice was calmer. "We didn't have any... obligations to each other."

"But I did!" she cried. "That week wasn't just because, Liam. I don't do that."

He knew that.

"And I know it... meant something to you, too, Liam, and I'm so, so sorry Gabe showed up the very next day, of all damn days."

He stared dully at the television, where kingdoms were won and lost on the word of a woman. He hated to feel this raw. "Thea," he said. "Figure out his place in your life. And then..." *What? Will you be waiting for her like some pathetic, faithful dog? Sitting on the front porch long after his owners have moved?* "Just... do that."

"But you had a place in my life. A good place. I wanted to... see where that would take us."

So had he. But he'd been forgetting about real life, about history and exes and lessons learned. And he was all done opening himself up. "It took us here, T," he said, his voice dull. "I don't reckon there's anywhere else to go, do you?"

He hung up.

♦

The next morning was excruciating. After a night of trying to cry silently so the boys wouldn't hear, Thea gave up and got up at five, sitting at the kitchen table with her coffee, staring into nothing, listening to the ticking clock on the wall that brought closer the moment she would see Liam again.

Jake came downstairs early as well, looking as rested as she. She made him some eggs, and he took a cup of coffee, which he never drank. His hair was spiked up again; she had gotten used to seeing his natural curls and mourned them, for all they made him look more like Gabe. The truth was, he'd looked more like himself, and now Gabe had made him retreat into this persona again.

At seven o'clock precisely, they heard the dull roar of the blue monster baby, and a quiet knock sounded on the front door. *Just don't look at him. Nothing good can come of it.*

Jake put his free arm, the one that wasn't carrying his mug, around her as she sat, and pressed his head to hers. "Bye, Mom."

"Bye, baby."

"It'll be okay," Jake said, and she was so touched by his comfort that she looked up at him. So she saw Liam's large frame through the window in the front door, and once she saw it, she couldn't look away.

Jake opened the door, blocking him from her view, but she'd seen him in the window, and he looked like a slab of granite, staring at her as if the week before had never happened. She could hardly believe it had herself.

Jake hustled himself out of the door with one brief backward glance at her, so she tried to smile and raise her hand, but when he was gone, she felt tears drying on her face. She hoped he hadn't seen them.

After that, she went into automaton mode. She got showered and dressed, woke Benji and fed him and dropped him off at the bus, and went into work. So far, so good. But work had always been slow, and today was no different.

While she waited for the phone to ring, she worked on her class assignments, spreading books out around her and shamelessly using the company's internet connection. She tried to focus on the words in front of her, but she kept getting stabbed by memories.

Stab. There was Gabriel, eyes soft, telling her he'd never stopped loving her.

Stab. Liam, above her. *I'm crazy about you, T.*

Stab. Gabe, with a job, with stability, promising a new swathe of wonderful things.

Stab. Liam, creating stillness and calm just by being in her house, even when he was rolling his eyes at a broken window.

By lunchtime, she'd shoved the books aside and just sat with her head in her hands.

"Is everything all right, Ms. Fielding?"

Dr. Marion was standing in front of her, some papers in his hand. She hadn't even heard him come up.

Dr. Marion came from the UK and he was young; he'd gotten his doctorate a couple of years ago and had worked here ever since. He'd only known Thea in student mode, and she liked him for that; he had no expectation that she would do anything other than study at her desk.

As she looked up at him, she was aware her face was probably still pinched from two nights of no sleep. "I'm fine, thank you for asking," she said.

"Studying hard, I see."

"Yes, but I have time if you need something."

He looked at the papers in his hands as if he'd forgotten they were there. "Oh! Yes. Could you write these up into Excel?"

"Sure."

"If you don't mind my saying so," he said, "you're looking a little peaked. Not quite the thing."

"Oh. Thank you. I'm okay. Not quite the thing today, maybe, but I'll be completely the thing tomorrow."

"There's a big difference between working for your bachelor's and your master's," he said. "More pressure, more research outside class. Are you sure you're not taking on too much?"

"No!" In all this craziness, the one thing she had to hold on to was her dream of teaching. "No, I'm fine, really. It's not the classes. Must have been a full moon the last couple of nights. Stopped me sleeping, that's all."

He looked at her with a scientist's skepticism for such a vague correlation. "All right, well, let us know if you need a rest."

"I don't! Thanks though!" She opened her eyes wide, trying to look as awake as possible, and flashed a big, fake Fielding smile at him. He smiled back and, thankfully, walked away.

Thea went back to her head-in-hands position. Dr. Marion's notes swam in front of her eyes.

Maybe she *was* trying to do too much. Maybe her ill-advised—but hot—week with Liam was a symptom of a mind driven mad by two years of studying and mothering and working and trying to do it all. But what was the alternative?

Find a rich husband.

Not really an option. She didn't have the looks or the confidence to sell herself that way. Oh, or the morals, of course, although some days, when they were eating hot dogs for the third time that week, she wondered.

Use the rest of the trust fund.

Sure, the boys wouldn't get to college. But they'd have a lot of fun for the next three to ten years. Live in the moment, the way Gabe used to.

Let Kane bail you out. Again.

Dammit. He already bailed them out, as witnessed by Jake's phone and Benji's tablet. And her job. And the house he and Cat had basically chosen for her.

Did she have any backbone at all?

Not right now. Just... not right now.

She squeezed her eyes shut, then opened them and began working on Dr. Marion's spreadsheets.

♦

At lunchtime, Thea called Gabriel. He'd programmed his number into her phone, knowing her password because she hadn't changed it for ten years, even as her phones had to be replaced. He picked up at once.

"I'm glad you called," he said.

Well, she wasn't. "Listen, Gabe. If you're serious about being there for the boys–"

"And you, darlin'."

"For the *boys*," she reiterated, "then we can figure out a schedule. You are welcome at my house if you are going to be a part of their lives again." She put emphasis on the word *my*. "If you have a place to live, they can come and stay with you. Stay, not live."

"I know that, pet. Like I said, that's what I'm asking. For now at least. I'm staying with Sean, but I'm moving into my own place at the end of the month. It's only a one-bedroom, though. I figured they could take the bed and I'd take the couch."

Sounded shitty, but at least he'd been thinking of how he could have them near him. "You have a ways to go before Jake, at least, will want to stay with you."

"I know," he said again. "I'll work on him."

"All right. I have a study group on Wednesday. You can take Benji out for dinner then."

"Great."

"Have him back before eight o'clock."

"Sure."

"Gabriel."

"Yes, pet?"

"If you fuck up this time, I will *end* you." The thought of her boys being hurt again brought a welcome adrenaline rush to her limbs, helping her break out of her stupor.

"I won't. You'll see."

Chapter 20

Liam and Jake worked on a crumbling pipe system in a derelict Victorian that morning. They weren't due at O'Brien's until after lunch. Jake was silent unless he absolutely had to speak. They'd gotten into a good enough rhythm before Jake had gone on vacation that this wasn't a problem, except for the reason for it. Jake wasn't exactly a talker at the best of times, but they'd shared some stories about basketball and other sports they liked.

"How was the Cape?" Liam tried.

"Wet."

That was that, he supposed.

Liam got them both sandwiches, and they sat in the back of the company van. The day was unseasonably cool and overcast, which fit. Jake looked up and scowled at the sky; Liam wanted to copy him.

But, oh yeah, that was right, he was the grown-up here. And he had something to say. "Jacob," he began.

"It's never good when you start with 'Jacob.'" A twist came to his mouth that might have been a smile.

"Jake, then." Liam didn't try to look at him. How the hell he was going to get this across without sounding insufferably patronizing and... and teacher-y? He'd already started with the dreaded full name.

"Are you firing me?" Jake burst out. "'Cause Mom said—"

"No!" Okay, so he'd better look at him. Shit, the kid looked terrified. "No, Jake, of course I'm not firing you." He put a hand on Jake's shoulder and shook it. "What I'm trying to say is that... whatever is happening in your life right now... however things turn out... I'm here if you ever want to... vent." He waited for Jake to roll his eyes and say, *yeah, right*, but the boy was silent. "Okay?"

"Did you and Mom break up? She's sorry we lied to you about my dad coming back."

Liam ran a hand down his beard. "What I'm saying to you is outside anything your mom and I have to sort through." Jake's eyes were downcast, staring at his Coke can. "Outside of your relationship with your dad. This is about you and Benji and me. And I want you to know I'm still here. If you need anything."

They both watched the Coke can now. Slowly it began to crumple inward, squeezed by Jake's fist. "I don't have a relationship with my dad," Jake said to the can. "His choice."

Liam nodded, though Jake couldn't see. "Eventually—not now, but someday—you might find it less... exhausting to make peace with him, if he means what he says about rebuilding that."

Jake ducked his head away, stood up, and threw the can with sudden violence into the bushes behind them. Some birds stopped singing and then cawed loudly.

"One more thing," Liam said, standing himself. "Don't take it out on others, okay? This is hard for everyone." He went over to the bushes to find the can. "Especially the environment." He looked back with a smile, and Jake was giving him a reluctant half smile back.

"Now quit lounging around and get back to work." Jake quickly put together the tools they needed to finish the day's piping while Liam threw the remains of their lunch in the dumpster.

"What are we working on now?" Jake said when they were on their way to Sean O'Brien's place later.

"It's a quote. I get the plans and walk the site, if there's any house there. Then I'll go home and do a takeoff of the plans. I'll show you, if you like."

"Yeah, sure."

Liam did some math. "I have to pick up your brother tonight. But we could go back to my house after that. I have a big dining table I can roll out the plans on."

"Okay." That was high enthusiasm from Jake.

"You'll like this contractor," Liam said. "He's one of the good guys. Off the boat Irish—took me about three years to understand what he was saying."

"Sounds like half my relatives. My Irish side."

Right. Liam had forgotten Jake's father had gone back to Ireland when he'd left them. Bad choice of subject.

"Then you won't have a problem with Sean."

He said that as he pulled into O'Brien's yard. The impressive warehouse-type building on one side ruled over a site with backhoes, excavators, flatbed trucks, and vans similar to the one Liam was driving but with *O'Brien Construction* and the cloverleaf logo on the side.

"Oh shit," Jake said. Liam turned to him. Jake was paper white, his eyes round and blue and... scared?

"What is it?" Then Liam remembered their conversation. "No way. He *is* your family?"

Jake nodded, his eyes and mouth round. "My da's—dad's—cousin. The one who gave him all the work he kept screwing up. I didn't know you were talking about O'Brien."

"Oh." Typical. Two million Irish in Massachusetts, and his job was now to impress the one whose cousin he already despised. "Do you see much of him? After..."

"After my dad left?" There was no compunction to say the words, just a caustic fatality to Jake's voice. "No. They were too embarrassed, Mom said."

"Do you want me to take you home? I can pick this stuff up later."

"No." In one jerky movement, Jake had the door open and was out, walking to the warehouse.

"Hold up!" Liam grabbed his notepad and phone and hopped out of the van himself, locking it as he ran to catch up with Jake.

He led Jake to the office door, around the corner from the showroom Sean had set up in the main warehouse. Up some much less impressive stairs and into the office area, which boasted beige walls and cubicles, some tired plants, and four or five men and women sitting at desks.

Liam stopped at the first one; Jake hung back, but Liam could feel him craning his neck around him. "Hi," he said, smiling at the woman who had looked up from her computer and taken off her glasses when he came in. "I'm from Pat the Plumber? For the Winter Hill multifamily?"

"Oh yeah," she said, smiling back at him. "How are ya? I'm Mary-Ann. I'm the CM on that sucker."

Liam introduced himself, and they shook hands. Her age was anywhere between thirty and fifty, and she was dressed like him—jeans and a company T-shirt. Her short brown hair was almost hidden under a Sox cap.

"I know your father," she said. Her accent was thicker even than his—not an R in sight. She regarded him with gray eyes that were assessing but not unwelcoming. "And who's this?" she asked, turning the assessing look on Jake.

"This is my..." *Assistant? Apprentice? Summer help?* "This is Jake. He's helping me out this summer."

"Nice to meet you, Jake." Liam saw the boy's arm wobble from the shoulder as Mary-Ann gave it a good firm shake. "You know your way around a set of blueprints?"

Jake looked a little panicky, so Liam answered for him. "He will in a little while."

"Good." Mary-Ann stood and walked them into a room in the back, which held racks of plans and high shelves filled with rolls of paper.

"Have you been here long?" Liam asked. He'd thought he would know all the construction managers.

"Coupla years." She was at the shelves, pulling out a set of prints. "I heard you'd left the business. You're back?"

"Just for the summer."

"How 'bout you, Jake? Pat scare you off plumbing yet?" She winked at Jake, who gave her an uncertain smile. She didn't seem to need an answer but held the plans out to Liam. "Only got so many of these; when can you get them back to me?"

"Tomorrow, first thing."

"Good." She shook hands again. "Tell your dad I said hi."

"I will."

They were almost out of the office, and Liam later believed he could tell Jake's breathing was easier, when Sean came in.

"Hello there!" he sang as he saw Liam, walking toward him with his hand outstretched. Then he saw Jake.

"Jakey?" Sean said. His hand dropped to his side.

Jake had gone white again. When he didn't answer, Sean closed the gap and said, "Sure and look how big you are! How old are you now?" His florid cheeks seemed to be turning even redder.

"Fifteen," Jake said through what sounded like gritted teeth.

"Jaysus, you've grown about a foot!" Sean went on in a forced jovial tone that made Liam wince. He'd never seen Sean out of his element before.

"Yeah, well," Jake muttered, his icy-blue eyes now focused on Sean. His mother's spirit, Liam thought. "That's what happens when you don't see someone for two years."

Sean gave a half laugh and made a big show of hoisting the sports bag he was carrying on his shoulder. "Well, you know, son, I..." He looked around the room. Everyone had stopped what they were doing and were now watching them. "Why don't we go into my office?"

He began to lead the way, but Jake wasn't moving. "No, thanks. Let's go, Liam."

Sean's eyes widened as he looked to Liam. "Liam?" he stammered. Liam could tell he had no ability to comprehend why his cousin's child was in his office and in the company of a man he knew only through work.

"Yeah," Jake snapped, walking to the staircase door. "My boss."

"What? Why—I thought you were here to see your father."

"Nope." Jake left it at that, but the bite in his voice was clear to everyone.

Liam didn't think he was going to help matters any, but he said, "We're picking up plans for the Winter Hill job."

"Oh." Sean had trouble switching from family to work. "Oh... okay. Jakey's working for you?"

"Uh-huh." Jake had already opened the fire door, so Liam followed him.

"I didn't know, Jakey," Sean called from the middle of the room. "If you'd wanted a construction job, I would have—"

But another voice sounded from the staircase. "Jake?"

Holy shit. Liam recognized that voice even though he'd heard it only once before, and that through a whirlwind of pain.

Jake froze in the doorway. Through the half-open door, Liam saw Gabriel come up the stairs. He couldn't see Jake's face, as it was turned toward his father.

"Jake," Gabriel said, smiling big. "I'm so pleased to see you."

"Well, I'm not pleased to see you," Jake retorted. "We're just leaving."

"No, wait." Gabe's smile fell off his face. "You came this far to see me, didn't you? How did you get here? Come on in and see—I've got an office and all now."

No one else moved. There was no way to make this end well for anyone. Gabe pulled the door open wider as he spoke and took Jake's arm to gently propel him in front of him.

Jake's face was a study in misery, anger, and fear. Dammit. Liam had no idea that this was where Jake's father worked. Why would he? He'd never heard of a Gabe working for Sean, which sounded about right, given what he did know of him. If he'd known there was the slightest chance Jake would meet his father here, he never would have brought him. Hell, he'd probably have avoided coming himself.

Well, he was here now, and the boy looked on the verge of collapse. Gabe didn't sound like the kind of guy who'd notice this, so Liam squared off in front of him. He didn't like that one of his hands was occupied with the roll of plans.

Between one step and the next, Gabe registered that Liam was blocking his way, and who Liam was. "Oh, it's you," he smirked, his voice completely different from the one he used with Jake. His twisted little smile was vindictive in perceived victory. "Got an eyeful the other night, didn't you?" He still had Jake's arm. Jake looked too limp to remove it. "What brings you here? Actually, you know what? I don't care. Excuse me, my son and I have to have a little talk."

That gave Jake the strength to wrench his arm away. "No, we don't." He scowled. "You have nothing to say to me. Liam, can we go now? Please?"

"Of course," Liam said as Gabe said, "What are you asking him for?" and the wheels turned almost visibly behind his eyes. Suddenly, he was leaping across the space, fists clenched and aiming for Liam's jaw.

It was Sean who caught him, but even his bulk wouldn't have been enough if Mary-Ann hadn't stepped in front of him and put her shoulder to his, grabbing one fist in her grip. "What are you doing, you idiot?" she said in an almost-conversational tone.

"That fucker's screwing my wife!" Gabriel shouted. No more smugness here, no engaging smiles and winning ways. Spittle flew, and Liam could see white all around his eyes.

"Get the boy out of here," Sean said, still holding a struggling Gabe. Liam didn't need to be told twice. He'd pushed Jake out of the way as soon as he'd seen Gabe lunge, and now Jake lay half-sprawled across Mary-Ann's desk. Liam grabbed the boy's arm, pulled him to his feet, and walked him to the door.

"This isn't over!" Gabe yelled over Sean's shoulder. "Not by a long shot! Just stay away from my wife!"

"Ex-wife," Liam was compelled to say. "One you left—"

"Is that what she told you?" Now Gabe had stopped struggling, and his face was triumphant. "Go on, Weasley. Ask her if she could forget about me long enough to divorce me."

Liam pushed Jake the last foot out the door, and they went down the stairs in silence. Jake was shaking. Liam felt like shaking himself. Thea had let *that* stay in her life for thirteen years? Fifteen years? Had she really not divorced him after more than a year of abandonment? Liam knew all the different forms of divorce from his own experience, and he knew she could have filed after a year of no contact.

Shit.

Still, Jake was more important now. Liam figured his best bet was to get him in the van and out of sight as quickly as possible, so he did. Jake folded up into the passenger seat and continued to shake all the way to Liam's house. Liam wanted to comfort him but figured touching him wouldn't help.

Jake only roused when Jake stopped the van. "Where are we?"

"My house. I figured I'd drop off the plans and then take you home. Unless you want to hang here while I go get Benji."

"No, I... I don't want to go home." Jake looked away from Liam, out of the window. Liam hoped like hell Gabe's words weren't echoing in his mind, but it was a slim chance. "Can I come with you to get Benji?"

"Sure. Let's get a cup of coffee first, huh?" He'd never seen Jake drink coffee, but he wanted to put some sugar and caffeine in the kid to counteract the shock. Maybe Jake didn't want to get out of the van because his legs were still shaking.

They stopped at a coffee shop, and Jake got a drink that was more cream and sugar than coffee. Liam got his usual and ordered them both huge cinnamon rolls. Jake wasn't the only one who could use some comfort food.

Chapter 21

"Hey, girl," came Sam's voice through the speakers as Thea drove home from work.

Thea had been dying for and dreading the call from her sister, favorite or not. *Well, at least she's not Cat.* "Hey."

"Haven't heard from you for eons. You okay?"

Thea hadn't called Sam since before her week with Liam, and Gabriel's arrival and all the chaos that had ensued.

"Well..." *Just get it over with.* Sam would get it out of her anyway; she'd never been able to lie to her. "Gabriel's back."

"*What?* That—" Sam went into a string of expletives that Benji would have loved to bring out at his next day camp assembly.

"Okay, okay," Thea interrupted her. "I know, but it doesn't help, Sam."

"I hope that was what you said to him when he showed up. How did it happen? Did he call you? Did you see his cousins?"

"He showed up on my doorstep."

"*Goddammit!* That... presumptuous, self-centered, useless *asshole!* I hope you kicked him down the stairs."

"He's the boys'—"

"Oh shit, T, don't give me that 'he's the boys' father' bullshit again! He hasn't been a father to those boys in years, and you know it!"

That was true, on paper. And then there were all the extra years of therapy the boys might need if she didn't let Gabe in.

"Why did he come back? Don't tell me. He wants to swan back into your bed like nothing ever happened."

Thea squirmed, but she couldn't deny it. "He says he's changed. He has a job now. I saw him driving a car from his cousin's company; I think on that point, anyway, he's telling the truth."

"Uh-huh. And what other 'truths' has he been snowing you with?"

"I'm not snowed. I'm just trying to do the right thing."

Sam's snort made Thea check her phone ear for spittle. She pictured Sam, sprawled over a camp chair somewhere in New Mexico, a tiny tank top and cargo shorts showing off her skinny, child-free stomach, lifting her heavy russet hair off her neck, probably with a man naked and asleep in the next room. It was so easy for Sam. Her life was uncomplicated. She had no ties, no responsibilities. She could earn whatever she liked and sleep with whomever she liked.

"T?"

"And I slept with someone."

Oops.

"*Thea!*"

"I didn't mean to say that out loud."

She imagined Sam's long legs moving from dangling over the side of the chair to sitting up straight. "Oh my God! Tell me *everything!* Was this before or after Gabe showed up? Tell me it was after—please tell me it was after."

"It was before."

"*Damn*, girl! About time! Who is he? Does this mean Gabe doesn't have a prayer? 'Cause Gabe doesn't have a prayer, right?"

She needed to answer that right away. Instead, she said, "He's a guy I met at school. We... got to know each other over the summer."

"What's his name?"

"Liam."

"Dammit, T, not another Irishman."

"No. Well, yes, obviously. I mean, we do live in Boston. But he's American. And anyway, quit tarring a whole nationality with Gabe's brush."

"Sorry." Sam didn't sound sorry. "So come on, more. Details."

"There aren't any—"

"Oh, dear, was he not very good?"

"No! He was—you know what? I'm not comfortable talking about this."

"T! Don't leave me hanging. Come on, I'm your sister. If you can't tell me, who else can you tell?"

"Uh, no one? 'Cause it's private?"

"I'm not going to tell—wait. Does Cat know? Oh *shit*! Does she know Gabe's back?"

"No, of course n—"

"Does Kane know? I think I might fly back just to see the first time those two meet again."

"You know, you are really a bloodthirsty creature."

"Damn right. Gabe deserves a couple of cracked ribs and a knee to the groin if anyone does."

"He says he wants back into the kids' lives. I can't treat him like shit—or have the family treat him like shit—in front of them. And don't tell Cat. Not yet. She'll tell Kane, and then Gabe'll have to explain a black eye again."

"Kane'll give him more than a black eye this time. Or maybe he'll have Ellen do it. She does boxing, doesn't she?"

Their sister-in-law was a certified ass-kicker, but again, Thea had to point out, "It wouldn't help. I have to try to trust him enough to let the kids get to know him again, but I'm keeping an eye on him, believe me."

"Uh-huh," Sam said again. "So is he keeping an eye on you? And what did this Liam say about him coming back?"

Thea winced. Liam's face through the screen door had haunted her all night. "He's not... in the picture."

"A one-night stand? All right, T!"

"Not really, but... that's how it might turn out."

"Because Gabe's back? Shit, T, do *not* tell me you're thinking of taking him back?"

"No, but—"

"I don't want to hear that 'but.'"

"If I let him back into the boys' lives, Sam, then by definition, he'll be in my life. I wouldn't ask another guy to get used to that."

"Sounds like this other guy is a wuss if he'll just step aside and let that asshole take over."

She thought of the muscles cording in Liam's arms, the thick lines of his neck. And the look on his face when he'd seen her with Gabe.

"He's not a wuss, Sam. It's just... it was new, and Gabe came back, and I can't deal with someone else's feelings when I don't know my own."

"So you are thinking of taking the asshole back! That's it. I'm coming up there and kicking *your* ass."

"Not taking him back," Thea assured her. "But if he can rebuild what he took away from Jake and Benji, then we all win."

"What about what he took away from you, T?"

She curled up in her chair, hugging a pillow to her. "I can't get that back," she whispered.

"Exactly. As long as you remember that." Sam obviously didn't hear the way her words sounded. Was Thea doomed never to regain happiness because Gabe had hurt her so many times?

"I'm going to have to touch base with you more often, obviously," Sam went on. "Don't you waver, kid."

"Don't call me kid. I'm eleven months older than you."

"Yeah, and you look it." Thea had to smile at the old joke. "Just kidding."

"It's true, though."

"Only 'cause you don't take care of yourself. The next time that dickhead tries to get near you, just think, 'What would Sam do?' In fact, I'll send you a bumper sticker. And remind yourself of what is out there by finding your Liam and pounding him some more."

"Jeez, Sam."

"See, this is what happens when you marry the first man you ever have sex with. Unbutton a little, T. You'll be amazed what happens. I love you, you dried-up old spinster."

"Love you too." She couldn't call Sam any names Sam hadn't already called herself. Especially since Sam was the spinster here. "Try not to sleep your way through all of Albuquerque before Christmas."

"No, not me. I've been seeing the same guy for three months. Well, on and off."

"Yeah, I guess you do have to get off him sometimes."

Sam cracked up, a deep laugh that warmed Thea. She had always thought of herself as boring compared to the dynamic Sam, and it was a treat to make her laugh. "That's the spirit. I gotta go. Bye, T."

"Bye, Sam." She didn't want Sam to hang up. Thea always felt that more was possible when she spoke to her sister. Without her unrelenting support and optimism, Thea remembered that she had boundaries, expectations, limits.

◆

Thea got back to Jake and Benji, but decidedly no Liam. She'd expected it, of course, but the knowledge of his absence, even before she opened the door, still hurt.

Lifting her chin, hoping that she could cling to a small thread of normalcy in front of the boys, Thea swept into the house, juggling two bags of groceries. "Hi, boys," she said. "Come put the groceries away."

The two boys, uncharacteristically playing a video game together, rolled their eyes and paused the game. In the kitchen, they got into their usual roles: Benji putting away chips and juice boxes, Jake taking the eggs and laundry detergent. Thea went out back to turn on the grill for hot dogs.

She was surprised when Jake followed her. "Mom."

"Oh God. What?" Her hand flew to her chest. She hated that tone.

"I saw Dad today."

"Oh." She kept her hand at her chest, scant protection for whatever he was going to say.

Jake didn't look as though there had been a touching reconciliation. His spiky hair seemed a little limp, trying its best but not really having the heart.

"He said..." Jake began. "He said you guys are still married. Is that true?"

"Oh, Jake." She was going to have to shut up with the *ohs*. But she did not want to have this conversation with him. "It's just a technicality, hon. I filed—"

"He said it to Liam."

Jake's voice was dead and flat, but he knew the significance of what he said. She couldn't unpack that right away, so she said, "How? When did he see Liam? How did he know where you were working?"

"We went to Sean's warehouse."

"Cousin Sean?" Jake nodded. "Crap. Did Liam know your dad and Sean were cousins?"

"No."

"And your dad is working there?" Again, Jake nodded. "Well, I guess at least we know he's not lying about that." Thea leaned back gingerly against the warming grill. She wanted so badly to ask what Liam had said, but she couldn't. Jake's face told her how the conversation had gone.

"I'm sorry, baby," she said again. She was going to be saying that until she was saying it front of his therapist in twenty years.

Jake's face tightened. "Don't be sorry. Be divorced. He said you haven't been able to forget about him. That's why you're not divorced."

Yep. Not a conversation she wanted to have. "I haven't forgotten about him because"—*because he saved my life*—"because he's your father."

"You swore," Jake growled. "You swore you're not taking him back."

"I'm not, Jake." The grill was getting hot to stand near. She straightened and put her arm around his shoulders. They were getting higher than hers every day. "But the only thing you have to concern yourself with is *your* relationship with him."

"I don't want a relationship with him!" Jake yelled, jumping away from her. "Why does everyone keep telling me to make nice? I don't want him! He's an asshole!"

Thea tried really, really hard to get the words No, *he isn't* out of her mouth. She failed.

"I'm not hungry," Jake said, pushing past her. "I'm going out."

"Where?" She hated that look. It was the one he'd had at the beginning of the summer. The one that said he didn't give a damn about anything, least of all himself.

"Into town."

"Jake, honey, not tonight." But he'd already slammed the screen door, and she heard him running up the stairs. Someday, she was going to have to have the conversation with him about what he and Zachary Benedetto's gang did every night. Funny how that discussion seemed easy compared to the one they'd just had.

Jake slammed out of the front door, and Benji came looking for her. That was when she realized she'd folded into a lawn chair and was staring into space, trying to find an answer to too many questions. Motherhood was hard, but this? She was never going to unravel this.

Chapter 22

"Ah, pet. I'm glad you called."

"I'm not. I hear you saw Jake today. And told him things you had no business telling him."

She was in the living room, the windows closed against the balmy summer evening, a full glass of wine in front of her for courage. Benji was in bed, and Jake hadn't come back yet. She'd closed the windows so her voice wouldn't drift up to Benji's bedroom, which was open to the breeze. Even so, she tried to keep her voice down.

"It is my business, darlin.'" His voice was different. It had taken on the sound she'd heard the night before—had it only been last night? She felt like she'd been awake for a week—a cold tone that bit into her. It was almost threatening. "Was it not my name on those papers you sent me?"

"Yes, of course it was. But Jake doesn't need to know—"

"That you've been lying about divorcing me? 'Cause you may as well give it up now, pet. We're not getting divorced and you know it."

Her hand tightened around the wineglass. "Is that the only reason you came back? Because those papers told you that you couldn't have your toy anymore?" Thea pulled her hair behind her head and tugged on it. "You expected me to be waiting here for you whenever you deigned to come back?"

"I already said sorry for all of that. I've changed; I told you."

"So have I, thank God."

"If you had, you'd have sent me those papers ages ago." She hated the certainty in his voice. He'd always been like this, and she'd been too embarrassed to admit to anyone that she'd bought into it.

"You know you belong with me," Gabe's voice trickled into her ear. It had taken her years to stop listening to that voice in her head, and now here it was on the other end of a line.

She firmed up her own voice. *You fought for yourself and the boys.*

Don't let him take it away again. "Listen, Gabe. You and I are not getting back together. What you have to focus on is rebuilding your relationship with the boys."

"Ah, I'm not worried about that. We have a great relationship already, so we do."

"So we don't, Gabe, and if you're going to keep living in fairyland, you might as well go back to Ireland right now."

"Sure I'll go back to Ireland. If you'll come with me."

She closed her eyes and reached for strength. "Didn't you tell me you have a job here now? A steady job? One that, for the first time, you're not going to fuck up?"

"I was just sayin'."

"Well, 'just say' that you're going to be a permanent part of the boys' lives from now on."

"That's all I want. And you, of course."

"That's not going to happen."

"Why not? We're a team, darlin'."

"God, Gabe, could you be that clueless? When were you ever a part of this team?"

"All right, I admit when it came to the finances, I fell down on the job for a while there—"

"For fifteen years, Gabe!"

"But those boys know who their father is, and that means a lot."

She pinched the bridge of her nose. "You spout that like I should thank you for just existing. They learned from you that being a father meant coming and going at will and never having to do any work and—"

"Jacob might be mad at me right now, but he knows who I am. He'll come around. He's like me, that lad."

"God, I hope not."

"I've changed, T. But you've got to admit, there was a side of that carefree lad you met at the bar that you liked." His voice got softer. "Didn't we have a lot of fun back then?"

He'd saved her life back then. And he'd played on that ever since.

"That's not what I—what we—need now. We need stability. We need to know what tomorrow brings. A father who shows the hell up."

"Is that what your other fella does?"

His voice had gone beyond the cool certainty of his first words. Now it was a sliver of ice. Thea took in a breath that made her chest hurt. Sure, she wouldn't put it past him to be jealous of Liam, and she'd never given him cause for jealousy before, but his voice made her feel that threat again.

She shivered.

When she didn't answer, he went on. "You know your ginger friend from last night? Seemed pretty surprised to see you with me. You didn't tell him I was back?"

She tried to recover, to not defend herself. "There's nothing to tell, Gabe. You left. You aren't back. Not for me, anyway. I seem to have to remind you of this every time we talk."

"Well, I sent him packing with a flea in his ear at any rate. He won't be back."

"He..." Gabe was probably right. "I... It's none of your business."

"It's my business if he's in my house pretending to be a father to my kids."

Again, the bite of hardness that scared her a little. It wasn't a physical threat. It was the promise, the certainty that he'd continue to do whatever the hell he liked, and Thea would never learn how to stop him.

She couldn't keep thinking like this. She'd clawed back too much. Setting her jaw, she said, "Do you want to see your children or not?"

He was silent, then said, "All right, T. We'll do this your way for now. But I'll tell you, I'm here for you, and I'm not going to give you up to some boring, soft-handed ginger."

"Oh, quit the jealousy crap," she snapped. "You gave up all rights to me that first time you skipped out. When I was pregnant. Remember?" He didn't answer. "Yes, I see you do. So, tomorrow? You'll take Benji out for dinner?"

"All right." He sounded sulky, which was more like the Gabe she knew.

"Great." She hung up. Then she held her hand to her chest, which was fluttering in some strange way as if she'd just avoided being mugged.

♦

She had to finish her class. This was one thought that remained constant, although there were periods in her day when she had trouble summoning the energy to care about school. School meant Liam.

Study group met the next night. She would normally have been happy to see her friends, but today they were merely an intrusion into her life, people in front of whom she would have to appear normal.

So much for that idea. Zahra had no sooner walked in the door than she held Thea by the shoulders and searched her face. "You okay?"

"Oh yeah," she said, willing herself not to look as wan and tired as she felt. "Just... life."

Zahra nodded. "It's a lot for you, working and school and the kids."

She'd done it for more than two years. Was she going to fall now, when the end was in sight, because Gabe made her feel like not trying?

The rest of them came in, and they'd been chatting for several minutes before Chloe said, "Liam's awfully late."

Thea swallowed the lump that appeared in her throat and said, in what she hoped was an even voice, "He's not coming."

Fail. She only had to see the immediate concern on Zahra's face for the tears to start in her eyes. "Oh, honey," Chloe said, and she leaped over the coffee table to sit next to her and hug her.

Thea flapped her away, not wanting to cry in front of the twins. "It's okay. Not a big deal." She grabbed a paper napkin to stem the not-a-big-deal tears that wouldn't quit.

"What happened?" Chloe asked at the same time as Zahra said, "You want to talk about it?"

When she hesitated, Seth said, "You don't have to." Obviously, he wasn't up for girly details.

"There's not much to tell," she finally said, grabbing her wine and taking a swig, hoping it would burn the tears away. "My ex is back."

A stunned silence followed.

"Bugger," Seth said.

In spite of the situation, Thea smiled. "That's what my sister-in-law would say. Will say when she finds out." Which was another thing. She thought she would have heard from Cat or Kane by now. Had Jake really not told his cousins yet? She wasn't sure what that meant.

"Our mom's English," David said. "So what about your ex? You're taking him back?"

"No." She didn't say anything else. She was so tired of explaining herself all over again.

"So did you tell Liam that?" said Chloe.

Had she? She thought so. But it was the hurt she'd done to him that she couldn't ask him to get past. Maybe one day, when his divorce wasn't so new, when the image had had a chance to fade... but by then he'd probably have found someone else.

She sighed. A big chunk of her future, one she'd only just begun to hope for, dissolved in front of her. "It's complicated."

"Not from what I saw," Chloe, ever the spade-caller, said. "And besides, what's he going to do about the class? He has to finish it, doesn't he?"

"He's not taking the class," David said.

"What?" the women all said together.

"Yes, he is," Zahra said. "I saw him on his laptop."

"He was faking it so he could be here. He wasn't enrolled in the master's program at all." David looked at his iced coffee, into which he'd poured a shot of Bailey's when they'd arrived. "After his divorce, he didn't have the money to go back to school. He was only auditing the language immersion class because he was going to be teaching in Zahra's neighborhood." He nodded at her. "Then he did the technology class so he could keep seeing Thea. 'Course, then he just started seeing her anyway."

Thea's mouth was open, her tears forgotten. "How do you know all this?"

"He asked me about loans that night we were out at his truck. I think he's found a way to get back to class, but he's going to be doing a... I can't remember what it's called, but it's for supervisory positions. You all said it when we first met him: he knows this stuff already. He's looking to be a principal, maybe a superintendent one day."

She'd known that much, at least.

"So..." Chloe said, shooting her green eyes at Thea. "The only reason he was here, all summer, was for you."

Thea gripped her glass's stem hard. "Oh."

"All. Summer," Chloe repeated.

"Yeah." Technically, they still had a month of summer to go. But there was only one class left after tonight, so it felt like the end was here.

"So tell me again why it matters that your ex is back?"

She couldn't tell them. She was cringing enough herself at the words *because he found me in Gabe's arms*; she couldn't bear to see the same expression on their faces. "Because I have to give him a chance to rebuild his relationship with the boys, and I can't ask Liam to stick around for that."

They all looked around, suddenly remembering that Benji was usually with them. But he was with his father tonight.

"That's a craptastic reason," Chloe said.

"I told you—it's complicated," Thea said miserably. "Can we get back to the lesson now?"

"Sure," Seth said kindly, but Chloe got up and a minute later came back with a tumbler filled with vodka and a splash of cranberry juice. At least, that was what it tasted like when she made Thea take a sip.

"I'll be drunk as a lord in about five minutes," she said, but she squeezed Chloe's hand. The burn of the liquor counteracted the ache in her chest better than the wine.

Gabe brought Benji back at eight thirty on the dot, as arranged. When the front door opened, Thea jumped up, as if trying to shelter the group from Gabe—or maybe him from them, she didn't know.

Benji, tired and overexcited, was pissed that he had to come home. His complaints covered the first awkward moments as Gabe took in the stony faces in the room. Everyone stared unashamedly at him. Thea might have laughed if she hadn't been so unnerved.

"You have to get your sleep," she said to Benji, not looking at Gabe. "You've got camp tomorrow."

"Why can't I hang out with Dad tomorrow?"

"Because he has a job, hon."

Benji pouted. "Jake gets to hang out with Liam at his job."

Thea held her breath. This time she did look at Gabe and just caught a fleeting glimpse of fury and... something else... in his eyes before he shuttered them into that bland expression of self-satisfaction he'd had since he'd arrived. Had the others seen it?

Interesting, that Benji didn't see any conflict between Liam and Gabe. To him, there was room in his and Jake's life for both of them. She was grateful for it, but the boy was only five and had no idea that the presence of one of the men in his life would probably mean the absence of the other.

"Jake is working for Liam," she reminded him now. "Dad can't babysit you all day. But"—she risked another look at Gabe, who perked up at the *but*—"maybe he can pick you up from the bus tomorrow afternoon."

"Yeah! You can, can't you, Da?"

"Sure I can," Gabe said, holding Thea's gaze. Then, a little late since he'd already promised, he added, "What time?"

"Five thirty. At St. Bernard's parking lot. You remember?"

"Of course I remember. I did live here for thirteen years." That was debatable, but he'd already turned to smile down at Benji. "I'll see you tomorrow."

"Yay!"

"Go get ready for bed," Thea said. "Say good night to everyone."

Benji grinned at them all and ran into the kitchen.

"Hello, all," Gabe said comfortably into the room.

Her friends, bless them, said nothing at all.

"So I guess from this warm reception that Thea's told you all about me," he went on, leaning on the doorframe like he was a fixture.

"Enough," Chloe muttered.

"Goodbye, Gabe," Thea said. "I'll see you tomorrow at the bus."

He turned his gray-blue gaze back to her. "Don't you trust me?"

"No. But even if I did, I have to sign a form for you to pick up Benji. They don't know you from Adam, you realize."

"I'm his da," he pronounced, as if that were enough evidence for anyone.

"Jesus, Gabe." She needed to put Benji to bed, but she pushed him out of the door instead, following him onto the porch and far away from the open window to the living room.

"Who are all your friends?" he said at once.

"My study group. Listen, Gabe—"

"Study group? You're at school?"

"Yes." She tried to raise her chin, to remember the pride that she'd gotten this far, no thanks to him.

"Ah, pet. What a mess." He put a hand around hers, but she pulled away. "You don't have to work anymore, don't you see? I'll take care of everything."

"You'll pay me back the years of child support you owe me?"

"Well, I—"

"You'll pay half the price of this house? The food? School supplies for the boys?" She was forgetting to keep her voice down.

"I'll take care of you. That's what I'm saying." He talked as though saying the words made it so. "You don't need to wear yourself out with school. What can they teach you there, anyway?"

"How to support myself because you never did!" she hissed.

"Bunch of abstract crap that doesn't help you figure out how to change a lightbulb or do your taxes."

She'd heard his tirade against higher education before. She'd been in such a dark place when she was with him, she'd believed him.

Anyway, it had all seemed too much to reach for when she was chasing around after the boys every day.

She rubbed a hand over her face and turned away. "Whatever. I'll see you tomorrow at the church."

But Gabe wasn't done. He grabbed her wrist again, harder this time. "Just remember," he said into the darkening sky. The shadow on the porch meant that she couldn't see his eyes, just hear that poisonous voice as he pulled her closer to him. "You belong with me. Your ginger friend is outta here. And who else would have you?"

He walked down the porch steps with a spring in his step. Thea stayed frozen for a second, breathing in the poison she'd thought she was free of.

They all left her with troubled faces that night. Her friends. In the fall, they'd be beginning classes in their own specialties and starting practicums in the winter. They would have to work hard to see each other again. And Thea couldn't think past the next day. She was so used to being alone, she assumed that she would be again.

Chapter 23

She had to talk to Liam again the next morning when he came to pick up Jake. She could have texted him, but it seemed ridiculous when he was right on the street. He didn't come to the door, but stayed in his truck. The blue monster baby's low roar was alarm enough for anyone.

Thea picked her way down the path, which was strewn, as usual, with the cracked concrete and weeds she'd become accustomed to. Somehow, today they merely highlighted all that was pointless about her, all that Liam was going to be able to walk away from so easily.

He wasn't expecting her, of course, and it was a few seconds before he reached over to lower the passenger window.

"I just wanted to tell you. You don't have to pick up Benji today."

His lips tightened. His eyes, which had been on her while he opened the window, slid away. "All right."

"Okay." She didn't have to explain why, but she did anyway. "Gabe's picking him up."

"Fine."

"It's good, Liam. If he wants to rebuild his—"

"Yep. I said it's fine."

And thank the moon and stars, Jake was behind her, waiting for her to get out of the way so he could climb in the truck. Jake said, "Bye, Mom," but Liam didn't say another word and peeled out, not trying to keep the blue monster baby's roar down.

♦

Liam and Jake were widening a channel for a sewer pipe at the house they'd visited on Jake's first day. Pat had come earlier with the backhoe and dug the main trench. He'd let Jake take a turn.

When an O'Brien Construction truck pulled up down the street, the hairs stood up on the back of Liam's neck. Jake didn't seem to have noticed. Liam didn't want to fight Gabe in front of the man's son, but he was in the kind of mood that made a man forget his lofty principles. He looked at the top of Jake's head as he wielded the shovel. His spikes were back; he must have gotten up at five to get them so angry. And whatever Jake put on them was putting up a good fight as the two of them sweated in the dirt.

"Listen," Liam said. "Remember that Cumby's around the corner? Go get us a couple of sandwiches." He pulled out a twenty. Jake wiped off his hands on his overalls. "Use the restroom first," Liam advised.

When Jake was safely out of sight, Liam approached the construction truck. He stood on the driver's side, arms folded, and waited.

Gabe wasn't slow to get out. It was a good thing he looked so much like Jake; it was a visual reminder not to pop him one.

The two men faced off in front of the truck, Liam with added breadth, Gabe with height and barely concealed rage. "What can I do for you, Gabriel?" Liam said, knowing his pleasant tone would piss the man off.

"You can stay the fuck away from my wife and my kids is what you can do, Weasley," Gabe said in a rush, as if he'd been forming the words for the last hour he'd been sitting watching them.

"Jake works for me."

"Fire him."

"No."

Gabe snarled. His fists clenched. There were oceans of things Liam wanted to say to him, preferably with his boot on the man's neck. But he forced himself to stay calm.

"One of these days," Gabe said through the snarl, "you won't have them to hide behind. When I've got them back and you're knee-deep in shit somewhere, you'll turn around and there I'll be. And I will pay you for how you made me look yesterday."

Only the tightness in Liam's jaw betrayed him when he said,

"You're pretty free with your fists, there, Donaghy. You ever use them on Thea?"

Gabe's reaction was too instinctive to be fake. His chin jutted upward. "Fuck off. I don't hit women."

Muscles Liam didn't know he'd tightened relaxed. "No, you just made her feel like she could never do any better than you, so she always took you back."

Gabe was on surer ground here. Liam hated that he'd given him the ammunition. "You think you know her? She's been my girl for fifteen years, Weasley. Of course she can't do better than me." He waved at Liam as if to prove his point. "The best she could do is some shit hauler working for his daddy. Fuck off and let the big boys take it from here."

I am going to hit him. I really am going to hit him. Liam kept his arms clamped tight across his chest. "Stop following me and Jake around. He's working for me for the next two weeks. Get over it."

"I'll go wherever I like."

"Fine. Come tell him what you just told me about his mother."

"You stay out of it." But Liam saw the hint of uncertainty in his eyes and used it as the excuse to disengage. The only thing he'd done by talking to Gabe was to enrage himself even more.

"So long, Donaghy," he said and turned his back, trusting the open street and twitching curtains to save him from an attack.

As he walked back to the house, Gabe said behind him, "Watch your back, McConnell." A few seconds later, the truck's engine started up, and when he turned to make sure Gabe wasn't about to run him over, the truck roared past him.

♦

Dr. Marion had let her leave work early without a whimper. Thea warred with gratitude and the knowledge that it was probably pity that kept them employing her at all. Pulling up in the church parking lot that afternoon, she saw a sedan with the name of Gabe's cousin Sean's construction company on the side, parked in front of the church. Gabe was leaning on the passenger door, facing the parking lot entrance. His ankles were crossed casually in front of him, and the afternoon sun shone on his black hair, giving it a gloss she remembered loving running her hands through. He looked up at the minivan's movement, and his eyes narrowed at her.

Thea parked next to him and rolled down her window. He was in a denim shirt that made his eyes a deeper blue, but today they weren't looking at her with that begging gaze she was accustomed to.

"Didn't think I'd show up, did you?" he said, his voice amused.

"Your track record isn't exactly faultless on this kind of thing, you know, Gabriel."

"I said I'd come, and I've come. You can trust me."

"Yeah, I know. You've changed."

The sarcasm in her voice hung between them. "You're not going to drive me away," he said.

"For Jake and Benji's sake, I'm not trying to," she said. "Just don't expect them to fall into your arms after three days."

"Benji has." He grinned. She wanted to hit him. "Anyway," he went on. "What about you? You fell after two."

She felt herself blushing. "I didn't 'fall.' You sat next to me. And I was drunk."

"Not that drunk, pet."

She wasn't going down this road again. She cut the engine and reached for her bag, which had fallen on the floor on the passenger side. When she straightened, Gabe was leaning in the window, his head right by hers.

He smelled the same, damn him. She almost wanted to freeze the moment so she could analyze how the smell of his musky cologne would affect her. Close to him, she saw his five o'clock shadow and the heavier cast to his jaw that he hadn't had last year. But she didn't look up as far as his eyes. She was afraid they might undo her.

"I'm here to stay, T," he said, and she watched his lips move. He had made her feel visible with those lips, once. And then, invisible.

"Gabe," she said, which wasn't what she'd planned to say.

His mouth, which was all she could see, smiled. "I love you, and you'll remember pretty soon that you love me, too. You're nothing without me."

And he took the last inch he needed and kissed her, a quick but firm pressure on her lips that even in that short time claimed her, and then he backed out of the car window and was watching the school bus arrive as if nothing had happened.

Benji was thrilled to see him. "That's my da!" he yelled to the camp counselor and pulled Gabe over to introduce him.

"Mr.... Donaghy?" the counselor asked, looking at the form Thea silently handed her.

Thea, still reeling from Gabe's kiss, tried to look as though presenting two men to the counselor in a month was normal.

"That's right." Gabe shook the counselor's hand, as if he were just another father and did this all the time, rather than a man who hadn't seen his son in two years. "Pleased to meet you."

His ready smile and those Cillian Murphy eyes charmed the girl as quickly as they'd charmed Thea. "You too," she said. "Benji's a great kid."

Gabe's chest swelled. Like he'd had anything to do with Benji being a good kid. "Thanks; we think so too."

Goddamn you. That's my kid. My kudos. You don't get to be proud of him. Not yet.

But what would she possibly say to the counselor? *Don't trust this man? He'll promise you one thing and deliver another? I can't even trust him to be here again next week?* Benji's face shone with pride, and Thea couldn't betray that.

She kissed Benji and got in her car while the bus disgorged more children and they were met by various parents and babysitters. Some parents she knew came over to the strange man standing with Benji, and Gabe contentedly introduced himself in the same way.

Thea seethed.

Benji was entirely taken up with his father, his face turned up to him and only him, talking a mile a minute while Gabe opened the back door of his car where a booster seat sat. *Dammit. He actually thought of that.* They drove away, the bus left, and Thea sat on.

Suddenly, she felt superfluous, useless. As if all her work thus far had been done only so she could deposit Benji into Gabe's arms and walk away.

◆

From across the road, his fists still clenched, Liam watched the bus pull away and Gabe help Benji into his seat. *He'd better have a booster in there. That kid isn't big enough to get in without one.*

Liam had no business here. But he disliked and distrusted Gabriel so much, he'd shown up, dropping Jake at home first. He'd forgotten Thea would have to be here too.

He'd seen Gabe lean down in Thea's window. Seen their chitchat. Seen him lean in farther. There could only be one reason he'd done that. Liam clenched his fists so hard, he broke open a wound on his knuckle he'd gotten at work that day. Thea and Gabe and the beloved child they shared had driven away long before Liam could move.

Chapter 24

Jake must have finally broken his radio silence with his cousins. Cat's voice seemed to shimmer red in front of Thea when she answered her call the next day.

"So, Thea. What's up?"

Thea sighed. "I have a feeling you know what's up."

"Me? Why should I know anything that happens in my family's lives?"

"All right, all right." Thea looked at the clock. "I'll pick up Benji and Jake and come see you tonight. Okay?"

"Don't put yourself out." Thea could have done a backstroke in the sarcasm.

She got out of the car at Cat's house with lead feet, gave a shave-and-a-haircut knock on the pocked wooden front door that was as old as the house, and pushed it open. "In the back!" her brother-in-law's voice called out, and she followed it to the comfortable family room with its ugly squashed chairs and couch and large-screen TV on the wall.

The boys piled onto the couch, where their cousins were playing a computer game. Thea was relieved to see that the game was appropriate for Benji's age. Antonio was good about that kind of thing. In seconds, they'd forgotten the adults existed. Thea was glad to see it. Jake needed a few hours just to be a regular teenager again.

Antonio, compact, square, and Italian, got out of his seat, abandoning a newspaper, and came over to hug her. "*Ciao, cara,*" he said.

"Ciao yourself," she replied. To her nephews she said, "Everyone enjoying your summer? Behaving yourselves?"

"Yes, of course." Antonio's dark eyes raked hers. "But someone perhaps has not?"

Here we go. She brought herself to her full height, which was taller than Antonio's, and opened her mouth, but he smiled. "I am not serious, Thea."

"How is she?" she asked.

He knew she meant Cat. "She would prefer to hear these things from you. So remember, when she is angry, it is because she loves you."

"Yeah, well, she must love me a whole lot."

Antonio smiled indulgently. "It is how she expresses it."

The man was nuts about her sister and had been for twenty years. Thea wondered what it was like to be able to rely on that kind of devotion.

I'm crazy about you, T.

She sighed. "Better get scratched sooner rather than later." Antonio didn't stop her from leaving the room.

Cat wasn't in the kitchen, the mudroom, the yard, or the formal living room. Thea went up the wide staircase, her hand running lovingly over the old wooden stair rail that had seen four generations of abuse from Fielding children. Cat and Antonio loved this house and had kept it in the family for all their sakes.

Cat had been all the mother she could be to Thea, even when Thea had stolen her thunder by becoming pregnant when Cat was. And when she'd had Benji and hit rock bottom, Cat had been there to pick her up and tell her she was doing the right thing by throwing Gabe out and trying to build a life without him.

She tried to remember all these things as she went to beard Cat in her own den: her bedroom. It was in the corner tower of the house, with a fine 180-degree view of the street from the bay windows. Cat was reading in the rocking chair that had belonged to their grandmother, the chair Thea had nursed Benji in until she moved into the house they'd found for her.

She put her arms around Cat from behind, embracing the chair at the same time. Cat didn't react at first. Thea hugged harder. "I'm going to squeeze a hello out of you," she said.

"You're jamming my shoulder blades into the chair!" Cat yelped.

But at least it had gotten her talking. Thea let go and took the other chair, a more modern easy chair their father had loved.

Cat had inherited the same coloring as the rest of them: thick, dark hair, dark-brown eyes, the expressive eyebrows, and, when she felt like it, the giant Fielding smile. Right now, though, she was all about glowering.

Thea felt like a chastened child but ignored it. She was thirty-five and well past being told off by Mother Cat. "Come on, then," she said. "Have at it."

"Have at what?" Cat looked out of the window. "I love hearing important details about your life from your children. Why would I want to know before they tell me?"

"I didn't know how to tell you. Or what to tell you."

She certainly wasn't going to tell her about Liam. Sam was one thing. Cat would complicate everything. She'd probably say Thea shouldn't be dating at all, with the boys so vulnerable. Not that Thea and Liam had dated. They'd just...

Sweated and moaned and held fast to each other and given each other everything... until I took it all away.

"Hey."

"What?" Crap. Cat had been talking.

Cat scowled. "I said, are you going to tell me now? You must have come up here for some damn reason."

Thea took a deep breath. "Okay. So he's back. He wants us back. He has a job he says is permanent. He's sorry."

"He's *sorry*?" Cat's voice rose to a squeak.

"Uh-huh. He's that sorry, so he is."

Thea's lips twitched, but Cat didn't think it was funny. "What in particular," she said icily, "out of all the stupid crap he's pulled for fifteen years, is he sorry for?"

"All of it. Apparently."

Cat gave a sound of disgust. "And what has he said to the boys? And what have the boys said to him?"

"In my presence, he hasn't said much to them. Benji's all over him. Jake ignores him. When he's not yelling at him."

"Someone better be yelling at him. I'll do it if you don't."

"I did." She flushed lightly, thinking of how ineffectual her yelling had been and how it had ended up.

"What's that?" Cat's sharp eyes caught the flush in her cheeks. "Why are you blushing?"

"Nothing! It's—I just—"

This was not a time to be lost for words. "Oh shit, T. Do not tell me you believe him."

"No... But I'm closer to it." Cat opened her mouth, but Thea preempted her. "I'm not saying I'm taking him back! But think of the boys. Wouldn't it be better for them to have their father back in their lives?"

"Not the way he was doing it. Besides, they've had Antonio. And Kane."

"Those are uncles. Fantastic uncles," she amended, nodding her thanks to her brother and brother-in-law's efforts over the years, "but not their father. They know the difference."

Liam was different. He watched the boys in a way their uncles couldn't, brought them out of themselves. Perhaps it was just that, with no children of his own, they'd known he had time for them.

Stop thinking about him. Every moment she remembered was a barb in her heart.

"All right. I see your point. But he can be back in their lives without being back in yours." Cat's tone became pleading. "Just tell me you're not going to take him back."

"No, of course not. I wish everyone would stop asking me that."

"'Cause I'm seeing something in your face I don't like, T. I've seen that dippy look before. You're too soft. You give everyone the benefit of the doubt. You gave that Gabriel"—she spat out his name as if it were Beelzebub—"the benefit of the doubt a hundred times, and he failed you every single time. Do me a favor and remember that."

Maybe after hardening her heart over the past few years, Liam had opened a crack in it, and she was vulnerable again.

"It's all very well for you," she said. "You can rely on Antonio. You have someone to wake up next to in the morning. Someone to hold on to when things are bad. When you don't have that, Cat, the world can be a wearing place."

Cat did what she did best: transformed in an instant from claws-out Mother Cat to the warm, loving sister Thea had relied on so much. She launched out of her chair and crouched by Thea's, wrapping her arms around Thea's legs, looking up at her. There was gray in her hair, Thea realized. She was getting older. They both were.

"I know, hon," Cat said. "God, I wish so hard for you to find what Antonio and I have. All the time. And listen, if Kane can find someone to put up with him, there's hope for everyone." She smiled the five-hundred-watt Fielding smile, and Thea returned it slowly. Making fun of Kane was their favorite pastime.

"Is he going to pay back the child support he owes you?" Cat went on, reverting to instructional mode.

"I don't see how he can," Thea said.

"At least you got that divorce from him. He can't get his hands on anything you've got."

Thea's smile faltered.

Cat's hands fell away from her legs. "Oh shit, T. You told me you'd served the papers!"

"I did! But he never signed them."

"Goddammit, Thea!" Cat unfolded herself from the floor and began to pace the room. "That's why he's back! Holy shit!"

Thea cringed. Cat was right, and she was feeling like such a schmuck for once again taking Gabe's words at face value.

"You can't get him for abandonment now that he's back, right?" Thea shook her head, the helplessness sweeping over her again. She would never be free of him. "You know he can get his hands on everything you have? The house, the trust fund, everything?"

"He won't. He was gone for so long. No judge is going to—"

"But he's back! I'm sure all he has to say is that he wants to make it up to you, and a judge—male judge, mark my words—will roll right over and let him take it all."

"I'll get a good lawyer. There's no way he'd have the balls to ask for money after all he owes us."

"God, you're an idiot, T." Cat strode back and forth in front of her and Antonio's bed. "Sorry, but you are. That's *exactly* what he's going to do! You're falling for it *again*! You should have filed those papers a year ago!" Cat came back to her and put a hand on the old rocking chair so she could point at Thea more forcefully with the other. "You can't keep drifting through life like this! You have to make some goddamn decisions for you and the boys to make your future safer!"

"Drifting?" Thea was on her feet now, too, shaking with her own anger. "*You're* the one drifting through life with your perfect fucking husband and perfect kids and this old house you never have to worry about being able to fix up, with time to kill judging other people! I have to fight every day to make our lives just a little bit stable! You know when Jake isn't here, he barely speaks to me or any other adult? And Benji is so desperate for a father, he was looking at Liam like he was a god until Gabe showed up—"

"Who," Cat interrupted, "is Liam?"

Shit. "It doesn't matter." Thea went to the door.

"Who's Liam?" Cat repeated as Thea went through it. She shut the door on the words, but sure enough, Cat followed her down the stairs. "Who in the living hell is Liam?" she said. Thea had gotten into the family room, hoping for safety behind her kids, perhaps.

The boys heard Cat. "Liam's Mom's friend," Benji said, not looking away from the TV.

"Mom's *boyfriend*," Jake added.

"Jake!" Thea snapped. "He's not—"

"He was until you pissed him off."

Cat actually stamped her foot. "Who the *hell* is Liam?"

Everyone finally looked away from the TV. Cat in full flow was not to be ignored.

Thea cast about for a way to describe him that would neutralize the spark coming from Cat's eyes. "You remember," she said. "The guy who fixed Kane's flood on the Fourth of July. Penny's cousin."

"Jake was working for him," Cat said. "What does he have to do with...?"

Thea saw the tumblers clicking into place in Cat's mind, the memory of how Benji skipped and danced around Liam, and Jake waited on his every word.

Thea closed her eyes, then opened them again. Everyone was looking at her. "It's the end of the summer now. Jake'll go back to school. We probably won't see him again."

"Oh," Benji said, disappointed. "He was going to let me use the power drill next time he came over."

"Yeah, Mom," Jake added. "How's his power drill?"

"Jacob!" The kid had lost all pretense at respect. "Just because you're mad at your dad doesn't mean you can disrespect me!"

"Yes, Jake." Antonio backed her up. "That was not appropriate."

Jake's shoulders hunched in the way she hated, the way that showed he was in a hostile world with very few weapons against it. He backed toward the French doors that led to the backyard. "How about a little respect for *me*, Mom?" he said. "Why aren't you two talking anymore? Now I have to work with him, and you're like a big elephant in the middle of every conversation we have." He opened the French doors behind him and walked out.

Cat didn't seem to know who to yell at first. Finally, she settled on, "Boys! Upstairs! You too, Benji!" They knew better than to argue.

Then she rounded on Thea. "Is this before or after Gabe showed up?"

"First of all," Thea said, making her stand, "and again, this is none of your business."

"It is when it affects my nephews!"

"They're my kids! Don't you think I worry constantly about what affects them? Why do you think I didn't encourage Liam or tell you about him?"

"The kids know him! They've hung out with him!"

"He's been teaching them how to fix up the house."

"Giving Benji power tools? Giving Jake a job?"

"Jesus, Cat, he hasn't given Benji anything of the kind. Now you're just not listening."

"'Cause you're not saying anything! And what about Gabe? Does this other guy know about him?"

Thea couldn't help the wince that went across her face, as usual, when she thought of Liam's face that night.

"I'll take that as a yes," Cat said. "And does Gabe know about him?"

"Yes! Yes, they know about each other. And Liam isn't my boyfriend. He's... out of the picture now."

"For Gabriel? Dammit, I knew you were going to take him back."

"I'm not! I just want my boys to come out of their childhoods not needing twenty years of therapy. And a second ago you were yelling at me for dating someone other than Gabe!"

"That's not what I said!"

Cat was still standing in the doorway. The breeze from the window blew in at that moment and brushed her hair across her mouth. In the pause she gained while Cat extricated it, Thea went to the French doors.

"I have to go ream out my son," she said with cold dignity. "Then I'm going home. When you decide to stop flaying me for decisions I made years and years ago, call me."

"Wait a minute! We're not done!" But only Cat's words followed her out into the yard. Thea was banking on Cat not coming out after her, on understanding that she had to talk to Jake alone.

Jake was walking down the tree-covered hill behind the house, toward the stream and the path that ran alongside it. "Jake!" she called. He sped up. "Dammit! Wait for me!" He didn't. "*Jacob Donaghy, right this second, stand still!*"

Somehow, that worked. *Huh. Looks like I found my teacher voice.* He stopped, a black spiky shadow among the brown and green of the woods. Thea caught up, her thin ballet flats sliding a little on the path's debris.

He was taller than her, standing on a small ridge, but as she got closer, she found her anger ebbing away. Wasn't understanding your kid one of the worst things about motherhood? She had to stop him from acting out, but her heart bled inside that he needed to.

"Jacob," she began, reaching out for his black-clad arm.

"I want to change my name," he said.

Surprised by the change in subject, she withdrew her hand. "What?"

"I'm not a Donaghy." His lower jaw stuck out as he nodded toward the house above them. "I'm a Fielding."

And her skinny, tough fifteen-year-old burst into tears.

They sat there in the leaves and rotten logs, and Thea held Jake to her as he cried and told her what had happened in Sean's office. Thea couldn't believe it—the physicality of it. Gabe might have been poison, but he'd never been violent.

"He was scary," he whispered.

"But he'd never hurt you," she said.

"I don't know anymore," he said. "He lost it, Mom. Totally lost his shit."

She didn't bother to reprimand him. "I'm sorry, baby."

He leaned away so he could mop his cheeks. They were far enough from the house that he didn't fear being overseen by his cousins.

She would no longer use the excuse that the boys needed time to rebuild their relationship with Gabe. Benji might still be able to spend time with him, but never again would she ask Jake to. He was fifteen and he already knew what was better for her than she did.

"You can change your name, honey," she said, "if it's important to you. But don't rub it in your dad's face. However much he's capable of it, he does love you."

Jake turned his face away. His cell phone beeped. He read it and said, "Can I go out tonight?"

"I thought you were going to hang out with your cousins."

"Mmm. Nah."

Whatever had come through on the text was more interesting than the video game, apparently.

"Listen, Jake," she began. "I don't like you hanging out with Zachary Benedetto and his crew."

"It's fine, Mom," he said at once, which meant it wasn't.

"What do you see in him, anyway? You're not a follower."

He looked insulted, as well he might. "I'm not 'following' him. We just... hang out. He's funny."

His face didn't look entirely untroubled, though. "Does he drink?"

"No."

"Drugs?"

A pause. "No."

"Jacob."

"Mom. I'm not an idiot." The ceasefire was over. He pulled away from her completely. Thea let her arms fall to her sides, mourning the loss of him.

"I know that, Jake, but sometimes, with the best will in the world, you can end up in situations you can't control."

"I won't."

"But you might."

"I won't, Mom. Can I go?"

Ah, the certainty of the teenager. Well, she was glad to see a little fire in his eyes, after the mess Gabe's outburst had left him in. "Yes, you can go." He leaped up. "Say goodbye to everyone first!" she called after him.

Thea got up more slowly and worked her way back through the trees. The back of Cat and Antonio's house was as familiar to her as her own hand. Thea's bedroom window that Sam would throw stones at late at night when she'd snuck out. The low roof over the sunroom that she could climb on when Thea let her in. The sun-faded green of the shingles, the wisteria that grew over the kitchen window every year. Cat hated it; Thea loved it. Staring at it, she began to feel a peace she hadn't experienced in years. Despite Gabe's return, despite Jake's pain and Benji's excitement and Cat's judgment and Sam's absence, Thea felt at peace. And it was because for the second time in a year, she knew exactly what she wanted.

She didn't have to cling to the memories of Gabe anymore; she could separate the gratitude she felt for his saving her from her anger at his defection. She could be genuinely thankful for their children, for what he had done for her, while not letting him get off scot-free for the things he hadn't. For the first time, she wasn't in love with him anymore.

And she was with Liam. Wholeheartedly, whole-body, screamingly in love with him.

She should find him and tell him. Hold on to him until he believed her. He might be home. She could go. Ask Cat to watch Benji, who probably wouldn't even notice, and just go.

But no. She needed to find the words. The words that had eluded her all week while Gabe tied her brain and her tongue in knots. She needed to sit quietly and figure out how to make her case. Like a lesson plan. To start with the basic theory and build on it, to make him see the future the way she wanted to, a future with her and the boys, negotiating each other's wants and needs, finding a center path they could share together.

And sex. She wanted a whole lot more sex with him.

Her thoughts drifted away from the esoteric and into the elemental. Yeah. She'd figure it out. And this time, she wasn't going to wait until the man figured out that he needed her.

Chapter 25

Liam sat in his favorite chair in front of his bay window, his head back so he could watch the stars come out, and tried to find the words to tell Thea she couldn't let Gabe back into her life.

He was pretty sure she wasn't going to. Pretty sure. The Thea he knew would never let someone treat her the way Gabe had. But then he thought of the divorce papers, not sent, and the two boys she and Gabe shared. And there were those five seconds, which felt like years, when he'd watched her fit so well into the man's arms. And that kiss, or whatever had happened through her car window.

He was really getting a taste for feeling sorry for himself. The sky was full dark and his beer was long empty before he reminded himself that he wasn't supposed to be dwelling on that night. She'd told him nothing had happened. Was he going to dismiss the weeks he'd gotten to know her for a few seconds that he might not have understood, just because his feelings had been poked?

Poked? Run over with a big truck. With spikes on the tires.

Anyway. This wasn't about him. This was about what was good for Thea.

A couple of blocks away, he could hear the sounds of Friday night coming from Main Street. He couldn't remember the last time he'd gone to a bar and just hung out with friends. The people he'd gone to college with were scattered across the state, and his cousins were busy with their own lives. His plumbing colleagues had always kept their distance from him because of his father. He'd never minded because he was an only child, used to his own company, and if he wanted more, he always had his cousins.

It occurred to him that he could have called Seth and David if he wanted to hang out, but their friendship was still new. Plus, they knew Thea. Looking at his watch, he saw that it was going on midnight. Too late for starting a night out, even for a man who'd only just said goodbye to his twenties.

His phone was still in his hand when it rang, making him jump and drop it into his lap. He almost dropped it again when he saw it was Jake. This could mean nothing good.

"Jake?"

"Liam. Can you come get me?"

"Sure." The response was automatic. Liam looked at his beer, which he'd finished hours ago and been too dispirited to replace. Then he was on his feet with his hands on his keys. "Where?"

Jake gave him an address of a neighborhood between his town and Thea's, where big houses backed onto an industrial park.

"Okay. It'll take me about fifteen minutes. Can you go somewhere safe?" He couldn't even spare the time to ask what was making Jake feel unsafe.

"Uh-huh. I think so. Just come, okay?"

"That was my front door slamming," Liam said, suiting action to words. "Hang tight. I'll be right there."

He started the blue monster baby and let the engine roar as he dodged the center of town to reach the highway.

The address was a perfect spot for clandestine parties because it wasn't in town proper, and some of the unscrupulous kids made use of this fact. Hell, Liam had been to some parties like that in his time. Though when everyone knew your dad, it was less fun. As a teacher, he knew the best and worst of what high school kids could do, and he kept his foot on the gas as hard as he dared, hoping that Jake hadn't fallen victim to the worst. He hadn't sounded drunk, just scared, a thin voice straining to stay cool.

But before Liam even got to the house, the flashing lights made his heart plummet into his shoes. He parked as quickly as he could and ran to the nearest police car. There were only two or three of them, and the house looked like it was still in one piece. He could smell pot and sour beer, and a couple of the lumps he'd taken for bushes groaned in the shadows. Liam took a breath and waited for the cop in the car to get off the radio.

"What happened?" he said as soon as the man looked at him.

The officer's eyes narrowed. "Are you a parent?"

"I—yes." What else was he going to say?

"Noise complaint. And then evidence of drugs."

"Crap." He looked at the house. Was Jake in there? What safe place had he found? Was he one of the drunken piles on the ground? "Are they inside?"

"No. They got arrested. There were minors in there."

Shit. This was getting worse by the second. "Everyone got arrested?"

"They're at the station." The officer was unperturbed by the panic in Liam's voice.

"But Jake... but my kid was sober. He called me."

The officer gave a disbelieving shrug but seemed to take pity on him. "They'll evaluate him there. You can go along and see him."

Liam turned on his heel and was several steps away before he remembered to shout "thanks" over his shoulder. He punched "police station" into his phone and got the address, then pulled up into a surprisingly empty parking lot. But he could hear the commotion inside from where he sat.

He called Thea. It was now well past midnight, and he expected to have to wait a few rings for her to pick up, but she did right away. "Liam! Is Jake with you?" she said.

Right. She would have been expecting him home. "In a manner of speaking," he said, hoping he sounded like the voice of calm. He still didn't know what had made Jake call him in the first place. And now that he thought about it, why had Jake called him and not his mother?

"He was at a party," he explained, "and he called me to get him out. But when I got there, they'd arrested everyone."

"Oh my God!" Her voice rose. "Is he okay? Is he drunk? Oh, God, I told him just this evening—"

"He didn't sound drunk. Or high." Liam walked to the building, giving her the address.

"But I have to—I have to get someone here for Benji. Goddammit!" He imagined her pacing her tiny bedroom.

"I can come."

"Yes! Thank you! No, wait." She might have slumped down onto the bed. "Stay there. See if you can get to see Jake. Tell them you're his dad. I'll call... someone else."

She hung up. He didn't blame her, though he had a whole slew of emotions he couldn't translate about the fact that she couldn't say Gabriel's name in front of him.

Liam went up to the station door and into the glass and fake-wood paneled space. Several officers, male and female, were standing behind the bulletproof glass that topped the counter, talking to the duty officers, who were furiously writing notes. A door behind them opened, and Liam could hear raucous shouts and cries from inside. None of them sounded like Jake, but the sound still made his stomach clench.

"I'm here to see Jake Donaghy," he said once someone came up to the counter. *You suck at this. You should have given him your last name.*

"You're quick. They only just arrived. Are you his parent or guardian?" the woman asked in a bored voice.

"Yes." At least, he'd guard the kid for the rest of his life, whatever happened between him and Thea.

"Name?"

"Liam McConnell." She raised her eyebrow but didn't address the difference in last names. "You'll have to wait while we get them all sorted out."

"But he wasn't—" he began. But what could he say? He didn't know what condition Jake was in. "Is he... safe back there?"

"Oh, yah," she said. "They're not violent. Just partying."

The one could turn into the other in a minute, but Liam wasn't in a position to argue. He found the waiting room, which was even more soulless than the reception desk, got himself a truly disgusting cup of coffee from a machine, and sat down to text Thea the update.

Megan is coming, she texted back. **I'll be there in a half hour**.

So, not Gabe. It gave Liam hope. She wasn't at the point of relying on her husband in emergencies.

Then he remembered and thumped his leg at his stupidity. She wasn't asking Gabe to babysit because she was probably telling him his son was in jail. Liam had been so caught up in his own worry about the boy, he'd forgotten that another man had more claim to Jake.

So the half hour passed painfully. More parents arrived, presumably called by their children as they were processed. The difference in attitude between parents was interesting to observe. Some came in ranting, insistent that this was overreach and their child was innocent. Some were tight-lipped and stoic, not looking the cops in the eye, filling out the paperwork in silence. Some apologized with profuse exclamations that "Johnny has never done anything like this before!"

Just as Liam was about to go to the desk to see what the holdup was with Jake's processing, Thea ran through the doors.

He hadn't seen her since yesterday morning, since she'd stood at his car and told him Gabe was picking up Benji. She looked about twenty, dressed as she was in light jeans with a rip in one knee and a big Boston College sweatshirt that fell off one shoulder. Her hair was messy, as though she'd been in bed five minutes ago. Utterly kissable, in other words. Liam's mouth went dry.

She ran toward him, and he almost put his arms out, the urge to hold her was so strong. But she halted a couple of feet away. "Have you seen him?" she said.

Her eyes were wide, afraid, luminous in the harsh fluorescent lights. "No. But they've been letting some of the kids go. I was just about to–"

She'd already turned away to hurry to the reception desk. "Jake Donaghy?" she asked the duty officer, who was filling out something on the computer and looked at her with one eyebrow raised. "Sorry," Thea said. Liam instinctively stood by her shoulder. "Please," she went on. "I'm sorry, but could you let me know about Jake Donaghy?"

The duty officer sighed, stopped typing, and spun around in her chair. "Tyrone?" she called to another man with his eyes on a computer. "You got a Jake Donahue there yet?"

"Donaghy," Liam and Thea said together.

"Donaghy," the woman repeated. "S'wat I said, Donaghy."

The man looked at his notebook. Liam could feel Thea quivering with tension in front of him, and he risked putting a hand on her waist. Immediately, she leaned into him, her back against his front. It wasn't a kiss, but it spoke volumes. He dropped a kiss on her hair, and Thea leaned into that, too.

Liam was just settling into feeling really good about tonight, on the whole, when two more people strode through the doors. Thea's brother and elder sister.

"T," Kane said, and Thea moved away from Liam to hug him. So Liam hated him. Hated that he was so much taller and that Thea easily went into his arms. *Great. Now you're jealous of her brother.*

The sister, Catherine, he thought her name was, scowled at him.

"Hi, Cat. You didn't need to come," Thea said.

"Yeah, right," Kane said. "Megan tells us Jake's in jail and we're not coming?"

Yeah. Because he's not your kid. But Liam didn't have any siblings. There must be a language between them he didn't understand because Thea didn't complain about their interference. She seemed grateful that they were there.

And just as she was maybe about to rely on me again.

Kane came up to the desk and threw a smile at the duty officer that set her blushing. *Oh, sure. Kiss up to the woman I've been trying to get information out of for an hour.*

"Hi," Kane said.

"Hi," the woman replied, her voice breathy. *Jesus H.*

"Can you give me the scoop?" Kane went on. "My nephew's in there. Has he been arrested?"

The duty officer's hand went to her throat, touching her collared shirt and tie uniform as though they were a set of pearls she wanted to run her fingers along. Fascinating, really, if Liam hadn't been so pissed off. "Let me see." This time she didn't even turn around or break eye contact with Kane. "Tyrone?"

"I don't have a Donaghy yet."

Kane leaned on the counter. "Any chance you could expedite him?" he asked in a low, intimate voice. "My sister has another kid at home."

"Okay," the woman said. Kane grinned at her and leaned back to nod at Thea. *This family.* Used to getting whatever they wanted. With their money and their looks, they always did.

"Tyrone!" the woman said.

"I'm going, I'm going," the man said and disappeared into the back, where the noise had lessened now that some of the children had gone home.

Kane, obviously used to being in charge, directed his sisters, and therefore Liam, to the waiting area. *I could have figured out sitting down on my own, thanks.* Although he wasn't sure how close to Thea he was going to be allowed to get, given the side-eye her sister was giving him.

"What are you doing here?" she asked baldly. *Okay, so maybe I won't try and sit next to Thea yet.*

"Jake called him," Thea said.

Cat and Kane took in this information. "But he's just his boss," Cat complained.

Thea's voice was exhausted, her posture slumped and fragile now that she had backup. She didn't look at Liam but said, "He knew he could trust Liam to help him."

"Oh." Kane and Cat were both looking at him very hard now. Liam folded his arms and stared right back.

Kane said, "Looks like you've been helping out a lot." Which could mean anything.

"Any chance I'm given," he replied, his voice cool. But Thea looked up at him from her seat between her siblings, and her smile gave him hope the way her lean-in had before.

Screw her family. Screw her ex. I'm not going anywhere.

The door to the back of the station opened and Tyrone came in, holding Jake by one arm. Everyone stood and rushed the desk, Cat only seeming to remember at the last second that it was Thea who had first dibs on her son.

He looked tired and disheartened, his hair spiky in some places but not others, his eyes shadowed. His shoulders were hunched, ready for battle, but all Thea said was his name.

"You have to sign some papers," the duty officer said, talking to Kane, of course.

"Sure," he said, giving her that smile again. What a calling card, that smile.

Tyrone, who was three times as wide as Jake, opened the half gate that separated the desk from the front and let Jake through it. Jake let Thea hug him, but she had enough presence of mind to know he wouldn't appreciate a full-blown cling at this particular time and place, and she backed off to run her eyes over his face. "You okay?"

"Yeah."

"He's shown no signs of intoxication, ma'am," Tyrone said. "Got swept up with the others. Can't be too careful. Kid got run over coming home drunk from a party in this neighborhood a few months ago."

Thea's eyes filled. "God."

Jake looked a little panicked at his mother's tears, and his gaze went to Liam. "You came," he said.

"You asked."

"Yeah." Jake was silent for a second, then he looked at his aunt and uncle. Thea moved away to sign the papers. "When did you get here?"

"Couple of minutes ago," Kane said. "What happened, Jake? What was so bad you couldn't call your mom?"

"It's not that, it's..." Jake looked at the police behind the counter. "Just... some sh—stuff was going down I didn't like. Ethan Standish had the party, but before that, we..."

He looked at Liam for help. "You may as well get it all out now, bud," Liam said. "Better now than later when someone else tells the story for you."

Jake's tone had kept the officers attentive, and now they both lasered in on Jake. "You want to make a statement, son?" Tyrone said in a kind voice.

Jake looked at Liam, then his mother. "Can I be with him?" Thea asked and was assured she could.

"And Liam?" Jake asked.

"One parent only."

Liam's stupid heart tugged for a second. But he had no time to indulge it. Thea and Jake had already disappeared into the room.

Chapter 26

The officer led Thea and Jake into an interrogation room—really not the most soothing of titles—and went to one side of the utilitarian metal table in the middle of the room. She and Jake sat on the other side. Jake was hunched in on himself, not looking at her or the police officer, just at his hands hanging between his knees.

Thea wanted to say so much, but didn't know where to begin. She thought she knew why Jake had called Liam instead of her. Her last words to him had been ringing in her ears ever since the phone call from Liam.

"Sometimes, with the best will in the world, you can end up in situations you can't control."

"I won't."

"But you might."

"I won't, Mom."

Yet it looked like he had. And since he couldn't admit it to her, he'd gone to the next adult he knew he could trust. Her heart swelled with the knowledge that he trusted Liam more than any other man in his life. Even his own uncles. Because Liam had earned that trust.

The officer turned on the tape recorder fastened to the table and gave it his initial speech with the date and time. He asked Jake's name and Thea's.

"How old are you, Jacob?" he said next.

"Fifteen."

"What is your address?"

Jake gave it.

"Okay, Jacob. What did you want to say?"

Jake hadn't looked up from his hands. Thea didn't speak, but she willed the strength into him.

"The swings. In the playpark," he mumbled. "I cut them up."

Thea closed her eyes. She'd known it. She'd ignored it. She hadn't wanted to deal with it, so she'd just let the kids do without their swings. Swings she'd pushed her own boys on a million years ago.

"And I was there when Zach cut the fence at the baseball field. But I didn't help."

"Zach?" Tyrone asked.

Jake took a big breath. For a moment it seemed he might go back on his decision. Then he said, as if pushing it out of him hurt, "Zachary Benedetto."

Tyrone nodded. "Anyone else with you?"

"Ethan Standish. Andrew Gallagher."

"Ethan whose house you were at tonight?"

"Yeah. His big brother set up the party. Their parents are away."

Now that he'd started talking, Jake's voice was becoming a monotone, the words losing emotion. She supposed it was a way to distance himself from them so he could get them out.

Tyrone excused himself for a moment, paused the tape, and left the room.

Jake kept his eyes on his hands. His knee had started jiggling, creating a rhythmic sound as money in his pockets shifted against itself.

"I'm so proud of you," Thea whispered, squeezing his other knee. "And so pissed at you."

Jake snorted. "Story of my life."

"Pretty much." She inclined her head to his. Heads touching, Thea's hand still on Jake's knee, they breathed.

"You've been very angry," she said.

"I was," he said, his voice vibrating through her head. "I knew getting in with Zach would be trouble, but... I guess I wanted trouble. I'm sick of being the responsible one."

Thea sighed. "You can take a break without resorting to vandalism. You could have talked to me about it."

"You were busy. And stressed. There wasn't much you did have time for but school and Benji."

That wasn't true, but it was to Jake. "I'm sorry, honey. You know

I think about you constantly, don't you? Even if I don't have time to talk to you sometimes?"

He thought about it and said, "I guess so."

They were silent again. Then Jake said, "I like Liam."

Thea's throat closed up. "I like him, too."

"He was great with Dad the other day. He even pushed me out of the way so I wouldn't get hurt. That was cool, right?"

"Yeah." Now she couldn't speak above a whisper.

"Then will you please start talking to him again? He defended you the other day. He's not that pissed or he wouldn't do that, would he?"

"I guess not." How hard would Thea have to grovel to make up for what Liam had seen? But now she knew she would. She knew that Jake had seen Liam's value better than she had and had acted on it. "I'll talk to him, baby."

"Okay."

They stayed in position, heads touching, breathing slow and even, while Thea looked for words, until Tyrone came back.

He started the tape again and said, "Okay, Jake. Anything else?"

For the first time, Jake looked at her. Or at least in her direction. "Before we got to the party, we walked from town through the graveyard, and... some of the guys pushed over some of the gravestones."

"Which guys?" Tyrone asked.

"Zach and Ethan. It's usually them."

"Did you join them?"

"No." Jake made himself even smaller, if that were possible. "That's not okay. Grandma and Grandpa are buried in that graveyard." Now he was brave enough to look Thea in the eye. She reached for his hand, but he didn't move it, so she grasped his knee instead. It was a small gesture of respect that he had shown, but he had shown it nonetheless.

"What did you do?"

"I told them to quit it." Jake chewed on his lip. "Not that it made any difference. They just said I'd gotten boring now that I had a real job."

"That's my kind of boring," Thea couldn't help but say. Jake rolled his eyes, but she felt it was a reflex. His body language included her in his ordeal, reached for her sympathy. He needed her love, and that was all.

♦

When they came out of the interrogation room, Kane and Cat were still in the waiting room.

"Where's Liam?" Jake asked at once, which Thea was grateful for. Without Liam there, she felt less able to make herself heard in front of her gorgeous, confident elder siblings. She could feel her voice being taken away while she looked at them, her throat being grabbed by that unseen, fifteen-year-old fist of uncertainty.

"I sent him home," Cat said proudly.

"Oh God, Cat. What did you say to him?"

"Hey," Cat bridled. "*You* told *me* you weren't together anymore."

"But I called him," Jake said. "It's nothing to do with you."

"Jacob!" Cat exclaimed. It was the rudest thing Thea had ever heard him say to his aunt.

"Why does everyone keep sending him away?" Jake went on. "First Mom, then Dad, now you." He scowled. "He'll never forgive Mom now if you two keep butting in."

The three adults looked at him in comical silence. Kane recovered first. "Don't hold back, Jake. Tell us how you really feel."

The choking feeling left Thea. Jake was saying all the things she should. "We're going home," she announced. "Thank you for coming to help, but we're fine."

"Wait a minute," Cat said. "You're not 'fine.' Your son almost got arrested tonight. And he's been—"

"Cat, you say one more word and I swear I will bar you from my home."

Another stunned silence. Neither of them were used to such a vehement tone from Thea, such conviction in her words.

"Okay, okay," Kane said. "It's late, and we're all upset. Let's just go get some sleep." He put a hand on Thea's shoulder, which she let him leave there out of habit. But it felt more patronizing than comforting tonight, and she was close to shaking him off.

They left the police station, Kane giving another big smile to the duty officer, who preened. Did he even know he was doing it? Well, hell. If it got Jake out of that police station, Kane could smile at the goddamn chief commissioner for all she cared.

Thea got Jake in her car. Cat walked to her own car without saying goodbye.

"Did you mean that?" Kane said, folding his long frame down to look through her window.

"I don't know." She was cold, despite the late summer night, and focused on turning on the heater rather than look at her brother.

"We love you, you know," he said.

"I know, Kane," she answered a little tartly, flashing him an angry glance. "Cat's version of that is just hard to take sometimes." She didn't add that his was, too. Kane had only started playing the dad when their own father died. Cat had always played the overbearing mother.

"Okay. Can we come check on you tomorrow? I'll bring bagels."

He'd just worry if she didn't let him. "Only if you come in the late morning and bring crumb cake as well."

"Donuts," Jake said next to her.

"Okay!" Kane laughed and let go of the windowsill. "Safe drive," he said, as he always did.

"You too." Dammit. She loved them. She was going to kick some ass tomorrow, but she loved them all.

Chapter 27

Kane appeared at ten o'clock the next day, laden down with the promised treats and his children. Ellen followed up with a bag full of milk and juice and fruit. Megan had slept on the couch and was thrilled with the bounty. Thea put on a fresh pot of coffee.

Jake was still in bed, but Benji had bounced up at his usual time, excited beyond belief that his beloved aunt had crept in during the night. He was curled up on the couch with her, watching cartoons and giggling, Megan refusing to talk in anything other than a Phineas voice. Thea had been sitting in the kitchen, working her way through a pot of coffee and thinking.

Cat arrived soon after the food was laid out. She looked snippy but hugged Thea and said, "I'm listening, next time you want to yell at me."

Thea smiled. "Good. Actually, I'm glad you're here. I just called Gabe and told him about last night."

Instantly, Cat was back in judgment mode. "Why'd you bother doing that?"

She wasn't going to trot out the old "because he's Jake's father" excuse this time. "Because if things were reversed, I would have wanted to know."

"Yeah." Cat snorted. "Which they never would be. Give me a cup of coffee, would ya?"

"Anyway," Thea went on, getting another mug. "He's on his way over."

"Shit. Kane's going to kill him."

Thea sipped her own mug. "Mmm." She tried to care, thought about Gabe attacking Liam in front of Jake, and stopped trying.

A knock came at the door. Thea and Cat looked at each other, and Thea moved toward the living room, where Kane and Ellen had moved the coffee table so their kids could play on the floor while

Benji and Megan stayed on the couch. Thea saw Kane's face first as he looked to the front door, but he didn't look mad, so she followed his gaze.

It was Liam.

The rush of feeling she got at seeing him at her threshold as he'd been two months ago took her breath away. He was taller, broader, hotter than she remembered. It was Cat who let him in, but he only looked at Thea, his blue eyes fixing her in her place. He wasn't smiling.

The room now had nine people in it and was very crowded. Liam stayed by the door. "Hello, Liam," Cat said, a touch of sarcasm in her voice. "What brings you here?"

"Hello, Catherine," he said.

Thea flinched. Megan sucked in her breath.

"My name," Cat said, blocking him from coming further in, "is Catriona."

"My apologies." Liam bowed at her, just a fraction, but how could Cat resist it? She opened the door, allowing him in.

"What are you doing here?" Cat asked again. Her voice was firm, but her shoulders relaxed.

He smiled at her, then turned his head and gave that smile to Thea.

Thea melted into the floor. Her. He'd come for her.

Another step sounded on the porch, a quick clatter of feet, and the screen door opened.

Liam turned as a voice said, "I've had about enough of you an' all," and then he was ducking and Megan cried out and Liam had a fist in Gabriel's ribs and Kane was on his feet. Gabe was off-balance, crashed into the door and broke a pane of glass, and Kane pushed him out of the door and followed him out, with Liam next to him. Everyone was shouting except Thea, who had stopped breathing, and Megan, who was holding Benji's head to her chest to hide his eyes.

Through the open door, Thea saw the scene play out. Gabe was bleeding from the mouth. Thea could bet that was Kane's doing.

"You dare come back here?" Kane was shouting, his voice deeper than Liam's but with a crack in it from the fire he'd been in a few years ago. "You *dare* try your shit again with her?"

"She's my wife!" Gabe roared. "You keep your fucking hands off her!"

Obviously his jealousy overrode his sense of self-preservation, because he wasn't even looking at Kane, the bigger danger, but at Liam.

"You left her," Liam said in the even tone Thea didn't know how he managed.

"What the fuck does that matter?" Gabe yelled. "She's *mine*. She'll have me back in a minute if you'll just fuck off."

Megan covered Benji's ears, but he was fighting her now and crying. Thea took in a great, gulping breath, and ran over to him herself. Hugging him close, she could still see the men though the window behind the couch.

Kane said, "Jesus Christ, man, have you no self-respect? No thought for your son, who's in there hearing every word you say?"

"Don't tell me how to be around my son!" was all Gabe had to say. "You set them against me from the beginning!"

"You managed that all by yourself," Liam said. "Go home, Gabriel. Go get some anger management counseling."

"You don't even get to talk to me," Gabe said, though he took one more step down the stairs. Kane took two corresponding steps forward.

"If I hear that you've been around Thea or your children in this kind of rage again," Liam went on in that calm voice, "I will have a restraining order put out against you. Now, if you mean it when you say you want a relationship with your kids, you'd better leave now and sort out your priorities."

Gabe sneered, and Kane said, "No. I want to kick his ass some more."

"I'll have you for assault!" Gabe shouted.

"And Thea will have you for abandonment," Liam said. "Deserting your wife and kids is a felony in this state, buddy."

She hadn't known that. Liam was standing a little behind Kane but square on to Gabe. His words, combined with Kane's banked anger, finally drove Gabe off the stairs. As he went, he dragged his hand down the stair-rail. "Shit!" he yelped, as a sliver jammed itself into his palm. Suddenly, Thea loved that stair rail.

He reached the bottom of the stairs, sucked on his palm, and looked up at them all. "She won't sue me," he said. Damn. Nothing cowed him. Thea cringed at his conviction, at his confidence that she was so weak she'd let him get away with anything.

"She doesn't have to," Liam said. "I just have to tell the cops you left her and the boys with no support, and they'll have your hide in jail by tonight."

There was a long, long silence.

"But if you agree to a no-fault divorce," Liam went on, "and you give up any rights to her money, maybe I won't make that call."

"That's blackmail."

"What was that cop's name that Jake talked to last night?" Liam asked Kane.

"Fuck." Gabe walked backward down the path and into the mailbox before righting himself.

"Bye!" Kane called, sounding much more cheerful, and he waved at Gabe's retreating back. "We'll be in touch!"

Thea hadn't realized she was shaking so much. Benji was crying into her chest, his sobs muffled. When she looked up she saw Megan's and Cat's eyes were both wide, their mouths half-open in shock. Ellen was shushing the baby, who had picked up on the mood and started crying too, while four-year-old Libby pressed in close to her side, sucking on a finger Thea supposed was sticky with donut sugar.

Jake was in the door to the kitchen. His hair was sticking up all over, his face dominated by his scared blue eyes. "Jake," she breathed, but he was still staring at the front door.

Kane and Liam walked back inside. Kane was saying, "How did you know about the abandonment?"

"I heard about it back when I was going through my divorce. I looked up the details last night."

"And he could really go to jail?"

"Yes." Liam came farther into the room, around Ellen and the kids on the floor, to stand in front of Thea. "I'm sorry, Benji," he said.

Benji turned his hot, wet face to him. "Is Daddy going to jail?"

"No, honey," Thea said. What would it help the boys if she called the cops on him?

"But he doesn't have to know that," Liam said in a low voice.

"No," she agreed.

He was there, after almost a week of not being near her, and Thea's heart was thumping out of her chest, despite holding a bedraggled six-year-old. Every line on his face, every hair on his beard was known to her, was precious to her. And he'd gone out of his way to help her in so many ways, even when she'd pushed him away. More importantly, he'd given her the confidence to have confidence in herself. He'd respected her opinions and reminded her to respect herself.

"Thea," he said. Almost without realizing she was doing it, she stood, turning to give Benji to Megan. Now she was at his height, and she could take in the breadth of his shoulders and remember the strength in his arms when he lay above her at night. When he held her son. When he stood up for her other son.

"I came over here," he began, "to tell you not to let him back in your life. Not to go back to believing what he said about you. You are stronger, more beautiful, more intelligent, more compassionate, and more worthy of happiness than you believe yourself to be. You are so much more and so much better than the woman who was his wife. I came to tell you that, just that."

He took in a breath. "But what I really want to say is: Choose me instead. I love you, Thea, you and the boys. I don't have a fancy accent, and I don't have a lot of money or a big house or big plans for the future, apart from marrying you one day."

Megan *eeped*. If Thea could have taken her eyes away from him for a millisecond, she might have thought that Cat was crying.

"The only thing I can promise you," Liam went on, "is that I will *be here.*" He pointed at the ground, which seemed to Thea right now only to exist because Liam stood on it. "I will show up every day, good days and bad. I will give you everything I have if you and Jake and Benji will let me share your life. I know you can all do just fine without me, but I'm asking you not to."

Oh, no, it was Thea who was crying. And while her family stood in their third stunned silence of the day, she wrapped her arms around Liam's neck and kissed him, a big, hard, passionate kiss that went way beyond propriety, beyond what her sons and nieces should be seeing, a kiss that prompted Liam to lift her up by the waist and hold her to him so tightly she could only deepen the kiss while her tears added to the taste of him and all that they were to each other.

"Shit, I think *I* love him," Megan said from very far away.

They both laughed, and it was enough to break the kiss, but Thea stayed close and Liam seemed to have no desire to put her down. Looking into those blue eyes, which had seen her so clearly from the very start, she whispered, "I love you back," and he grinned and kissed her once more.

"That's good," he said. "That's really, really good."

Epilogue

One Year Later

The minimum number of Mahoneys and McConnells who were allowed into a wedding of any one of them was one hundred. The Fielding side was smaller but augmented nicely this time by the friends Thea had made: Zahra, in a pale-gold tunic and hijab that glowed in the early summer sun, with her husband and three children; Chloe and her wife, Stephanie, the famous photographer who had handpicked the person discreetly taking pictures over to the side; and Seth and David, in matching light khaki suits and vivid ties. David had brought a girl.

The beach at the Cape was pristine today, needing little decoration apart from the huge sprays of baby's breath placed on either side of the justice of the peace. The shimmering blue of the New England sky met the sand, which at this time of year was still cool enough for the guests to enjoy burying their bare feet in as they waited for the wedding party.

Liam and his best men came forward first, all in matching khaki pants and waistcoats. Benji was thinner this year and taller, and Jake at sixteen was filling out, his basketball training now extending into the spring with weight training and track. Benji had his hand in his pocket, where he was afraid to let go of the rings.

There was some sort of scuffle at the back of the path leading from the hotel to the beach, and then Thea and her chaperone began to walk down. Chaperones. Because none of her siblings wanted to miss out on walking her down the aisle. But it was Sam, finally back from New Mexico to see her favorite sister get married, who linked arms with Thea and drew her down the beach to her man.

Preview of Stand

Sam, Thea's kickass younger sister, is too independent to need a man in her life. Right? Right? But what happens when she meets a man who needs her in *his* life? And when she falls in love with his kids? Catch a sneak peak at STAND, Sam's story.

◆

Part I

Chapter 1

That was *it*. Sam was getting the hell away from this house, its people, and all its memories.

"Come on, Cairo," she said. Her German shepherd leaped up from his spot under the kitchen table to meet her in the front hall.

"Samantha!" her older sister yelled from behind her. "Get back here! You can't walk away every—"

"Don't call me Samantha!" she yelled back, clipping on Cairo's leash. She should never have come back. Coming back only turned her back into an angry, childish seventeen-year-old who hated her name. Instead of an independent thirty-five-year-old with her own career and her own home and a state on the other side of the country that she missed like crazy.

"Sam!" her younger sister, Megan, called. "It's raining!"

"I won't melt!"

Sam slammed the ancient oak front door of her family home and took the steps down from the porch in one leap, Cairo happily jumping alongside her. The old house seemed to groan in protest. Yeah, yeah. She'd upset the status quo. Again. When Cat called her "Samantha," she was really in trouble.

She took long strides away from the house, down the street she'd grown up on, the trees that had been venerable thirty years ago now creaking with old age and the weight of rain on their summer leaves. The town was late in cutting back the overhanging branches. She let them hit her in the face, punishing herself for her moment of weakness.

"I tell ya, Cai," she grumbled aloud, "I shouldn't have come back at all. Not even for Thea's wedding. Not even to meet Kane's babies." They weren't babies anymore; the oldest was four. She winced.

Cairo matched his long legs to her strides and looked up at her, his brown face grinning happily at the walk. Sam took another tree branch to the face as she looked down at him. She didn't want him to cheer her up. She didn't want to see how thrilled he was with the new smells and new people he'd met.

"I guess you wouldn't have gotten your road trip though, huh, buddy?" she conceded, reaching down to scratch between his ears. He'd loved the three-day drive so much, sniffing the air through the crack in the window, visiting national parks, and sleeping on her bed at pet-friendly hotels. Had it been worth it just for that?

No. "Not for *nothing*. Shoulda packed up the car and gone back home right after the wedding."

Her feet took her down a couple of side streets and through a short back alley to the public footpath in the woods. The slick mud oozing into her sandals soothed her. She knelt down and smeared some on her hands, too. There. That was more like the Sam she knew.

Had her love for exploration started here? The family home's backyard was like many in this cookie-cutter suburb of Boston: small, dominated by the house, a detached garage and a long driveway for the many cars that had come and gone through the years. So she and her four siblings—Catriona, the oldest, the mother hen; Kane, the only boy, handsome and carefree until their father had died; Thea, studious and quiet, laughing at Sam's jokes; and Megan, the baby, running to keep up—had often come to this trail, racing each other through the trees to the stream that ran through the middle of the woods and reflected the seasons.

Sam knew every curve, every eddy, every inch of that stream. She'd learned about erosion from watching it curl around a tree root until the root became exposed and the tree fell across the water.

She'd crawled in and out of the old farmer's cottage that had fallen to ruin in the middle of a thicket of brambles, not caring about the scratches when she found an old wooden bucket and rusty ladle. She'd learned about foundations and strata and decomposition alongside how to navigate her sisters' moods and weaknesses. And which of her brother's friends were worth getting to know.

Well, that had been years ago, when their lives were simple. Before they'd lost their father and then their mother and Sam had lost all faith in men being there when they were needed.

She sat down on one of the slick rocks near the tiny waterfall the town had aggrandized with its own name, and stuck her feet, sandals and all, into the rush of water. When she let Cairo's leash out to its farthest extent, he hopped down to sip from the cool current.

Lifting her heavy hair from the nape of her neck, she raised her face to the rain coming through the trees and tried to blank out her mind.

But Cairo gave his warning bark, and then she heard the voices.

"It's raining. Can we go back now?"

"No. We just got here."

"Ugh. Dad, this is so lame."

"No, it isn't. This is family. This is what we do."

"Lame family."

"Well, it's all you got, so suck it up and look at the falls."

Sam opened her eyes. Two children with faces as uninspired as the weather had appeared on the other side of the narrow stream. Sam had three sixteen-year-old nephews, and the boy looked about their age, though he wore a hoodie that covered half his face. The girl might have been younger; she was in flip-flops, which couldn't have been useful on the rocky path down to the water.

Behind them, their father had a scowl on his face that he quickly rearranged when he saw her. From where she was sitting, he looked tall, taller than her own five foot eleven. The calves she could see below his Bermudas were strong. He either ran or rode a bike on a regular basis.

He looked familiar. The rainy shadows slanting through the trees across his face reminded her of something.

She squinted across the stream. The bike. The blond. "Tyler?"

He took off his sunglasses. The long, thin face of the teenager she'd known had become chiseled cheekbones and a strong jawline, but his ocean-blue eyes were the same.

He didn't recognize her. Not surprising. After years spent outside, she was permanently tan, and her sleek, dark hair had lightened and coarsened in the sun. "It's Sam Fielding," she said awkwardly. "From... school."

His eyes widened at first, but then they narrowed, his lips thinned, and he said, "Oh. Sam," and it sounded as if her name hurt him to say.

Unsurprising, really, given the last time she'd been near him.

Her half smile faltered and died. His kids stopped their desultory exploration of the falls and stared at them. "You know each other?" the boy asked.

"Yep," Tyler said, biting off the word.

From the way their eyes narrowed at her, the kids could sense he wasn't happy. "Uh..." Sam said. "How are you?"

He shot a glance at his kids. Thank God he wasn't about to follow up that scowl with a trip down memory lane. "Fine," he said. Then, after a pause, he added, "Did you move back to town?"

"God, no," she said before she could stop herself. "I mean... no. I live in New Mexico."

The girl's eyes widened just as her father's had. "Cool," she said, then she looked at Tyler. "Like Uncle Noah?"

Sam recalled a kid who'd hung out with Tyler in high school, with the same emo fashion sense, the same reputation for being a great artist but otherwise not worth her time. "You're still friends with Noah Tran?"

He looked away, then back. "Yep."

"Do you live in Taos?" the girl went on. "That's where Noah lives."

Sam couldn't be as reticent as Tyler, not in front of this girl's enthusiasm. "I'm in Albuquerque, but right now I live near the Zuni Pueblo. Do you know what that is?"

"Where the Native Americans lived?"

"Uh-huh." Ignoring the dislike Ty was quite understandably radiating at her, she went on. "Many of them still live there. My company helps them save the ancient sites they were driven out of. Find artifacts, that kind of thing."

"So are you an archaeologist or an anthropologist?" the girl asked, obviously knowing her stuff.

"Both. My doctorate was in archaeology, my bachelor's in anthropology."

"You have a PhD?" Tyler interrupted.

"Yeah." Sam couldn't help herself. She lifted her chin. "Surprised?"

"No. Just..."

"I want to be a psychologist," the girl interrupted. "Or a psychiatrist. I haven't decided."

"You don't have to decide yet," Sam assured her. "That's what college is for."

The girl wore her hair in a fat braid down her back, and now that Sam focused on her, she saw a thick purple stripe on one side of her hair. Sam smiled at her. "Cool hair."

The girl beamed. "Can I pet your dog?" she asked.

"Sure. Do you know how to approach him?"

"Of course." The girl walked into the stream. Her father opened his mouth, but she said, "I'm fine, Dad," before he could speak, and continued to pick her way through the shallow water toward Sam.

Sam had given Cairo the "stay" hand command, and now she aimed a radiating welcome at the girl so Cairo would know she was safe. "Cai, say hello."

The girl held out the back of her hand in a fist and let Cairo come the last few inches to sniff her. Cai did so, then looked at Sam. "Okay," Sam said, and Cai wagged his fuzzy tail and stepped forward, his whole backside swaying at meeting a new friend. He looked scary but was a big old mush, really.

"His name's Cai?" the girl asked.

"Cairo. And I'm Sam. And you are...?"

"Alyssa." Alyssa was on her haunches now, rubbing Cairo's long ears while he panted with joy. "Cairo, like the city?"

"Uh-huh. Nice to meet you."

"He's perfect."

"Thanks. Yes, he is."

"So why are you back?" Tyler asked, reminding her of his presence.

"My sister got married." Guilt twisted in her stomach. Thea would want her to be at home right now, apologizing to Cat. Pretending there was nothing missing in their lives.

"Which sister?"

He remembered she had a bunch of sisters. She'd rather that than the other things he knew about her. "Thea. She was a year ahead of us." The one who'd driven Sam to school for two years, until their father had died and everything had changed.

Tyler looked at her for a moment longer, his pinched expression screaming dislike. *I'm not that girl any more*, she wanted to tell him. *I'm not ashamed of most of it, but I'm different now.* She couldn't say it, not in front of his kids, not in these few startled seconds.

"All right, guys, we should go," he said, turning back to his children.

"We just got here!" complained the boy. His frown made him look just like his father. Their pale skin was even tanned to the same light biscuit.

Even Sam had to hide a smile at the exasperation on Tyler's face as he turned to his son. "You were just saying you wanted to—"

"Sam!" a voice called from behind her. "Sam?"

It was Megan, sent to find her. "Yeah, Meg!" she called back, still looking at Tyler. Cairo leaped away from Alyssa's hands and over to greet his auntie.

Megan came through the trees. She, of course, looked perfect, even for a casual family Sunday lunch. The clothes horse of the family, dressed like she was on her way to a photo shoot. Her white skirt floated beautifully off her slim hips, and she somehow owned rainboots that still looked chic by matching her black embroidered blouse.

"Hey, puppy," she said lovingly to Cairo, then, "Hi!" to the other three, whose bright clothes stood out in the shade of the wet trees. They were all unashamedly staring at her. She gave them the full-wattage Fielding smile. "Nice day, isn't it?" She held a hand up to the rain.

"Hello," Tyler said. He didn't know Megan; she'd still been in middle school when they'd graduated. His son was staring at her, his Adam's apple bobbing up and down. Megan tended to do that to people. Sam gave Tyler credit for not staring too.

What was the protocol here? "This is my sister, Megan," Sam said. "This is Tyler Cavanaugh. We were in high school together."

"Not together," he said and turned away from the women. He put his sunglasses on and raised his voice a little to the kids. "Let's go." This time, they didn't complain. "Nice to meet you," he said over his shoulder to Megan as they began to walk back up the opposite bank. "'Bye, Sam," he added with the merest flicker of his eyes toward her. The trio disappeared into the woods.

"What the hell did you do to him?" Megan immediately demanded.

Sam lifted her hair off her neck again. Those last couple of years of high school... well, she didn't think about them. If she did, it was to remember with bravado the nights of drinking, making out with boys she forgot the next day, or her first time with Brennan Caplan and how she'd made him wear two condoms. Which was *not* a good idea.

She liked to think Megan didn't know any of this. "We were in different circles. I met him a couple of times."

"Oh." Megan clearly had other things on her mind. "Okay. Let's go back. Mother Cat's had another glass of wine and Kane's asking her opinion on the company, so she's in a much better mood."

Looking over the stream again before they turned to go home, Sam imagined Tyler as he'd been in high school: bony, wearing glasses, his hair cut in some painfully homegrown way. She flinched a little as she wrapped Cairo's leash around her hand.

"Oh, come on," said Megan, who'd seen her wince. "We're not that bad."

"I wasn't thinking about—" Sam finished the sentence by butting Megan's shoulder with hers. "Yeah, you are."

Megan butted back. "You just say stuff to piss Cat off."

"It's my favorite pastime. And a good reason why I don't visit."

Megan sobered as they came out of the woods and onto the sidewalk. "Did you have to bring up Dad, though?"

Sam folded her arms, the familiar bullheadedness taking over. "Why not? Is he like an inverse Voldemort or something? He Who Was Too Perfect To Be Named?"

"No," Megan said, her tone even, but Sam already felt like shit. "He was just Dad. But he was the only one we had, Sam."

Megan had been only ten when their father had died. Sam had no business tainting her memories of him with her own anger at his pointless death and the mess he'd left the family in when he'd gone. She put an arm around her little sister's shoulders, which were as tall as her own. "Sorry."

At Cat's house, things were chaotic but normal. The adults pretended nothing had happened. The rain stopped, so the kids recognized fresh meat and dragged Sam and Cairo out into the yard to play catch. The family golden retrievers dropped soggy bones at Cairo's feet and shook the rain off their fur.

After a little while, Kane's daughter came up to show off the half-eaten dinosaur she'd dug out of the sandbox. Sam crouched down and talked to the little girl about T. rexes. Thea's younger son, Benji, and the friend whom he was about to have a sleepover with while Thea was on her honeymoon, joined the group to listen.

Megan came up behind her and nearly knocked her into the sand by hugging her from the back.

"Get off!" Sam said in a muffled voice, her face smooshed into her knees.

"I just wanted to say I'm sooo glad you came home," Meg said into her back.

"Only for Thea," Sam said crossly, but she squeezed the hands that had wrapped themselves around her neck. "And Libby. And maybe you a little bit. Now get the hell off me."

"Get the hell off me!" four-year-old Libby echoed. Seven-year-old Benji and his buddy gulped with shock and delight.

"You're the worst aunt in the world." Meg laughed, easing up on Sam's neck. "Don't talk like your auntie, Libby."

Sam's other nephews had forgotten they were hip and cool sixteen-year-olds and were having a loud game of basketball in the driveway. Jake was now spiking the basketball like it was a football while Paolo or Mateo—her twin nephews would have to stand still for her to be able to figure out who was who—tried to jump on his back.

"Now that you've broken the ice," Meg said, "will you come see us more often?"

Sam looked at her. They had the same dark-brown eyes, same strong eyebrows, same toothy smile. She hadn't been in Meg's life since Meg had left high school. It suddenly occurred to Sam that her baby sister could have used a friend in those years.

"I'll try," she said.

Acknowledgments

Thank you, first and foremost, to the readers who got into Kane and Ellen's world and demanded I write about Kane's sisters. I loved all four of them so much; it's a treat to give them their own HEAs. Perhaps most especially Thea's.

To Julie Sturgeon, editor extraordinaire, who fixed all my weird word orders and still said she liked the book at the end. To Jess Verdi, who ushered Breathe into the world and without whom I wouldn't be here. Wow, that's a lot of w's. I need an editor for these acknowledgments, clearly. To Kimberly Dawn, who fixed my commas and my hyphens and good-naturedly listened to my complaints about parentheses.

To my critique partners and friends who read this and/or other books in this series: Michelle Bond, Victoria Farhat, Delores Stewart, Lena Pinto, Michael DeMarco, Kim Katil, and Margaret Dudonis. I am so very lucky to know you all. And to everyone who encouraged me to self-publish, most absolutely especially Lori Matthews and Stacey Wilk. You guys are my rock.

To my girls, who encourage me and roll their eyes at me in almost equal measure. And finally but not leastly to Donn, who rides the waves of my crazy career with me and is always there at the end to dry me off and fix me a dark and stormy. I love you so much.

About the Author

Kimberley Ash is a British expat who has lived in and loved New Jersey for 30 years. She writes fish-out-of-water stories about people who find home where they least expect it. When not writing contemporary romance or romantic women's fiction, she can usually be found cleaning up after her two big furry dogs and slightly less furry children.

Other Books by Kimberley Ash

The Fieldings

Breathe

Stand

Rise

The Van Allen Brothers

Forgive Me

Forget Me

Free Me

Standalones:

Champion

Connect with Kimberley

I hope you loved Thea and Liam and *Hold!* Join my Facebook Group, Read Your Ash Off, sign up for my newsletter, and follow me to get the latest info on my new releases and events. I look forward to meeting you!

Website: www.kimberleyash.com
Bookbub: @KimberleyAsh
Instagram: @KAshAuthor
Goodreads: Kimberley Ash
Facebook Page: Kimberley Ash Books
Twitter: @KAshAuthor